STORM
RIDER

Also by Cassie Edwards

STORM RIDER

Cassie Edwards

A SIGNET BOOK

SIGNET
Published by New American Library, a division of
Penguin Putnam Inc., 375 Hudson Street,
New York, New York 10014, U.S.A.
Penguin Books Ltd, 80 Strand,
London WC2R 0RL, England
Penguin Books Australia Ltd, Ringwood,
Victoria, Australia
Penguin Books Canada Ltd, 10 Alcorn Avenue,
Toronto, Ontario, Canada M4V 3B2
Penguin Books (N.Z.) Ltd, 182–190 Wairau Road,
Auckland 10, New Zealand

Penguin Books Ltd, Registered Offices:
Harmondsworth, Middlesex, England

ISBN 0-7394-3069-6

First published by Signet, an imprint of New American Library,
a division of Penguin Putnam Inc.

PUBLISHER'S NOTE
This is a work of fiction. Names, characters, places, and incidents either are
the product of the author's imagination or are used fictitiously, and any
resemblance to actual persons, living or dead, business establishments,
events, or locales is entirely coincidental.

I dedicate *Storm Rider* to Rita Robinson, a dear friend.
Always,
Cassie Edwards

I'm searching for my love at every turn,
When I think of him, my body yearns.
His raven-black hair, and sun-kissed skin,
Start fires to burning from deep within.
Have you seen him on the rise?
I search for him in the skies.
Tell him I'm waiting, waiting in the shadows,
When he sees me, his heart will know.

—Diane Collett

Prologue

1837

Five-year-old Tabitha June Daniel couldn't help but feel uncomfortable as her parents argued on the top deck of the paddle wheeler making its way down the Missouri River toward Saint Louis. She clung to the ship's rail and tried not to hear the heated words between her mother and father. Yet there it was— anger she could not get away from.

Her pretty floor-length, puffed-sleeve yellow dress, with its fully gathered skirt and lacy petticoat beneath, fluttered in the breeze. Her tiny black patent-leather shoes caught the gleam of the early-afternoon sun. She glanced up at her mother's lovely face, which was flushed pink with anger as she ranted at Tabitha's father.

Tabitha winced as the words got more intense. She was embarrassed that their argument was drawing the attention of other passengers strolling leisurely on the top deck, or standing at the rail to take in the view along the riverbank.

"William, this is the last time I will accompany you to that dreaded heathen land where redskins lurk in every shadow," Mildred said. Her voice caught with emotion. "Lord, William, your physician father left everything to you when he died. We're wealthy enough for you to settle down in Saint Louis and enjoy things like the opera or the symphony, instead of running back and forth between civilization and the wilderness, risking all of our necks for your so-called fur trade."

"Mildred, please keep your voice down," William said. He looked nervously over his shoulder at those who were gaping at the argument. He slid his hands into the pockets of his expensive black wool suit coat. A diamond glistened in the folds of his velveteen ascot.

"I have been patient long enough," Mildred fumed, ignoring how her husband's right cheek twitched from a barely subdued anger.

She gazed up at him. His six-foot height towered over hers. His slicked-down black hair framed a handsome face with a beard and mustache and eyes that were as black as night. He was as dark-skinned as any Indian, but only because he was an outdoorsman as well as a businessman.

Mildred could see how he looked down at her with controlled irritation. She wished that he saw her as that young, pretty, golden-haired woman he had married ten years ago. But she knew that when he looked at her now, he saw only an annoyance.

She tried to hold back her tears at the thought that she had nagged him so much, he perhaps did not even love her anymore.

But still, she could not stop speaking her mind, especially now. Tabitha June would soon be six and entering school. Mildred wanted her daughter to have a normal life, not one accompanying a father who traded with the Indians for their expensive pelts, robes, and other items that he could bring back to the Saint Louis markets. Indian goods brought a big price on the banks of the Mississippi.

"William, must I remind you of our daughter's need for roots so that when she starts school, she can have the same friends from year to year?" Mildred said. "And must I remind you of the risks of taking supplies back and forth in steamers? The boats can get snagged in the river and sink. Some have even caught fire and burned—not only the cargo, but also the passengers."

"Must *I* remind *you* that the loss of one boatload of robes can cost a trader ten thousand dollars?" William argued back. "So do you think I would board a paddle wheeler that I didn't trust? Relax, Mildred; enjoy the day. It's beautiful. Just smell the fresh river air and wildflowers. Can't you enjoy anything anymore, instead of finding things to nag about?"

"I know . . . you have told me more than once that the chance of loss is worth the risk given the possible gains over a period of ten years, even though your family is forced to take up residence at that filthy Fort Union, while you trade with the redskins," Mildred said, sighing heavily.

"You can call Fort Union filthy after I saw to it that you had the best cabin there?" William asked. "This fort is the principal and handsomest trading post on the Missouri River. And it is situated about six and a half miles above the mouth of the Yellowstone River, which is beautiful country, and well suited for such an establishment."

He sighed, raked his fingers through his thick black hair, and looked out at the wilderness slowly passing by. "It was a good trade this year," he said. "There is pile after pile of expensive pelts in the hold of the ship."

"Have you heard anything I've said, William?" Mildred said with a huff. "Don't you care?"

William looked at her, then turned and walked away, leaving Tabitha and her mother alone at the rail.

"Mommy, don't be mad at Daddy," Tabitha said, tugging on the velveteen skirt of her mother's dress. "We'll be home soon."

"Yes, I know," Mildred said. But her words were

cut short by a sudden explosion that ripped the deck in half and quickly spread flames everywhere.

"Lord, no!" Mildred cried, her eyes wild with fear. She grabbed Tabitha into her arms just before half of the boat tipped and threw them into the water. Near them other people thrashed around, screaming and yelling.

"Mommy, Mommy!" Tabitha cried, grabbing desperately at her mother as her mother tried just as desperately to keep hold of her.

"I can't swim, Tabitha," Mildred cried. "I can't swim!"

Just before her mother sank beneath the surface of the water, she managed to shove Tabitha onto a piece of ship debris.

Tabitha floated downstream, crying out for her mother and father, who remained with the destruction and death behind her.

Burning pelts and debris floated dangerously close to her.

Exhausted and afraid, Tabitha drifted on the plank for what seemed forever. Clinging to it for dear life, she still searched in the river for her mother and father, even as she feared they were gone forever. Tabitha felt frighteningly alone.

She was glad when the plank ran aground, tipping over and depositing her on the riverbank as though the hand of God were helping her.

Her whole body was weak from the ordeal, and

she shivered from cold and dampness. She crawled farther from the river into clean, dry grass, then collapsed.

She soon fell thankfully into a deep sleep where—for a while, at least—she couldn't relive the horrors of watching her mother sinking before her very eyes, and knowing that her father had sunk as well somewhere in the hungry jaws of the river.

When Tabitha awakened, she found herself in a tepee with an Indian man and woman.

She wasn't afraid, for at Fort Union she had become acquainted with Indians when they came to trade. They were friendly with white people.

A pretty woman with long black braids and wearing a beaded white doeskin dress knelt beside Tabitha and gently touched her face. "*Hohahe*, hello, child. I am *kola*, a friend. I am called River Song," she murmured. "You are in the lodge of Chief Blue Thunder, who is my *mihigna*, husband. We are of the Crow nation. My husband and I saw a great fire in the river from a distance and knew that it must be a white man's boat. We went to investigate. We found no survivors. As we returned from the place of disaster, we went for some distance, and then came upon you asleep next to the river. We assumed you were from the boat, and had lost your loved ones in the tragedy. We brought you home with us. You are safe here."

"My name is Tabitha, and . . . and . . . my mommy

saved me," Tabitha said. She burst into tears as she recalled the moment her mother had pushed her onto the plank. "Then . . . then she went away from me deep in the water. My daddy was also on the boat and . . . and must have also gone away. I have no more family. I . . . I am all alone now."

River Song lifted Tabitha onto her lap and rocked her slowly as the child trustingly clung to her. "No, little one, you are not alone," she said in the English language her people had learned in order to trade with the white eyes. "You can stay with me and my chieftain husband."

River Song could not help but feel blessed this day by having found the child, sent to her, she felt, from the heavens, since River Song was barren. She had been blessed, too, by having a husband who loved her too much to take a second wife only for the children she might bear him.

"Thank you," Tabitha said, a sob lodging in her throat. "But what about my mommy and daddy? How can I be sure they . . . they are really gone? I want to see them. I loved them so."

"My husband will send warriors out once more to see if your mother and father might still be alive," River Song said softly. "But do not have too much hope if they still cannot be found."

"I'm sleepy . . ." Tabitha said. She snuggled closer to River Song. She closed her eyes. "I'm . . . so . . . sleepy."

"*Istima*, sleep, little one," River Song murmured. She hummed a soft song and continued to rock Tabitha in her arms until she saw that the child was again fast asleep.

River Song then gazed over at her husband, who sat beside the fire, watching his wife and the child together.

"*Mihigna*, my husband, I have never seen such a beautiful child, red-skinned or white," she murmured. She reached a hand to Tabitha's golden hair. "She has the hair of sunshine and eyes the color of the sky. She has a face of perfection."

She turned her gaze toward her husband again. "I want her, husband," she said. "I wish to protect her, to love her, and to raise her as ours. Without us, she is so *isna*, alone."

"*Hoye*, I agree, and I see your happiness as you hold the child and speak with her," Chief Blue Thunder said. He smiled warmly at his wife. "I shall send warriors out to search for her parents once again, and if they cannot be found, then, my wife, I vow to you never to let anyone take the child from you."

"Your words bring such joy to this wife's heart," River Song murmured. "But I do know that if her true parents can be found, I must relinquish her to them."

"*Mitawin*, wife, you know as well as I that they are gone from this earth forever, for were they still alive, we would have found them on our other two searches," Chief Blue Thunder said. "But as you promised the child, I will send warriors again to search so that I can assure her that we did."

"Talking Rain," River Song blurted out. "If she can be with you and me in our hearts and home, I would like to call her Talking Rain, for when the adorable child talks, it sounds like a softly falling rain in spring."

Chief Blue Thunder nodded. "Yes, I, too, see that name as right for the child," he said. "Yes . . . Talking Rain . . ."

Chapter 1

Thirteen Years Later
September—Chan-pah-sap-ah-wee,
Moon of Black Cherries

The sun was high today, sending its golden rays down upon the soldiers' council house, a lodge as big as three skin lodges formed into one. It made an area twenty-four feet in diameter, and could easily accommodate sixty to eighty warriors.

The soldiers' lodge was pitched in the center of the village. The whole body of warriors was called only when the *gauche*, chief, wished a public meeting, or when their hunting regulations were to be decided upon.

This was the state house of the Fox band of the *As-see-nee-poi-tuca*, Assiniboine Indians. Their name meant "our people," and they had only recently moved to this area to make their new permanent camp. All business relative to the camp and other nations was transacted in this lodge, and all strangers and visitors lodged there when they stayed overnight.

Today they were in the state house to have council with a neighboring band of Crow Indians, whose encampment lay not far from theirs.

Chief Storm Rider, a young *gauche* of twenty-five winters dressed in heavily beaded, tight-fitting fringed buckskin attire and moccasins, was in charge of this meeting.

After he and his Assiniboine people were established at their new home for several weeks, Storm Rider had sent an offering of tobacco and an eagle feather with its lower end painted red—his band's calling card—to the Red Root band of Crow, inviting them to have council and discuss how they would have friendly relationships. Also, Chief Storm Rider hoped they could work together against the enemy renegade Crow called the Snake, and his allied warriors who were terrorizing the area.

At his young age, Storm Rider had raised himself to distinction quickly, and was generally loved and admired by his people. He was a handsome, honorable, sensible man, judicious in governing his band, and had been named chief because of his bravery in war excursions against *toka*, enemy tribes.

Although the title and position of chief was not hereditary, that honor had been granted to Storm Rider upon the death of his chieftain father in a raid when Storm Rider had just turned twenty winters of age. Storm Rider was now doing all in his power to protect his band against such raids again.

Chief Blue Thunder, the Crow chief, was glad to have special attention from the powerful young Assiniboine leader. His own Crow people were not as wealthy as they used to be due to illness, as well as endless raids by the Snake. Blue Thunder had come eagerly today with twenty of his favored warriors to hear what Chief Storm Rider had to offer.

The Crow warriors and their chief assembled on one side of the huge soldiers' council house, the Assiniboine on the other. They faced each other with only a slow-burning lodge fire separating them.

Storm Rider sat with his best friend and confidant, Fast Wolf, at his side as he looked across the fire at Chief Blue Thunder. He felt good about his decision to invite the older chief there for council. Storm Rider had not doubted that the Crow chief would accept the peaceful overtures he planned to offer him, even though the two tribes shared a history of bloody warfare.

But that was far in the past.

This was now.

Storm Rider's band being a rich people, the Crow band would have much to gain from a friendship. Their numbers, strength, and power had decreased significantly because of the very man that Storm

Rider wanted to fight—and eliminate—if at all possible.

The Snake.

Even the name caused bitterness in Storm Rider's heart, for it was that evil man who had sent a deadly poisoned arrow into his father's heart, and then his mother's.

Storm Rider had vowed then to hunt him down and end his reign of terror. He hoped that by bringing his people to this part of Wyoming, where the Snake was known to roam, Storm Rider would at long last see the Snake dead, along with those who allied themselves with him.

Today Storm Rider hoped to end the council with the older chief as his friend and ally. Hopefully, together they could achieve what, working alone, they had not.

As was usual, Storm Rider opened the council in a solemn and orderly way.

The pipe was central to all ceremonies, and its motions varied with the occasions.

Today the real calumet was to be used. The pipe was always kept packed in many layers of cloths and skins, making a roll as thick as a man's thigh.

Not to be opened until the full council was assembled, it had been placed before Storm Rider, its present owner, on a piece of scarlet cloth. Everyone became quiet and watched Storm Rider open the ceremony by unrolling the pipe. With each layer of skin and cloth, he always uttered different words.

Laying aside the first layer, he said, "Peace we wish."

With the second, he said, "Look over us, *Wah-con-tun-ga*, Great Medicine."

With the third, he said, "This to the sun."

Lastly, as he rolled aside the fourth layer, he said, "This to the earth."

Each declaration gave value to each layer of cloth and skin, until the pipe and stem appeared with a tobacco sack, then a bunch of sweet-smelling grass, a probe for the pipe, and a small sack containing a charm.

Chief Storm Rider filled the pipe from the tobacco sack, but did not yet light it.

He rose from the blankets and pelts and stood beside the large central fire. He solemnly presented the pipe to the east, singing a gentle and harmonious song, then presented it south, west, north, to the sky, and lastly to the earth, repeating the song at each presentation.

In conclusion, he turned the pipe slowly three times. All there responded by saying, *"Hoo-o-oo,"* when Storm Rider placed the pipe on a scarlet cloth beside him. Storm Rider lifted the pipe again and lit it with a piece of the sweet-smelling grass.

For nearly a half hour the pipe was passed around in silence, handed from mouth to mouth, making its full circuit. Storm Rider then laid it down again and opened the meeting by stating his reason for gathering the two tribes.

"My Crow friends, welcome to the soldiers' lodge of my people," Storm Rider said.

He looked from man to man, his eyes stopping at the older Crow chief.

"Chief Blue Thunder," he said. "I am a mild-mannered man, who has been a chief for five of my twenty-five winters. For these years I have searched for the killer of so many of our Assiniboine people, including my beloved parents. Chief Blue Thunder, I have called you and your chosen warriors together to sit with me and my warriors in council. I am honored that you are willing to sit and smoke with us."

"It is good to be here, and *pila-maye*, thank you, for this opportunity to hear what you have in your heart," Chief Blue Thunder said, his gray hair hanging in two tight braids down his thin back.

He wore only a breechclout, revealing shoulders and a chest that once were muscled, but now were thinning, having grown gaunt with age.

"I see the importance of peace between your people and mine, and I do welcome you to the area," Chief Blue Thunder said in a low, dignified voice. "My band of Crow are not as powerful and as self-sufficient as they once were. As friends, our bands should feel at liberty to hunt on both of our lands.

Speak of what else you have on your mind, my brother."

"It is known that you have the same *toka*, enemy, as my people," Storm Rider said. "Of course I speak of the Snake. With your band of Crow working with my band of Assiniboine, we can finally rid all lands of the vermin who has, until now, eluded capture. Together we would outnumber that serpent of a man and those who ride with him. Also, as friends, we would have one less enemy to contend with and guard our herds from. We can travel safely on each other's land to the Gros Ventres villages in quest of corn, a staple for us both. And we can winter together in peace and run buffalo and share the meat and skins. Do you see how much better off we would be as friends? What do you say, Chief Blue Thunder, to my suggestion?"

Everyone listened as Blue Thunder, who did not hesitate at speaking his mind, responded. "For my people's part, I will say that we welcome your offer of friendship, and are willing to aid your hunt for the renegade who has taken so much from my people, as well," he said tightly. "Good, wise men such as you are scarce. Being so, they should be listened to and loved. Chief Storm Rider, I speak for all of my people when I say that we welcome you as our ally. We *are* better off as friends than enemies. I vow to you to look elsewhere when the hunger for stealing horses heats my warrior's blood. If any of my warriors goes back on my word and steals from you, he will pay dearly. The act of stealing from you, our new ally, will be punishable by death."

"I vow to you the same," Storm Rider said. He squared his shoulders proudly, knowing that he had won a victory with a Crow leader who had at one time been his own father's enemy.

But times had changed.

Alliances needed to be made, and Storm Rider saw in the older chief's midnight eyes an honesty and truth that years ago might not have been there.

Today was different.

The old chief saw the need for such honesty and truth for his small band of Crow to continue to exist.

"I remember your *ahte,* father, well," Chief Blue Thunder said, a sudden glint coming into his eyes. He leaned forward so that the flames of the fire made shadows across his thinning face. "Your *ahte,* was a *wicasa-iyotanyapi,* an honorable man. We went against each other often in warring, but not to kill. It was the challenge of stealing horses, not the actual fight, that we enjoyed. I could never have aimed an arrow at your father, nor he at me. The challenges that brought us together made us more friends than enemies, yet we made certain none of our warriors were aware of this. It would have taken away from the joy of the chase. Do you see what I am saying, Storm Rider? Do you feel the same way sometimes when you come up against a foe? That you would do anything to keep him alive in order to continue the opportunity to challenge him?"

Storm Rider was stunned to hear the old chief admit truths that his own *ahte* never had.

It made him feel a sudden, strange bond with this old chief.

He smiled at the chief. "Feelings between men as you have just described are rare," he said. "I am glad to know that you had such a relationship with my *ahte*, and no, I have never shared the same feelings with any foe. You see, I have tried hard not to make many foes. My goal in life has been to keep peace so that my people could live long, prosperous lives."

"But there is this one common *toka* between us," Blue Thunder said. He folded his arms across his bare chest. "The Snake. I hope for the day I will see him writhing on the ground as the snake he is, not only in name, but in deed. He is not someone I would ever keep alive for the challenge of besting him. His challenges are not in horse stealing, but in terrorizing people, then killing them."

"It is good that your men and mine will come together as one in finding the Snake and giving him his final, well-deserved punishment," Storm Rider said. He nodded. "And that we will, Blue Thunder. In the memory of my father, we will!"

Storm Rider stood up and smiled from man to man. "Today's council was *waste*—good, very good—but it will be the best possible only once we have shared in food!" he proclaimed. "Come outside, where our women have prepared a feast! We shall eat, sing, and talk more of success in the hunt, and I do not speak of hunt for buffalo. This hunt is for the Snake and his evil, murdering cohorts!"

The response from everyone was a loud, abrupt, "*Hoo-o-oo!*"

Chapter 2

Wanting to acquaint himself more with the lay of this new land, Storm Rider rode his magnificent strawberry roan in a slow lope through knee-high waving grass.

He was entranced by the loveliness all around him: the mountains, the bluffs, the trees with their autumn leaves a patchwork of color, and the cool, clear water of the streams and rivers.

The water was so clear and unspoiled, he could see fish clearly as they swam along the rocky bottom, looking like the slow movements of moonbeams, or at other times darting as suddenly as a lightning strike.

Yes, he was glad he had brought his people here to live, to prosper. And now that his relationship with the neighboring Crow encampment seemed secure, he hoped that the Snake would finally be apprehended and killed.

He was determined to seek the demon out, and this time realize the vow that he had whispered over the grave of his beloved chieftain father—a vow to hunt down and destroy the man who had murdered his parents and so many more of their Assiniboine people.

By nature, Storm Rider was not a vengeful person, but after the deaths of his parents and so many other loved ones at the hand of the Snake, he now lived for vengeance.

Storm Rider had even postponed taking a woman into his lodge as a *mitawin*, wife, because he put his need for revenge before the needs of his body.

Prayer had gotten him through the bodily hungers he felt, as prayer had helped him through these weeks, months, and years since his parents' deaths.

Prayer had led him to this place where everything seemed too beautiful for any evil to be lurking in it.

But he had learned tragically that someone with a deranged mind was always out there ready to terrorize, to kill, to frighten, to taunt.

And where there was such a man, there had to be someone to put a stop to his evil ways.

Storm Rider was that man!

Soon the Snake's evil deeds would be a thing of the past. Then, and only then, could Storm Rider think of other things . . . most important, having a woman in his blankets to love, to cherish.

And then there would be children!

His thoughts came to a quick halt when he saw a horse on the ground a short distance away, obviously dead.

Storm Rider brought his own steed to an abrupt stop and drew his rifle from its gun boot. The downed animal was the color of a red cloud.

He focused on the arrow imbedded in the horse's side. Blood pooled from the wound onto the ground beneath it.

Storm Rider looked cautiously from side to side, then peered more intently into a thick stand of aspen trees at his left, in case anyone lurked in the shadows.

He saw nothing, and heard only the rustling of the tree's golden leaves like the sound of a slow, falling rain.

Again he gazed at the fallen steed, its dark eyes locked in a death stare.

Slowly, mindful of everything around him, Storm Rider rode toward the horse.

When he reached it, he dismounted.

He made sure that he kept his rifle ready to fire should a sound from somewhere nearby alert Storm Rider that he could be the next victim.

Still there was only the rustling of the leaves, and the heaving breaths of his steed that seemed more labored as it sensed the presence of death, evil, and danger.

Concentrating again only on the downed animal, Storm Rider noticed a painting of the likeness of a black snake on the shaft of the arrow in its side. The feathers of the arrow were also black, taken from a raven.

"He is near," Storm Rider whispered to himself, his heart pounding with the anticipation of possibly coming face-to-face with his enemy today.

Ah, he had waited so long. . . .

"The Snake is so near that I can smell his stench," Storm Rider said aloud with a snarl. If the evil one was close enough, he would hear the hate and determination in his voice.

But Storm Rider had to think of something else now, as well. Where there was a horse, there had to have been a rider. Where was the one who had been in this horse's saddle, riding across the land the same as Storm Rider, too trustingly?

Out of nowhere the Snake had emerged and had shot the horse. But what of the person who rode it?

Where could he be? Had he been wounded? Had he crawled off to die? Or had the Snake downed the horse and then taken the innocent one captive?

The sudden sound of a whimper made Storm Rider's shoulder tighten. He took in shallow, guarded breaths.

A trap! he thought suddenly.

Could this be a trap?

Was the Snake hiding close by and pretending to

be wounded? Or was it someone else, the rider who had saddled this horse this morning, who had more than likely stroked its thick mane and spoke loving words into its ear, as Storm Rider did every morning to his beloved, faithful horse?

Out of nowhere had tragedy struck again, as it had so many times with the Snake?

Storm Rider knew this was one of his enemy's tactics. He would come out of hiding to strike fear in the hearts of innocent ones. Then his victims could no longer live each day in peace and quiet. The Snake knew that sometimes this was just as devastating as the actual slaying.

Surely the man lay in his blankets at night laughing at those he had brutalized, planning to kill them perhaps the next day, or the next.

Yes, Storm Rider did believe that today's dark deed was done for that purpose, and that it was not the Snake lying in the tall grasses, pretending to be weeping from pain. It was his victim, and Storm Rider had to find him and offer help.

Still keeping his rifle ready should his assumptions prove wrong this morning, Storm Rider looped his horse's reins over a low tree limb, secured them, then walked stealthily onward. Again, he heard the sound of someone in pain which led him through the golden-leafed aspens.

He carefully wove himself in and around the

lovely, white-barked trees, then stopped and stared disbelievingly at what he saw a short distance away.

It was not a man the Snake had harmed today.

It was a woman! She sat beneath a tree, holding her ankle. She tried to stand and put weight on it, but winced with pain.

His heart leaped in his chest when he recognized the victim. It was Talking Rain, the mystical *hinzi-win*, yellow-haired white woman he had heard so much about since his arrival to this area.

Finally he could meet her, the woman known to perform valorous acts usually done only by a brave warrior, such as stealing horses, having a huge success on the buffalo hunt, and many more feats. She was known to be a good huntress, both on foot and on horseback.

Of course he had thought that all the talk was exaggerated, for what woman could ever do as was rumored about Talking Rain?

Yet even so, he was intrigued by her and eager to meet her. Myths were created from stories like hers and carried on and on through the years, as they were about heroic chiefs.

He smiled, wondering how she must feel to inspire such tales. Did she feel proud? Foolish? Or conceited?

Yes, finally he could see her up close. One time he had spotted her riding below him as he sat on a bluff overlooking his new land. He had been exploring as he was today.

Now, this close, he was in awe of her utter loveliness.

From a distance he had noticed her long, golden hair blowing in the wind as she rode, and a body well hidden beneath the buckskin clothes of a man.

Her face, streaked with paint when he had seen her before, was now marred by the tears of a woman.

Having learned to use all of her senses keenly, Talking Rain heard the faint snap of a twig as Storm Rider took a step closer.

With the quickness of a snake's lethal strike, she leaped to her feet momentarily forgetting the pain in her ankle. Her knife was like a streak of lightning as she drew it from its sheath at her side.

"*Ahpe*, wait. Remain calm," Storm Rider urged. He was stunned at the speed with which she had moved to her feet. This proved that she was not injured seriously, which was good.

"I am a *kola*, friend," Storm Rider said guardedly. "I am Storm Rider of the Assiniboine nation. We are friends to your Crow people."

Talking Rain recognized his name, for she was awed by everything she had heard about him. Glad to finally meet him face-to-face, Talking Rain lowered her knife to her side.

"I know you," she said, her eyes fixed on his.

"My adopted chieftain father had recent council with you."

"Yes, that is so, and I am also aware of you," he said.

He was still captivated by her beauty, her thick golden lashes and gently sculpted features. Her lips were luscious, full, and inviting. Her blue eyes seemed to be looking right into his soul, as though she could read his every thought, especially one he had forced to lie dormant for far too long . . . desire.

Desire for a woman!

With her shapely figure so enticing, her soft voice matching her beautiful name, how could Storm Rider not see her as a woman, rather than the warrior she so obviously tried to portray?

"How do you know of me?" Talking Rain asked.

She realized that this man was seeing more of her than she wanted to reveal, and she was observing more of him than she wished. He was perhaps the most *owanyake-wasten*, handsome warrior, she had ever known, and his voice was filled with such a gentle warmth.

And his muscles!

Even though he was fully clothed in fringed buckskin, the cords of his muscles strained beneath the fabric, confirming the rumors—he was a man of endurance, strength, and pride.

Her thoughts were stilled when he spoke again.

"How do I know of you?" Storm Rider repeated.

A small smile quivered across his full lips. "Does anyone not know of this mystical woman who is white, yet lives as though she is red-skinned, and who has ridden with warriors on horse-stealing expeditions and buffalo hunts as though she were a man?"

He paused and took a step closer. He could tell his words had made her stiffen, and had brought a flash of daring into her lovely blue eyes.

He liked the spirit in her, the difference.

And he saw the defiance in her eyes, so could the rumors possibly be true? Was she as strong and courageous as she had been made out to be? If so, he wanted to discover what made her different from every other woman he had ever known.

Yes, a woman like her was rare . . . rare indeed.

"You know how unusual it is for a woman to do these things," he continued. "In fact, you are the first. As we all know, a woman's true place is at home doing womanly duties and chores."

He paused and gave her a closer, lengthier gaze.

"Why are you so different?" he suddenly blurted. "And how is it that a white woman has adapted so well to feats that Indian women would never want to brag about were they even capable of them?"

Her own people had accepted her chosen style of behavior, so she had never before been questioned at such depth about her skill. Insulted, Talking Rain lifted her chin defiantly.

"I owe neither you nor anyone else an explanation of why I do what I do," she said, her voice tight. "I am my own person, as you are yours."

She tried to stay composed beneath the searching eyes of this Assiniboine chief, yet it was hard. At times like this, when she was reminded of her skin color, she was catapulted back in time to when she was called Tabitha June, and had a white mother and father.

She ached inwardly, momentarily haunted by that day when her world was changed in treacherous waters—when she saw her true mother that last time before she was swallowed by the river.

It did pain her so to remember.

Choosing the life that she had, that of valor and strength, had been her way of fighting off such memories. Staying busy with present challenges kept those of her past locked away. And after seeing her true mother unable to even swim, Talking Rain had sworn from that day forth to be strong in every way.

She had lived through the one horrible ordeal of her life. She would endure anything else that stood in the way of her happiness . . . even handsome chiefs who dared to enter her domain, and who made her feel something deeply within herself that no man had before.

She suddenly wanted to prove herself to him, so

that he would know that what he had heard about her was not rumor, but truth.

And she did not want any man, ever. She would always remember how her parents had constantly argued . . . how they loved yet hated one another.

How could she ever forget that final day with them? During their last moments together before the explosion, they had been ranting and raving at each other.

Her parents' loud, angry voices rang in Talking Rain's ears even now, reminding her that to fall in love with a man was a trap. To love was to hate . . . and to fight.

No, she did not want a life like that. She didn't want to bring children into such a world. She wanted no man to war with.

And although she had seen a different sort of relationship between her adopted parents, who shared only sweet words of love, she could not believe it would ever be the same for her. Her true parents' blood ran through her veins, and surely their inability to love each other would be her legacy from them. She might not ever be able to love a man with a gentle sweetness.

She winced as pain shot through her ankle again. It reminded her that she had been taken off guard today. Because of her carelessness, she had lost her beloved horse, and was momentarily rendered almost helpless.

The loss of her horse was far more hurtful than her ankle, though. An ankle would heal. The ache in her heart over the loss of her horse never would.

"I see that you are hurt," Storm Rider said when he saw her flinch. She had not been able to camouflage her pain, even for a moment.

"No, I am not," Talking Rain said, telling an obvious lie. She hoped that he hadn't heard her crying earlier. She hoped her face wasn't streaked by the tears she had shed—tears more for her horse than the pain of her injured ankle. She wanted no man to see the weak side of her, or believe her to be like any other woman.

"I found a downed steed," Storm Rider said. He was trying to choose his words more carefully, since this woman so obviously guarded her responses. "Is it yours?"

Again the regret at her carelessness, which had caused the death of her horse, made Talking Rain fight back more tears.

She didn't respond to his question, for she knew that if she did, her voice would reveal the hurt she felt so deeply.

"Did you see who shot the arrow that killed your horse?" Storm Rider asked, ignoring her refusal to admit that the horse was hers. He knew that it was.

Again she didn't respond. She needed a few moments more to regain her composure and speak without emotion in her voice.

Storm Rider found it hard to understand why she was purposely being stubborn. Was she embarrassed by having been found looking weak and alone? Or was it because she did not want to discuss someone besting her?

"I saw the arrow with the drawing of the snake on its shaft," Storm Rider said. "I know of only one man who uses that figure to identify himself. The Snake. The Snake killed your horse, yet spared your life. Do you understand the meaning behind such a decision?"

"Yes, the Snake did it," Talking Rain admitted. "The coward that he is, he shot from the cover of the trees. But I saw him ride away. I heard his crazed laughter. He is insane!"

"Yes, an insane man who enjoys spreading fear, death, and destruction wherever he goes," Storm Rider said.

He stepped closer to Talking Rain.

"Do you see why he did this today, why he only toyed with you, instead of killing you?" he asked. "Since you are known for bravery, he did this to scare you."

"Or he might have done it as a warning of things to come," she murmured, swallowing hard.

"He *kakis-niyapi*, torments, taunts, then kills," Storm Rider said.

He knew that his bluntness would be frightening to any other woman, but surely not Talking Rain.

She did not seem to be the sort who would fear anyone or anything, or she was good at pretending.

Inside her heart she might be afraid, as would anyone who had come face-to-face with death and luckily survived. Even a man would feel those emotions.

"You should no longer be alone," he stated. "I will escort you to your village. The Snake might be waiting to attack you now that you are injured and horseless and no longer able to fend for yourself. Let me see you safely home."

He glanced down and noticed that she still stood without putting any pressure on the one ankle. He could tell that she was still in quite a bit of pain.

His gaze moved to her face. "But first, let me take a look at that ankle," he said.

"I must decline both of your offers," Talking Rain replied stubbornly. "I can see to my own safe return. And our village shaman will see to my injury, not you. You are a stranger to me."

Talking Rain couldn't help but resent this man, because his band of Assiniboine was stronger than her Crow band. She had seen how eager her father was to ally himself with him and felt it was wrong.

The Crow had suffered losses for as long as she had lived with them. But they always came back again strong enough not to ask for favors elsewhere.

She found it hard to believe that her father had allowed this young chief to look more powerful in front of the warriors who had sat in council with him.

Had she been there, a part of the council, she would have spoken her mind.

She would have discouraged her father from accepting help, and in doing so revealing just how much help he did need in his people's time of trouble. Yet she knew that sometimes pride could get in the way of progress, and it was evident that her people were suffering.

She just hated that her father had sought help from such a young chief . . . a young chief who knew how to insult women, then in the very next breath be kind and decent to them.

Yes, she had never met a man who confused her as much as Storm Rider, or who made her feel strangely foreign to herself. He awakened feelings in her that were so very new.

"And how can you get home when you can hardly even stand, and without a *mitasunke,* a horse?" Storm Rider said, arching an eyebrow.

He had never met anyone as stubborn. She was so anxious to prove that she was capable of fending for herself, even though she had already been bested today by someone.

"*Huka,* I am not afraid. I can walk well enough to find a horse to steal, and then I will manage well enough to get home by myself," she said.

She smiled almost wickedly into his wondering

eyes. "So you see, *gauche,* chief, I am *not* as other women," she said, her eyes daring him. "What you have heard about me is not rumors. Everything you heard is true, told by my people who know me, not by those who only guess about me. I have always found ways to see to my own welfare. I learned the necessity of doing that on the day my mother died. She did not know enough of swimming to save herself from drowning in the river."

"I have heard tales of you stealing horses, but still I cannot help but feel that those stories—your reputation—are exaggerated," Storm Rider said, his lips lifting into a slight, teasing smile.

Talking Rain gasped, for this man would not stop insulting her. She could feel the heat of anger in her cheeks. The audacity of this man, practically calling her a liar! She curled her fingers into tight fists at her sides.

"You . . ." she said, finding it strangely hard to find words in her anger. Usually she was a match for any man in heated dialogue!

Her eyes widened in disbelief when Storm Rider suddenly reached out and whisked her fully into his arms.

"What do you think you are doing?" she yelled, as he began carrying her through the aspens to his tethered steed.

She pushed at his chest and squirmed in an effort to get free.

"Put me down," she commanded. "Stop. Let me go. Do you hear? Wait until I tell my father how you have not only insulted, but manhandled me as well."

Storm Rider gazed into her angry face. "Now you are sounding like a little girl who needs protection from a father, not a fiery woman who tries to prove that she is more man than woman," he said, his eyes twinkling. "Which are you? A girl-woman? Or a man-woman?"

Another sharp pain shooting through her ankle made Talking Rain momentarily forget what he was saying. She quit struggling and reached out for her ankle. Just touching it made her feel suddenly nauseous.

She had to fight hard against crying again. She would rather die than let Storm Rider see her cry. He was infuriating, yet there was no denying that she found him handsome and noble, a man of such strength.

Oh, how could she allow herself to feel these things about him? She had never been this way before about any other man. Why now? Why him?

"I know that you are in pain," Storm Rider said, his voice now soft with understanding. "Why not stop putting on such a tough front and allow me to take you home? You know the dangers of being left alone, especially without a horse. The Snake could be waiting to finish what he started. Your life is in

37

danger, Talking Rain. Let me give you the protection you need, at least until you are safely at your home."

He hoped that she couldn't hear the thudding of his heart, for she would know that it beat that way because of her. He had been that quickly taken with her, a woman who was born white, yet now lived the life of a redskin.

Yes, he was attracted to her but did not know how to feel about a woman who acted so untraditionally.

When he thought of marriage and whom he would choose to be his bride, never had he considered anyone like this woman. Yet, surely so much of how she behaved was pretense. Anyone as beautiful as she had to be harboring a woman's needs and passions deep within her.

He would love to test her, to see.

She struggled again, then sighed. She gazed at him. "Please say no more," she said. "I know how foolish it is to be alone. I do need a way home. Please do take me home."

She couldn't believe that she had given in to him and asked to be taken home, but she truly had no choice.

And she could not deny that his presence did affect her. He had awakened feelings in her that proved she was all woman, feelings she desperately wished to ignore.

He was so obviously astute about certain things

that she was afraid he could see into her heart. Then he would know that when she looked past his insults, she found he stirred delicious feelings inside her, which no man before him had been able to accomplish.

She decided there and then to end the infatuation with this man. A man was the last thing she wanted in her life. A man would steal away everything that she really enjoyed—her freedom to hunt, to go on horse raids, and to do everything else that had given her reason to get up each morning and made life so exciting and worth living.

Could a man actually make a woman forget such things? Could a woman desire a man so much that he became all she wanted of life?

No!

She willed herself not to notice how wonderful it felt to be in his arms, or how enticing his body smelled, or how his voice stirred her sweetly and sensually.

As he gently placed her on his horse, their eyes momentarily meeting, she knew that the beating of her heart was proof that she had a much different battle to win this time.

"I will get you safely home," Storm Rider said. He reached a gentle hand to her cheek. "And then . . ."

She slapped his hand away. "There will be no 'and then,' " she said angrily.

She squared her shoulders and forced herself to look straight ahead, yet was unable to deny that it made her melt when he mounted the steed behind her. His body was there, touching hers. She had never been this close to a man before in such a way.

Then one of his arms snaked around her waist and held her against him as he rode off on his beautiful horse at a steady lope. She knew that she was in trouble.

Her heart was pounding like thunder!

High on a bluff, a tall, very lean man with a snake tattooed on each upper arm sat on his black horse, his dark eyes gleaming as he watched Storm Rider ride through the tall grass with Talking Rain.

The Snake laughed menacingly under his breath. "*Anhe*," he whispered with self-satisfaction. "*Waste-wasteste*, good, very good."

Yes, his plan had worked far better than he had hoped. He had managed today to lure two enemies into a trap, and even though he had an easy opportunity to kill them now, he decided he wasn't ready to do it just yet. He was enjoying toying with them too much.

The waiting only enhanced his pleasure, for in the end, there was no doubt in his mind that he would be the victor.

First Storm Rider would die, then Talking Rain, and then Chief Blue Thunder!

Chapter 3

As Storm Rider rode into the Crow village with Talking Rain on his horse with him, everyone stopped their chores and stared.

Talking Rain saw the wonder in the eyes of her people and was embarrassed by it, for this was the first time they had seen her helpless. She was even seated on a horse with a warrior instead of riding her own.

Oh, how she detested the very thought of the Snake, and hoped that she would somehow have a role in his death. She would love to be the one who sent an arrow through his dark heart.

Now achieving that goal was more important than before. She had something to prove to this man whose arm was still wrapped around her waist. If he witnessed her shooting the murderous demon, would not that finally prove once and for all that her reputation was real and not simply rumor?

Her thoughts were stilled when she saw her

mother rush from her tepee, then stop at the sight of her daughter on Storm Rider's horse.

Talking Rain sighed, for she knew that her mother was not only wondering why she had to be brought back on someone else's steed, but was perhaps just a mite pleased that she had to ask the aid of a man.

Her mother had tried hard to change her into someone Talking Rain did not wish to be—a woman who did a woman's tasks, who did not get joy from hunting and stealing horses.

Did her mother see this one slipup as the beginning of a change in her daughter? Could her mother see that something in Talking Rain had changed? That a man had captured her heart when no other man ever had?

Although River Song had long ago given up convincing Talking Rain to take on a more traditional female role, Talking Rain loved her Indian mother very much and admired her in that role. Her adopted mother never raised her voice to her husband, but, at the same time, never cowered before him either.

In truth, Talking Rain envied her mother's traits. But still she could not allow herself to be anything but strong and independent. After being made so quickly defenseless as a child that day long ago, Talking Rain *did* want to remain strong, not frail like most women her age. She would never allow what happened today to happen again.

Her eyes softened when her *ahte* stepped from his large chieftain lodge and stood beside her *ina*, mother. He was a man who understood her in every respect and admired her for what she did.

Perhaps a small part of him would have loved a more timid, cuddly daughter, yet his eyes always showed that he was proud of the difference in her. He had never tried to change her an iota. She had to wonder what he would think of her weakness today, allowing the Snake to best her.

Above all else, her mother and father would share two feelings—gladness that their daughter was still alive, and gratitude to Storm Rider for having delivered her safely home to them and their Crow people.

Storm Rider rode onward, then drew a tight rein before Chief Blue Thunder and his wife, River Song. He saw the puzzlement in both parents' eyes and understood, for they were surely seeing their daughter in a much different light than ever before.

She was a woman who had accepted help from a man.

"Chief Blue Thunder, I have brought your daughter home safely to you," Storm Rider said, not yet dismounting. He was waiting to see what Talking Rain was going to say or do. "She fell victim to our mutual enemy, the Snake."

"The Snake?" River Song gasped, her face suddenly stricken with alarm. Her eyes filled with tears as she rushed to Talking Rain and took a hand in hers. "Daughter, tell us what happened. Where is your horse?"

"Mother, Red Cloud is dead," Talking Rain said solemnly. She had to fight hard to keep down the sob she felt lodged in her throat. "The Snake . . . he was suddenly there. He killed Red Cloud, yet spared me."

"I am saddened over the loss of your prized steed, but so thankful that you are all right," River Song said. She brought Talking Rain's hand to her lips and pressed a soft kiss on its palm.

"Daughter, daughter, what am I going to do with you?" she then said, still holding Talking Rain's hand. "You should never be alone. Never. Yet you stubbornly do as you please."

"Daughter, you look well enough, but are you?" Chief Blue Thunder asked, his eyes moving slowly over her.

"When I was thrown from Red Cloud I fell on my right ankle, *ahte*," Talking Rain answered. She reached her arms out for her father. "*Ahte*, please take me inside our lodge. I will tell you everything then."

Chief Blue Thunder eased her from the horse.

He frowned when her foot grazed against his body and she cried out with pain.

"Is it broken?" he quickly asked.

"I hope only sprained," Talking Rain said, her arms around his neck. She gave Storm Rider a glance; then her eyes lingered as Chief Blue Thunder gazed at him with a smile.

"*Pila-maye*, thank you, kind friend, for bringing our daughter safely home to us," Blue Thunder said. "*Hakamya-upo*, come. Come inside and share food and talk. It is the least that we can do for you after seeing so kindly to our daughter's safety."

Storm Rider turned his eyes slowly to Talking Rain. He couldn't tell by her expression whether she wished for him to stay or leave. Though he found it hard to guess her feelings for him, it was very obvious that she resented him in some way—perhaps because he had openly doubted her abilities to hunt and to steal horses.

He hoped that he had not started a rivalry that would end in tragedy, for if she felt the need to prove herself to him, to what lengths might she go? She had managed to stay alive today, when she could so easily have been killed. If she tried to do something valorous now only to prove herself worthy of the tales told about her, she could so easily be the next victim of the Snake.

Storm Rider wondered if he should leave, so that her resentment would not be made to grow in his presence.

Although . . .

"Come, you must rest in our lodge before going on your way," River Song suddenly said. She smiled sweetly up at Storm Rider. "We owe you so much, Chief Storm Rider. We will never forget the generosity you showed our daughter today."

"Yes, do stay awhile," Blue Thunder said, smiling also. "At our last council, we achieved much, but dwelled on the serious side of life. Let us come together today to strengthen our friendship in a more lighthearted way. My wife and I are indebted to you, Storm Rider. You would honor us with your presence in our lodge."

Realizing that it would be an insult to refuse, Storm Rider returned the smile. He avoided Talking Rain's brooding mood as she was carried into her father's lodge, her mother following.

Storm Rider joined them after he dismounted his steed. A young brave took his reins and led his horse behind Blue Thunder's large tepee, where the chief's own steeds were corralled.

After everyone was seated around the lodge fire and fresh logs burned in the center of rocks, platters of food were placed close at hand. Storm Rider watched River Song tend to Talking Rain's swollen ankle, as Chief Blue Thunder left momentarily to summon his warriors on a search for the Snake.

"*Micinksi*, daughter, you must not do these foolish, dangerous things ever again," River Song scolded as she wrapped the ankle with soft white doeskin. "Today should be warning enough that the Snake has something more in mind than scaring you and killing your steed. Until he is dead, you must not leave again unless escorted."

"*Ina*, you know that I cannot promise that," Talking Rain said. Her mother made a final knot in the buckskin to secure the binding over her aching ankle. "I love my freedom too much to allow that weasel of a man to interfere in my daily life. But I promise that I shall be warier of my surroundings. I shall never ever again let down my guard."

"It is done," Chief Blue Thunder said as he came back into the lodge. "Many warriors have left to search for the Snake." He sat opposite the fire from Storm Rider. "I hope you do not mind that I told them to go to your village and ask assistance of your warriors. The more we send out, the easier it will be to find and stop him."

"It is good that you did that, for yes, I agree with you. The more who search for that man, the easier and sooner he will be found and made to pay," Storm Rider said.

He nodded a thank-you as River Song gave him a wooden dish on which lay several slices of baked rabbit meat and bread. He glanced over at Talking Rain. He was very aware that she purposely avoided looking at him. At times he would catch her glancing his way, but she would look quickly away when he returned her gaze.

Her behavior told him that she had something in mind that would prove her skills. He hoped that he was wrong, and simply reading too much into her angry glances, that she would harbor her resentment now, and then soon forget it.

He wanted to know her better, as a man wants to know a woman. But he doubted that she would allow such feelings between them. He forced himself to look away from her.

He listened to River Song as she sat beside her husband and began telling how Talking Rain became a part of their lives. It was a tale of a little girl found on a riverbank, and how they had taken her in and made her their own. She was their daughter in all ways other than birth.

"She is a *ie-wakan-lake*, precocious, headstrong daughter," Blue Thunder said, softly chuckling. "And because we love her so much we have allowed her to do what she wished. We never held our daughter back when she showed an interest and found joy in activities that were not usual for girls. I, more than her mother, have enjoyed seeing the independence in her. But she was born white, of a white community. Perhaps allowing her to do as she pleased among her Indian people will keep her from hungering to return to the life of a white person?"

Blue Thunder's eyes twinkled as he looked over at Talking Rain. "Yes, I will be the first to admit that she is spoiled," he said. "But she is still a special person who cares for others, especially our Crow people."

Talking Rain sighed heavily. "*Ahte,* please quit talking about me as though I am not here," she said. "I am certain that you are boring Chief Storm Rider. And . . . surely he has things to do besides sit here listening to a father brag about a daughter."

"Storm Rider, I do hope I have not bored you," Blue Thunder said. He glanced away when he heard movement at the entrance flap, and then smiled when his other two children came into the lodge.

"I fear, Storm Rider, that I must brag a little more of my family, and then I shall see you to your horse, for I do understand that you have duties awaiting you at your village, as mine always await me," Blue Thunder said. He gathered a child into each of his arms.

"So I see you have more children than Talking Rain," Storm Rider said. He turned and smiled at the young brave and maiden. "It would please me to make their acquaintance."

"Then I will introduce my daughter, Dancing Wings, and my son, Young Elk," Blue Thunder said, pride gleaming in his eyes. "They are twins, twelve years of age, and were quite a surprise to their mother and father. Over the years, my wife had no success at conceiving."

"But I relaxed after Talking Rain came into our lives. Enjoying our daughter somehow helped me conceive," River Song said. She laughed softly. "I forgot to worry over being unable to have a child, for we finally had a daughter. And like a miracle, I did become pregnant and gave birth to not one child, but two. Twins. We are such a happy family now."

Everyone continued to talk and laugh and speak of the twins and of Talking Rain—still as though she weren't there. Talking Rain was quiet, trying hard to fight the strange, sweet feelings that Storm Rider caused inside her. His very nearness and deep masculine voice prompted a warm quivering in her stomach.

She so badly wanted not to care about him. He was a threat to a life she adored, for she knew how women behaved when they allowed themselves to love too easily. They became prisoners of their own hearts.

And that insult!

How could she forget his scoffing at her ability to hunt and steal horses as well as he!

She suddenly decided that she had to do something to Storm Rider to get past her infatuation with him. At the same time she would prove that he was wrong about her—she absolutely could perform the feats she claimed. Stealing horses was certainly a skill he did not believe her capable of.

Yes!

She would teach him a thing or two about discounting the person she wanted to continue being . . . and that wasn't a woman with a woman's desires!

Yes, she would steal a horse, all right, even if her ankle killed her while doing it. She would steal a horse from his personal corral.

She knew that friends did not steal from friends, but this time she would ignore that, for she had a point to make. And she had to look past the pact her father had made with Chief Storm Rider: that if anyone of their Assiniboine or Crow people stole from the other, the act was punishable by death.

All she could think about was besting Storm Rider and setting herself back on the path that would surely lead her away from these sensual feelings.

Again she was back in that thrashing water, with death and destruction all around her, remembering how scared she had been after seeing her mother sinking into the black void of the river. She had to make certain that nothing ever scared her again; she had to remain strong.

She especially wanted to look strong in the eyes of this man, yet deep down she wondered why it was so important to her, why it even mattered.

She watched Storm Rider and her father leave the lodge. She then listened as Storm Rider rode off on his steed, her memories strong of how it had felt to be on that horse with his muscled arm around her waist.

"Daughter, where have your thoughts taken you? What are you thinking about?"

Her mother's voice brought Talking Rain back to the present.

She smiled sheepishly, and was glad when her brother and sister began asking her about her encounter with the Snake.

"He is just that," Talking Rain said, her eyes darkened with sudden anger at the thought of her beloved steed lying on the cold ground with an arrow in its side. "That terrible, coldhearted renegade *is* a snake, a low-down, cowardly snake. And he is going to pay dearly for what he did today."

Chapter 4

Unable to sleep, Storm Rider rose from his bed of blankets and, in a brief breechclout, went to sit beside his lodge fire.

He wrapped his arms around his knees as he stared into the last glowing embers in his firepit. The logs had burned down to almost nothing.

He flinched when he saw instead of the embers, the lovely face of a woman . . . one he could not get off his mind. This was a mystery to him, for never had a woman lingered so long in his thoughts.

But this was not just any woman.

She had the gentle name Talking Rain and was so intriguing, how could he forget her?

He kept seeing her beguiling blue eyes, flowing golden hair, full, tempting lips, and a body that made him want to undress her and roam his hands over her silken flesh. Even thinking of doing that made his loins ache with heat.

Never before had his mind nor his body betrayed

him in such a way. Why now? Was it because she did not fit the pattern of what a woman should be?

Yes, he was totally confused by Talking Rain . . . why anyone so beautiful wouldn't want to dress in lovely doeskin and wear necklaces around her long neck.

The fact that she was white by birth had nothing to do with his intrigue. In all respects that counted, she was an Indian.

But he could not understand why she didn't realize that every time she rode alone, she put herself at risk.

The Snake was a danger—he could abduct her, rape her, then kill her. And there were others who could be lured into doing the same, who would be tempted by a woman riding alone so daringly free and without the escort of a man to protect her.

"I have got to stop this!" Storm Rider said.

He leaped to his feet and went outside.

He inhaled the fresh night air and stared up at a hauntingly lovely full moon. As he stood there, he tried to force his thoughts from Talking Rain. She behaved differently than any woman he had ever known, yet this only intrigued him more. It had been easy to pretend that he did not believe the tales about her, while all along he knew they were true.

He just had not wanted to imagine that someone so lovely could want to do such manly things when she was in reality feminine in all ways that mattered to a man.

Frustrated, Storm Rider circled his hands into tight fists at his sides.

"Forget her," he whispered harshly to himself. "Think of something else!"

Yes, if he did not send his thoughts down another path tonight, he would not get a wink of sleep. In his mind he would still be picturing her. Obviously she saw him as a danger, too, but he had not missed how she had looked at him when she thought he wasn't noticing.

Yes, when she let her guard down and forgot to be so angry at him, he saw an interest that could be attraction under other circumstances. Were she a woman searching for companionship in a man, she might be sending a silent message that she wanted that man to be him.

"The moon," he whispered to himself.

Yes, he would concentrate on the moon, not the woman, for was it not full and beautiful this night?

He bent down and rested on his haunches, lost in the memory of a night when he was only a child gazing in wonder at that bright, white ball in the black sky. When he questioned his mother about it, she had lovingly taken him on her lap. As they sat on a blanket outside of their tepee, watching that bright light in the dark heavens, she had told him a story that he would one day tell his own children.

His mother explained that this mystery in the sky was called the moon, and that *Wah-con-tun-ga*, the Great Medicine, caused a new moon to grow every time the old one was destroyed.

When Storm Rider asked how the old moon got destroyed, she told him that it was eaten up monthly by a great number of moles, which were known by the name *we-as-poo-gah*, Moon Nibblers.

She had said that the Moon Nibblers were all over the land . . . on mountains, along the prairies, and anywhere that man could travel.

He asked how would he know them if he saw them, and she explained that the Moon Nibblers had pointed noses, and burrowed and hid in the ground when they were not eating away pieces of the moon.

He smiled, recalling his deep relief when his mother had said that no one actually saw the Moon Nibblers, so he did not have to be afraid of ever coming face-to-face with one himself.

The moon, she had gone on to say, was generous—except for nights when clouds covered it, it lent its light for people traveling at night. Stars were sisters and brothers to the moon, and were home to the spirits of ancestors who had left this earth.

His mother had then warned him not to talk to others about the moon and stars, because they were sacred, but assured him that it was a mother's or father's duty to explain this to their children so that the bright light in the sky would no longer be a mystery to them.

She said to think of the moon from then on as having been placed in the heavens by the Great Medicine to give light by night.

He had used this light often on his horse-stealing expeditions and had silently given thanks for its generosity—

His thoughts were suddenly jolted by a sound that made his stomach clench.

His horses.

More than one of his prized steeds were whinnying in his private corral that sat directly behind his tepee.

Just as he should be at this late midnight hour, his horses should be asleep. If they weren't, that could mean only that someone or something was near his corral, or possibly even in it. But surely a person wouldn't be crazy enough to steal one of Storm Rider's horses out of his private stock.

It was natural to steal from a tribe's larger herd, generally corralled beyond the perimeter of their village. But only a loony person would come this close, unless he had something to prove at any cost!

But who? Besides the Snake he had no true enemy, certainly not anyone with so great a need to best him, unless . . .

But no.

Surely not.

Not only injured was she, but she knew the penalty for stealing from his band.

If someone from the Crow Red Root band was caught stealing from the Fox band of Assiniboine, the act was punishable by death!

Yet there it was again . . . evidence that his horses were disturbed as first one nickered, then another.

His heart pounding, he hurriedly grabbed the hatchet that he always left just inside the entrance to his lodge in case of emergencies. He was skilled at using the hatchet, especially if someone was trying to ride away on one of his steeds. He could throw the hatchet and hit a direct target even without the assistance of the moon. The movement in the dark was all he needed to down a thief.

He moved stealthily to the back of his tepee, his eyes and ears alert and the hatchet poised for throwing. He tried to envision the thief as anyone but Talking Rain.

Yet she was the only one who came to mind . . . the way she had glared at him too many times when he had found her and taken her home. Those glares were born of resentment . . . a resentment that surely came from his doubt of her ability to steal horses.

Would she still want to prove her point to him knowing the penalty of doing so? She would want him to know that she was responsible, or why would she go to the trouble? Especially tonight, when he knew her ankle still pained her.

As he reached the back of his tepee and saw who was leading the strawberry roan, his favorite steed, from the corral, he knew that he had been right. Talking Rain would go to any lengths to prove to him that she was as talented at stealing as her reputation boasted.

He lowered his hatchet to his side.

Just as Talking Rain started to mount his steed, he spoke her name. Startled, she stumbled and fell to the ground on her back. Storm Rider slid the handle of his hatchet into the waistband of his breechclout and went to Talking Rain. He stood over her, his feet anchored on either side of her body.

The light of the moon revealed a woman not afraid, but instead filled with a cold, quiet resentment. She glared up at him.

"Your *ahte* was right. You are *ie-wakan-lake*, precocious. Why would you attempt such a foolish thing as this?" Storm Rider said.

She continued to lie there. No muscle in her lithe body moved; nor did her eyes. They were locked in battle with Storm Rider's.

"Talking Rain, must I remind you that this act is punishable by death?" Storm Rider then said.

"The vows exchanged between my father's Red Root band of Crow and the Fox band of Assiniboine stated that no *man* can steal without such a punishment as a result," Talking Rain hissed out. "Nothing was said about a *woman*."

Storm Rider slowly stepped away from her.

He then knelt beside her. She still had not moved so much as a hair since her embarrassing fall to the ground.

"You find it too convenient to use gender when it most benefits you. Are you not working hard to prove that you are a man?" Storm Rider replied sarcastically. "Do you wish people to ignore the beautiful woman that you are, and see only that side of you that pretends to be male? If so, why do you tonight use your womanhood to ward off the punishment that you know that you have earned?"

"It matters not to me who calls me what, and as for tonight, I did it for a purpose," Talking Rain said, defiantly, though she now regretted her decision. She knew what she did was wrong and that he could kill her this moment and be justified in doing it.

But there was no denying that she was not ready to die. She had too many other goals to pursue!

And she resented Storm Rider more than before because she had not been able to achieve her goal tonight.

"You did this for a purpose?" Storm Rider said, arching an eyebrow. Although he almost knew for certain what her reason was, he wanted to hear her say it. "What purpose?"

"I had something to prove to myself, and . . . and to you," Talking Rain said, hating that she had actually admitted this to Storm Rider.

She wished now that she had stayed in her blankets and had tried another means of proving her worth to Storm Rider, and on another night.

As it was, Storm Rider had caught her red-handed, and she doubted that she would ever get another chance to prove anything to him.

It was in his right to condemn her to death, or even to kill her himself.

Or . . . to take her as his captive.

But surely he wouldn't do any of those things. He had to know he would make a sudden enemy of her father, and it was in both of their best interests to stay allies, at least until the Snake was found and killed.

"Explain to me why you need to prove something to me, and what you are trying to prove to yourself," Storm Rider asked, surprised that she had not yet attempted to rise from the ground.

He was not yet ready to help her up.

He wanted answers first, which would help him decide what he was to do about her crime tonight.

Certainly he could not let her get away without some sort of punishment. The longer she lay there, the longer he had to think about what he would do with her now that she was a thief.

With Storm Rider's eyes on her, awaiting her

reply, and truly not knowing what to say, Talking Rain looked away.

Storm Rider waited a moment longer. Then, utterly frustrated with her, he took her by the wrists and yanked her to her feet.

"You took my horse from the corral, so it is your job to put it back," Storm Rider said flatly.

He stepped away from her and placed his fists on his hips.

She gave him a glance. Limping on her obviously painful ankle, she led his steed back inside the corral and then turned and gave Storm Rider a defiant stare.

"Now what will you do with me?" she asked, her voice tight with what sounded like hate, even as she knew that she could never hate this man.

She found herself taken in by the mystique of this young *gauche* who was loved by so many people. The longer she was with him, the more she felt for him. She fought against these emotions with every fiber of her being, yet the longer he looked into her eyes, the weaker her defenses became.

"What will I do with you?" Storm Rider said.

He stepped closer to her.

He bent down, his face so close to hers that they both felt each other's warm breath.

"What do you believe you deserve as punishment for tonight's crime?" he asked, their eyes locked. "Death? Or life?"

That word *death* stopped Talking Rain's heart as though it had been pierced by an arrow. She swallowed hard, and then forced herself to straighten her back and look past him.

"And so you will not wager a guess, will you, as to what I am going to do with you?" Storm Rider said. "Then you shall wait until I am ready to tell you."

He took her by a wrist and led her from the corral, around his tepee, and then inside his lodge.

He pointed to a blanket spread beside the fire.

"Sit," he commanded.

Having no choice but to do as he said, Talking Rain sighed heavily, then eased down onto the blanket. When a pain shot through her ankle, she tried not to cry out or grab for it.

She had only walked from where she had left her own horse hidden in the shadows to his corral, and then from the corral to his lodge. But that was enough to have inflicted pain on her ankle. It throbbed, and she could see it had swollen even more beneath its bandages. She forced herself not to feel it, nor to look at it.

She gazed over the glowing embers of the fire and past Storm Rider, where he sat opposite the firepit from her.

"What am I to do with you?" Storm Rider said. He was struck by her loveliness, even though her face was marred by a stubborn frown. "If you were a man caught red-handed stealing my favorite steed, you would already be dead. But as it is, you most certainly are a woman, and the Crow chief's daughter."

He paused thoughtfully then said, "Yes, because I have made a pact of friendship with your *ahte*, I must be careful about how I make you pay for the crime you almost succeeded in committing."

He waited for her to say something, or to at least look at him.

But she persisted in staring stoically past him, her lips pursed tightly. She refused to respond to anything he said or did.

"For now, until I decide your fate, you are my *winu*, captive woman," Storm Rider suddenly said.

Finally he got a reaction out of her. He saw her flinch and knew that his words had at last touched a nerve. Slowly he would break through the barrier that she was trying so hard to place between them, for he knew that she did not truly hate him.

He never would forget those moments after he had taken her home, when he had caught her looking at him with something other than resentment. He realized then that the woman in her was trying to take over her heart, and she was fighting this with all of her might!

He glanced at her ankle. "You do know that it was foolish to use your ankle so soon after such an injury," he said. "But, of course, tonight you have done more than one foolish thing, have you not?"

She turned flashing eyes toward him. "Nothing keeps me down for long, and absolutely no one can keep me *winu*, captive," she spat out. "*No* one."

"Must I remind you that I am not just anyone?" he said. His eyes gleamed into hers. "I did not get the title of *gauche*, chief, *otancan*, the principal leader of my people, for making poor decisions, especially about whom I do or do not take captive, or when I might give them their freedom . . . if ever."

Talking Rain's eyes wavered as Storm Rider looked directly into them.

He tried not to weaken in his determination to make her pay for what she had done. But more than that, he wanted to find a way to bring out the true woman in her.

If holding her captive was the answer, so be it!

Chapter 5

A full night had passed well into the next day, and still Talking Rain had not allowed herself to go to sleep since being forced into captivity by Storm Rider.

She wanted to prove to Storm Rider that her endurance outmatched even his. So far, she had won.

He had given in to sleep shortly after securing her wrists behind her with buckskin ties, and binding her ankles with his so that she could not get up and run away as he slept. One movement and he would be awake.

She smiled as she recalled having devilishly toyed with him through the night. She had purposely yanked on the ropes many times to awaken him.

When his eyes had met hers, she knew that he saw her defiance even at that late hour, when most women would be asleep. She had given him a prideful smile, glad that at least in this, she was besting him.

But it was when he fell asleep the last time that her resolve had weakened, for she had foolishly gazed at him at length without his knowledge.

She had even crawled closer, so that she could look more easily at his face, her pulse racing at his handsomeness.

And up that close, she smelled his manliness, which caused a strange sort of ache between her thighs.

Realizing how their proximity continued to affect her, she had crawled as far away from him as the ankle rope would allow.

For the rest of the night she sat stubbornly erect, even though her eyelids had grown heavy with the need to sleep.

Just as she had almost given in to her exhaustion, the sun had risen in the morning sky and cast its golden glow down the smoke hole and onto Storm Rider's face, awakening him.

That was a short while ago.

Talking Rain had just now returned from bathing in the river with the other women, having been told that should she try to flee, the women would catch her and bring her back to Storm Rider's lodge. She felt refreshed. She wore a clean dress that one of the women had given to her. The same woman had even loaned Talking Rain her brush made from porcupine quills. Her hair now lay in lustrous golden waves down her back.

For the moment she was alone in Storm Rider's large lodge, and thankful to be free of bonds. But she knew that did not give her any chance to escape. Two warriors were posted outside the tepee on each side of the entranceway.

But at least being untied made her captivity easier to accept.

"Though for how long shall I be forced to *stay* captive?" she whispered as she sat closer to the lodge fire.

The river had been colder than usual, due to snows that had fallen much earlier this year in the higher mountains, and laced the runoff with cold.

She knew that winter was not that far away. She had listened to her *ahte* say that if they wanted to find and kill the Snake, they had to do it now, or get stopped by the heavy snows that come not long after the autumn leaves fall from the trees.

So surely Storm Rider would return her home when he went to meet with Blue Thunder to discuss strategies for the manhunt.

Perhaps even today . . . ?

The distinct smell of food turned Talking Rain's head just as Storm Rider shoved the entrance flap aside and came into the tepee carrying an assortment of cooked meats and slices of apples that she knew he had taken from the orchard not far from her own village.

It was said that long ago white people had spread

apple trees on their journey west. After devouring the delicious fruit they had brought with them from their former homes, they had thrown apple cores away and thus left the seeds to take root.

Trees had sprung up everywhere. The delicious red fruit was enjoyed by her people every autumn.

"Did you find the river warm enough for your bath?" Storm Rider asked as he knelt and placed the tray of food beside her. "The snows came early this year in the mountains, which means winter is not far off."

"The river is never too cold for my bath," Talking Rain said, lifting her chin. "Even in the middle of the winter, when I can find a place in the river not blanketed with ice, I will take delight in bathing in it. And you? Do you bathe, as well, when the waters are cold? Or do you do as most *women* do . . . bring the river water and warm it over the fire before washing?"

Storm Rider found her admission quite ludicrous, for he had never seen any woman bathe in the river when it was even partially covered in ice. He found her attempt at insulting him humorous. So again he gave her a half smile and said nothing. He would avoid insulting her all over again by letting on that he didn't believe her.

"All right, I can tell that you don't believe me again," Talking Rain blurted out. "And do you think I care? All I want to know is when I will be free to go. You plan to take me home to my father today, do you not? You do not plan on punishing me for what I did, or attempted to do, last night. I would have never kept your horse. I just wanted to prove to you that I was capable of stealing it."

"And so your tales go on and on, do they?" Storm Rider said, his eyes twinkling. "If you are really known for stealing horses, you would never consider giving one back. So you would be much better off saying nothing if you cannot say something I will believe."

She was taken aback by just how much he didn't trust her. She wished she could rush to her feet, run past him, and at least try to escape. Listening to his insults was worse than the captivity itself.

But she stayed her ground.

The low grumbling of her stomach made her realize how hungry she was, and her eyelids were getting heavier by the minute from want of sleep.

Her fatigue and hunger made her feel even more trapped. She had to get him to release her, to escape not only his annoying comments about her, but also her obvious growing fascination with him. Sometimes, when she let down her guard, Storm Rider's handsomeness almost took her breath away.

Yes, she must eat and sleep so that she would be revitalized and could devise a clearer plan to free herself.

She grabbed a piece of meat and stuffed it into

her mouth, followed by sweet bites of apple. She ate until she was comfortably full. But the food had made her even sleepier. She couldn't stop herself from yawning, nor could she keep her eyes open.

"Enough is enough," she said to Storm Rider. Again she yawned and stretched her arms above her head. "Do you not think it is time to stop playing this game and let me return home? My mother and father will be sending warriors to search for me. Do you really wish them to find me held captive by you?"

"You have eaten; now you can sleep, for it is obvious that by stubbornly refusing to sleep last night, you cannot stay awake much longer," Storm Rider said. He wiped his mouth clean with the back of a hand. "Lie down. *Istima,* sleep. I have my own morning bath to see to."

He glanced toward the entrance flap, then gave her a soft smile. "Do not try to leave, for you will be stopped the minute you set your feet outside my entrance flap," he said, standing. "Rest now, Talking Rain. Perhaps when you wake up you will accept your captivity and decide to behave better in my presence. Behaving badly gains you nothing, absolutely nothing."

"Are you saying that I am a true . . . true *winu,* captive . . . that you are not going to let me return home?" Talking Rain said, her voice drawn and weary. "How can you? And what of my *ahte*? He will despise you. You will have him not as an ally, but as a bitter enemy forever."

"When your father learns of your wrongdoing, he will understand my choice. He would expect worse . . ." Storm Rider said. "Now go to sleep. When you awaken, I do expect you to be more accepting of the fate you brought onto yourself."

"You won't get away with this!" Talking Rain cried.

She tried to leap to her feet and force her way past him, but her ankle made her crumple onto the blankets and pelts in pain.

"Rest and allow that ankle to heal," Storm Rider said firmly.

She watched him leave, then turned onto her stomach and began crying in frustration. But crying made her even sleepier. Finally she drifted off, then awakened a while later when she heard a movement in the lodge.

She turned slowly to one side and saw Storm Rider standing beside the lodge fire. She could not help but stare at him. He was sleek and wet from his bath in the river. His raven-black hair hung damp and loose across his shoulders and down his back.

He left the lodge and came back only moments later, his chest and arm muscles straining as he carried in an armload of firewood and dropped it on the opposite side of the fire from where she lay.

Her heart pounded as she watched him position

logs amidst the slow-burning flames. His every movement proved how strong he was.

He suddenly looked her way and caught her watching him. Their eyes locked and she could tell by the mischief in his that he knew what she was thinking, and the true effect he had on her.

For Storm Rider, it would be so easy to forget that Talking Rain was a thief and to treat her like the woman he knew existed beneath her tough exterior. His heart's desire was to carry her to his bed and show her exactly how it felt to be a woman.

But he had never forced himself on any woman.

He would not start now.

He turned from her, pushed his mane of hair back from his shoulders as he rose to his feet, and left the tepee.

Outside he sucked in a deep breath. Having her there and not pulling her into his arms was going to be perhaps more of a challenge than stopping the Snake!

He gazed at the soldiers' council house.

He was glad that he had a meeting awaiting him there, for he needed something to distract him from the woman . . . if anything ever could!

With determination he stamped to the council house and entered.

As his warriors watched wordlessly, he sat beside the lodge fire and stared into it, silent and moody. His warriors shared wondering glances.

*   *   *

Talking Rain sat up and watched the buckskin entrance flap sway with the breeze.

She had noticed the haste with which Storm Rider had left the lodge, and she understood. Yes, he was finding himself drawn to her, as she was to him.

"Oh, why did I get myself in this mess?" she whispered harshly to herself. "This isn't the way it was supposed to be."

She gazed pensively into the flames of the fire.

She had always made careful plans. Never had she anticipated that proving herself to Storm Rider might end up proving more to him than she wanted—that she was falling under his spell!

Chapter 6

Talking Rain sat uneasily beside Storm Rider in the soldiers' council house. After she had awakened from her nap, Storm Rider had taken her here, where he was now in the process of gambling.

She knew that it was rare for a woman to be present in the council house when gambling was the late afternoon's entertainment.

Women were normally forbidden to be around the men while they gambled, smoked, laughed, and sometimes even partook in a drink that made them slightly intoxicated.

She could not believe that Storm Rider brought her there simply because he did not trust her enough to leave her at his lodge. She was afraid that she might be used as a pawn in the gambling ... that Storm Rider might toy with her, making her believe that he planned to gamble her away. In truth, though, she couldn't see that happening.

Talking Rain knew from the way Storm Rider looked at her when they were alone that he wanted her as a man wanted a woman. Yet might that be why he chose to gamble over her? To prove that he didn't care what happened to her?

She was torn and hated being there, and the men gave her glances that made her more uncomfortable by the minute.

She wanted to plead with Storm Rider to return her to his lodge, but her pride would not allow it. Whatever he chose to do today, so be it. She would prove to him that she was not a whining baby, that she was just as strong in her convictions as she had thus far shown herself to be.

Smoke from the men's pipes swirled around her. She forced herself not to cough, but to endure this, as well, while the man who brought her there seemed to have momentarily forgotten her presence.

She glared at him as he continued with his game. She knew that most of the Crow warriors' leisure time, either at night or during the day, was devoted to gambling in various ways. Even back at her village, when the soldiers' lodge was not occupied by business matters, the men entertained themselves gambling.

The rattle of the bowl dice could be heard in many private lodges too.

Some women were as addicted to the practice as men, though their games were different. And not being in possession of much property, their losses, although considerable to them, were not as distressing as the men's.

The warriors gambled for more serious prizes. Wives were even known to be played for when all else was gambled for and lost by a particular warrior.

Talking Rain recalled how a few moons ago one warrior of her village had killed another when he refused to gamble his wife.

That had led to a ban on gambling for a while, but the warriors had such an appetite for it that it soon resumed as their primary pastime.

So now she believed that the Assiniboine warriors were the same in this respect. They obviously enjoyed the game of chance as well.

The Assiniboine's principal game was the same as the Crow's—that of the bowl, or *Cos-soo*, which involved a wooden bowl, highly polished inside and out, with a flat bottom a foot or less in diameter. The rim turned up about two inches.

Today several were involved in the game, which would continue until one of the warriors had to give up everything in his possession to those who had bested him.

A man held the bowl inside the rim by the tips of four fingers, his thumb underneath. Dice were placed in the bowl and were thrown up a few inches when the man struck the bottom of the bowl on the ground, so that each die made several revolutions. It was a game of complete chance, and no one could take advantage in making the throws.

Suddenly a commotion outside the lodge caused the gamblers to stop and set down the bowl.

Chief Storm Rider stood and went to the entrance flap to see what was happening.

Talking Rain was too curious to sit and wait to know, herself, and did not want to sit among the warriors without Storm Rider at her side. She pushed herself up from the blankets and, limping, went to Storm Rider.

Just as they stepped outside, she heard a familiar voice.

It was her younger brother! Young Elk had come into the Assiniboine village for the first time.

She wondered why he had arrived alone. She knew that he did go horseback riding on his own, but had been warned against it, since the Snake was so close and eager to harm anyone who crossed his path.

But nothing would keep her headstrong twelve-year-old brother from doing as he pleased.

His father had been as understanding with him as he had with Talking Rain. Young Elk was free to follow his dreams and desires. Blue Thunder had taught all of his children the importance of independence.

Storm Rider glanced down at Talking Rain. "Is not that your brother, Young Elk?" he asked, then faced Young Elk as he approached, holding his horse's reins.

"Yes, that is my brother," Talking Rain said. She lifted her chin proudly. "Somehow he knew that I was here and has come for me."

Before Storm Rider had the chance to respond, Young Elk stepped up before him. His eyes, though, were on Talking Rain, not on the powerful Assiniboine chief.

"Talking Rain, Father has sent many warriors out searching for you since you went missing last night," Young Elk said. "I separated from them and searched in my own fashion for you. Big Sister, you taught me the art of tracking. I followed the path of your horse's hooves and they led me here. Why are you here? Why did you stay the night instead of returning home so that our parents would not be worried? It is not like you to stay a full night from our village and home."

"Ask *him*," Talking Rain said tightly, giving Storm Rider an angry glance. "Ask him, little brother, and see what he has to say to explain my presence here."

Young Elk's gaze shifted to Storm Rider. "I sense that my sister is not here because she wants to be," he said. He squared his youthful bare shoulders, his only attire a brief breechclout and moccasins. "Why is that, Chief Storm Rider?"

Storm Rider looked over at Talking Rain. "Do you really wish me to tell him about your failure as a horse thief, or would you rather confess to it?" he said, his eyes locked with hers.

"You tried to steal a horse? You failed?" Young Elk said, his eyes wide. "Whose, sister? Whose did you attempt to steal, and what does it have to do with Chief Storm Rider?"

"It was his horse, Young Elk," Talking Rain said, sighing heavily. "I attempted to steal Storm Rider's favorite steed."

"Why would you do that?" Young Elk gasped, his eyes darting again to Storm Rider. "And what is her punishment?"

"She said that she was stealing my favored steed to prove something to someone," Storm Rider said.

"To whom?" Young Elk asked, looking anxiously from his sister to Storm Rider.

"That does not matter now," Storm Rider said. "But what does is that your sister must pay for her crime. Both she and you know of the pact agreed upon between myself and your father: should anyone from either of our bands steal from the other, the act would be punishable by death."

"Death?" Young Elk gasped as he took an unsteady step away from Talking Rain and Storm Rider. "You will kill my sister for attempting to steal your horse? You . . . would do that?"

"No, Young Elk, he does not plan to kill me, but he is holding me *winu*, captive," Talking Rain said. She then gave Storm Rider an angry look. "He is probably even planning to gamble me away to the one who wins *Cos-soo* today," she said sarcastically. "The game had just begun when we heard the commotion of your arrival in the village."

"You would gamble for my sister in such a way?" Young Elk said, obviously stunned by the whole situation. "My *ahte*—"

"Your *ahte* will understand that I have the right to deal with your sister in whichever way I choose, for the pact between us was a serious one," Storm Rider replied tersely. "Now, Young Elk, be on your way. When you arrive at your village, relate to your *ahte* how it is that I have your sister. Tell him that she will remain my *winu* until I decide otherwise."

Young Elk placed a hand at the knife sheathed at his side. He glared at Storm Rider. "I demand you release my sister to me now," he said angrily. "She is to go home with me. If not, my *ahte* will send many warriors to get her, and then the peace will be gone as quickly as it was achieved between you and my band of Crow."

"I think not," Storm Rider said, his eyes dancing. He admired this young man's spunk. It matched his sister's, and Storm Rider realized at this moment that when he had his own children, he wanted them to be as strong and independent as these two. He admired these traits.

But he did not admire the threat that accompanied this young man's show of bravery.

"Young Elk, you know the art of gambling well, for *ahte* has taught you," Talking Rain said quickly. "Little Brother, offer to gamble with Storm Rider to see who will truly have me. When you win, you can take me home. Then all of this nonsense will be behind us."

"There will be no gambling between your brother and myself, not now, not *ever*," Storm Rider said. He glared down at Talking Rain. "You are mine. I do not need to gamble with anyone to prove it."

He turned angrily to Young Elk. "Leave now," he said. "Go to your *ahte* and tell him that Talking Rain is no longer a part of the Crow people. She lost that identity when she tried to steal my prized steed. She is now mine. She is my *winu*."

"She is no one's captive," Young Elk shouted as he doubled his hands into tight fists at his sides. "Release her now, or I swear to you that I will return soon with many warriors and get her. Should you try and stop us, do not be surprised if many of your people die in the process. Right now, my only concern is the welfare of my sister."

"Young brave, you are lucky that your sister did not die instantly when I found her stealing my horse," Storm Rider said heatedly. "You tell your *ahte* that I urge him to understand and not resort to violence over this, for anyone who sat in council the day we Assiniboine and Crow vowed friendship and decided upon the payment for the crime of horse stealing between our two bands will know that I am within my rights to keep this woman and to do with her as I please, even if she *is* the daughter of the proud Crow chief."

A strange silence ensued as Talking Rain and Young Elk stared disbelievingly at Storm Rider. Then Young Elk gave Talking Rain a quiet, apologetic look, turned, and walked toward his waiting steed.

"Young Elk, *ahpe*, wait, no . . ." Talking Rain said in a whisper as she reached her hands out for him.

She watched him ride from the village at a hard gallop, soon to be lost from her view.

She turned angrily to Storm Rider. "You will be sorry you did that," she said, her voice catching. "My *ahte* will not allow me to stay here with you another night. He will never allow you to keep me as your captive. You will see. You will see soon."

Then she lifted her chin boldly, her eyes narrowed. "*I* would like to join your gambling game," she said, her voice filled with determination. "I want to play for my release, for, Storm Rider, I know that I can play *Coo-soo* as well as you."

"And why am I not surprised to hear you say that?" Storm Rider said, chuckling. "Of course you do everything as well as a man, do you not? If so, in what other ways do you think that you can best me, warrior to warrior?"

"Just name it," Talking Rain said. She smiled wickedly and placed her fists on her hips.

"For now, all games are over," Storm Rider said. His smile turned into an irritated frown. "It was wise of me to take you to the gambling game today, for had I left you alone in my lodge, you would have seen your brother's arrival and run to him in an effort to escape, only to get you both hurt when my warriors would have been forced to stop you."

He gave her another frown, then reached a hand out for her. "*Hakamya-upo,* come," he said firmly. "I am taking you to my lodge. I will have to think about today's confrontation with your brother and prepare for however your father might choose to react to the news of your captivity."

"There is no question in my heart how he will react," Talking Rain said hotly.

She winced when he grabbed her by a wrist tightly, so much that it pained her, and walked her toward his lodge. She stifled a cry of pain when her ankle began hurting again.

"I would not be too quick to judge a father's re-action to losing a horse thief to an avowed friend," Storm Rider said.

He half shoved her through the entranceway and into his lodge when they reached it.

"Go," he grumbled. "Sit. And be quiet."

She gave him a hard look.

Then, knowing that she had no other choice than

to do what he said, she went and sat beside the lodge fire.

She tried to envision Young Elk's entrance into the Crow village, and her father's reaction to the news of her captivity.

She sighed heavily when she thought of what her mother's might be.

Her mother would be filled with an instant despair.

That alone made her regret what she had done.

Chapter 7

"How can he do this? This is *sheetsha, sheetsha,* bad, bad!" Chief Blue Thunder shouted as he paced back and forth in his soldiers' council house.

He stopped, his long bearskin robe swishing around his legs as he turned abruptly toward Young Elk.

His brow furrowed, he gazed down at his young son. "Tell me again what Chief Storm Rider said," he demanded. "Tell me again the attitude of your sister."

"*Ahte,* Chief Storm Rider said that I was to tell you that he is within his rights to hold my sister, your daughter, captive, and that you should understand his reasoning for this. She was caught stealing his prized steed," Young Elk said.

He was very aware of how his father kept clasping and unclasping his hands—folding his fingers into tight fists, then releasing them, only to make tight fists again. He had seen his father angry many times before. But never had he seen his *ahte* this angry. And he had good reason.

Young Elk was just as upset and angry.

"Continue," Blue Thunder said in a growl when he saw that his young son was having difficulty relaying the full message again. "My son, I must hear it once more; then I shall decide what actions we will take."

"*Ahte*, Chief Storm Rider told me to tell you that Talking Rain is no longer a part of the Crow people, that she lost that identity when she placed a hand on his prized steed," Young Elk said, his voice drawn.

"*Ahte*, he said . . . that my sister is his," Young Elk repeated. "And although he said that she was his *winu*, the way he said 'mine' made me believe that he has more in mind than keeping her captive. I believe, *ahte*, that he might see her now as his woman. Do you think that he would marry her even though he thinks her nothing more than a horse thief? Is he taking advantage of her being there because he might have decided to . . . ?"

"What brings you two together alone in the soldiers' council house?" River Song asked as she rushed into the lodge. "Is it about Talking Rain? Young Elk, did you discover the whereabouts of your sister?"

She stopped and looked from her husband to her son, and saw their worried expressions.

She grabbed Blue Thunder by an arm. "*Mihigna,* husband, tell me what causes such a frown on your face?" she asked, her eyes wide. "Why don't you or Young Elk respond to my questions?"

Her face suddenly draining of color, she slowly dropped her hand down away from him and took a step backward. "No," she said in a gasp. She stared wild-eyed up at Blue Thunder. "Do not tell me that Young Elk brings bad news to us about our daughter."

Again she reached out and grabbed Blue Thunder's arm. "Please do not tell me she is . . ."

Blue Thunder placed his hands gently on her shoulders. "No, our daughter is not dead," he reassured her. "But Young Elk did discover where she is. Wife, she is safe, but . . ."

"But?" she cried, searching his eyes for answers. "What do you mean? What are you finding hard to say? Where is Talking Rain? If she is safe, why is she not safe here, at her own home, with her family?"

She yanked herself away from Blue Thunder, and turned to Young Elk.

"Son, tell me where Talking Rain is and why you did not bring her home," she said, her voice catching.

Young Elk made no reply.

"Why am I not to know?" she cried. "Why are you being so cruel to this mother who loves her daughter so much, as much as had she been carried inside my womb?" Her voice broke. "I would die for her, Blue Thunder. *Die!*"

He suddenly grabbed her into his arms. "It is not easy to tell you this," he said, his own powerful voice weary. He held her close. "But the important thing is that she is not harmed in any way, and that she could not be any more safe here than there."

"You still talk to me in circles!" River Song cried as she wrenched herself free of her husband's embrace. "Tell me the truth about our daughter, or I shall despise you forever for this moment."

Blue Thunder was taken aback by his usually genteel wife behaving so unlike herself. He stared at her disbelievingly.

"She is in the possession of Chief Storm Rider as his captive," he rushed out. "She is safe there, so at least be happy for that, my wife. She was not harmed in any way when she was caught stealing Storm Rider's horse, except for her pride. She has never before been caught in the act of stealing a horse, until now."

River Song gasped and took an unsteady step away from Blue Thunder. Young Elk reached out for her. She just as quickly brushed his arm away.

She swallowed hard. "She is being held captive?" she repeated, her voice wavering. "She was stealing a horse . . . the young chief's horse?"

Then she spoke much more loudly. "I do not understand why she would do this," she said hoarsely.

"And even then, I do not understand why Chief Storm Rider would treat her so harshly."

She paused, her eyes filling with tears. "And I sat with her beside her bed of blankets last night until she was asleep," she murmured. "She seemed in such pain with her injured ankle. She seemed so innocent, like a small child again as I sat there looking at her. I love her so much. Was she planning all along to do this terrible thing while I watched her devotedly? Was she not even asleep after all? Was she waiting for me to leave so that she could carry out her scheme? No. I do not understand any of this. How? Why . . . ?"

"Did you not see how Storm Rider seemed to rankle our daughter's nerves so easily when he brought her home to us?" Blue Thunder said.

He sighed as he took River Song by a hand and led her down onto a pallet of pelts and blankets beside the lodge fire.

Young Elk joined them, choosing to sit beside his mother, who seemed to him to be in a slight state of shock.

"Yes, but I found it hard to understand, especially since he was kind enough to bring her back after discovering her horseless and wounded," River Song said.

Again she searched her husband's eyes. "Husband, I am finding all of this so hard to understand. That word 'captive' . . . How can our daughter be treated as though she were a vicious criminal by the very man you made an alliance with only a few short moons ago?"

"She is being treated as a criminal because, my *mitawin,* she *is,*" Blue Thunder said.

"But it is valorous to steal horses, to strengthen our own herd," she argued.

"You did not sit in council with me and Storm Rider, nor hear the determination with which our alliance was made. Even horse stealing was discussed between us," Blue Thunder said. He inhaled deeply before continuing.

"*Mitawin,* wife," he then said, "we agreed that there would be no horse stealing between our Red Root band and their Fox band, and that if any of our warriors were caught stealing from the other, the act was punishable by death."

"Death . . . ?" River Song gasped. Her shoulders swayed as she felt instantly faint.

"No," she said on a sob. "Not our daughter . . ."

"No, that will certainly not be our daughter's fate," Blue Thunder reassured her. "But, *mitawin,* our daughter was aware of the punishment for stealing horses. Any warrior caught in the act could face a death sentence, and she attempted to steal Storm Rider's steed anyway."

"No," River Song cried. Then she grabbed Blue Thunder by the arm. "But, husband, did you not say that if a warrior stole, *he* could be condemned to die? You did not say that a woman would suffer the same punishment. That being so, couldn't our daughter be set free to come home to us?"

"Do you forget so easily? Our daughter has always walked in a man's moccasins more than a woman's, and she has tried to prove this in every way possible. So why would she not be made to suffer the same punishment as the warriors she emulates?" Blue Thunder said, his voice drawn.

He paused and sighed, then said, "It was her choice to master horse stealing over making moccasins. So, in the eyes of those she has wronged, she is as much of a threat as any warrior."

He paused again, then added, "This time she was again trying to prove herself and was caught and bested by a man . . . and not just any man, but a young chief whose pride will not allow him to set her free as though she has done nothing wrong."

"And so what is his plan for her besides . . . besides holding her *winu*?" River Song asked. "Where will this lead, husband? Where?"

She leaned toward him. "And what are you going to do about it?" she asked solemnly.

He framed her face between his hands. "*Mitawin*, have you not always trusted my judgment in all things?" he said.

"Yes," she murmured, reaching up to cover one of his hands with hers. "In everything."

"Then trust me with this," he said softly. "I must think carefully before I act."

"Do not take long," River Song said, her voice low and urgent. "This time your decision involves our daughter . . . a daughter who is no longer in the loving hands of her family, but instead . . . a *man's*." She added, "Yes, a man who until recently was a total stranger to us. It was you who sat in council with him, not I. You had the opportunity to guess his true worth, and whether or not he was trustworthy."

"Yes, and I studied him well and learned through his words he could be trusted in all ways important to our Crow people," he said. "I saw him as a good man with a good heart whose intentions are pure and honest. Together we hope to stop the Snake's evil. Alone, it has not been possible. But together we are large enough in number to hunt him down and kill him."

"But this has nothing to do with the Snake," River Song said, her voice breaking. "This is our *micinksi*, daughter. And she is being held captive." She lowered her eyes and visibly shuddered. "Captive . . ."

"I think there is more on this young chief's mind than holding our daughter captive," Blue Thunder said. "I saw how he looked at her the other day. He saw in her the woman that any man would be blind not to notice. After all, she is very beautiful . . ."

"Husband, you do not believe that he will claim her as his wife, do you?" River Song gasped out, aghast at anything being forced upon her daughter, especially marriage.

River Song had wanted her daughter to eventually put aside her foolish desire to hunt, steal horses, and all the other skills she had perfected since she began challenging boys, and then men, her age.

River Song had hoped that Talking Rain would feel the call in her heart to be a wife and a mother. If Talking Rain put as much effort into these roles as she had into the other activities that River Song had been forced to accept so long ago, then she would be a wonderful wife and mother!

But to have marriage forced upon her?

By a stranger?

The thought sickened her.

"Think about what our daughter did," Blue Thunder said. He slowly rubbed his chin. "She must have been stealing that horse for some other purpose than simply to add it to her corral—she can already boast of having many. And she did this under the poorest of circumstances. To go in the dark of night, alone, injured, and knowing that the Snake could still be waiting for the chance to abduct her, says to me that stealing this particular man's horse meant more to her than even the fear of danger."

He continued. "And why do you think she would want this so badly knowing she was forbidden to steal a horse from our new allies? Perhaps it was because she is infatuated with the one she stole from and wanted to impress him. Maybe she saw her feelings as a threat to life as she has known it, and she needed to send him a message: that she would chance getting caught to prove to him that she is capable of doing anything she chooses."

"Husband, you are talking in riddles. I find it hard to understand your logic. Our daughter could not care for a total stranger so much that she would risk her life foolishly, trying to impress him, or to make him loathe her so that he would not pursue her," River Song said. "Husband, you must go and demand her release."

"I have thought this through, over and over again, and still nothing explains the foolishness of our daughter's deed last night. It does not make logical sense to me, either," Blue Thunder grumbled. "I have to find a way to make Storm Rider release her, so that our alliance will not be broken, not when we have so much to gain by remaining friends."

He kneaded his chin some more, thinking that perhaps *he* should be the one to go to any length to keep a lasting peace between his people and Storm Rider's.

He slowly smiled at a thought that did make some sense, but he did not speak it aloud to his wife. If Storm Rider was so adamant about having

Talking Rain, surely it was for other reasons than to imprison her.

Maybe Storm Rider had fallen beneath the spell of her loveliness and decided to take her as his wife. Yes, the more he considered it, the more he approved of such a prospect. Would that not solve many problems, especially for his daughter?

He avoided his wife's searching gaze, for she would not agree with what he had just decided to do. She had already voiced her opinion about the young chief keeping Talking Rain for a very private, selfish reason—to marry her!

There came a time in a father's life when he wanted his daughter to marry a fine man and bear children so that he could enjoy grandchildren before his time on this earth was over.

Yes, he did hope that a man like Storm Rider could tame Talking Rain and bring out that part of her that Blue Thunder knew was gentle and sweet . . . and feminine.

His decision was made, and he would not tell his wife just yet. He would wait for her to adjust to Talking Rain's absence, for all mothers had to eventually give up their motherly ties to their daughters.

This time it would happen in a most unconventional way, yet the more Blue Thunder thought about it, the more it seemed the best solution for his daughter, and for ensuring a safe, trusting relationship between the Red Root band of Crow and the Fox band of Assiniboine.

He and Storm Rider now had not just one common goal—to find the Snake—but also to make sure that Talking Rain was happy. Had not seeing to Talking Rain's happiness been Blue Thunder's goal since the day he had found the half-drowned waif lying beside the river?

He did believe that a man was the answer to his daughter's lasting, true happiness, and he now knew that was Storm Rider.

Chapter 8

"My *ina* will be devastated," Talking Rain blurted out. She looked over at Storm Rider as he slid another log into the fire. "It is not fair to make her suffer for something I did. I will not beg you, but I will ask once again to allow me to go home so that my mother will not have to agonize over my safety. She does not know you. How can she trust that you will do me no harm?"

"You should have considered her feelings before you foolishly attempted to steal from me," Storm Rider said. He settled onto his haunches beside her. "You made a very bad decision coming to my private corral instead of going where the rest of my people's herd is kept. Your chances of success were far less stealing so near to my lodge, where you should have known that I would hear you. Like all Assiniboine, I was trained as a child to be alert to all sounds."

He leaned closer so that their eyes were even with each other's. "It is as though you planned to get caught," he said, his lips tugging into a slight, teasing smile. "Is that not true? You wished for me to find you in the act of stealing?"

His eyes twinkled into hers. "If so, tell me why that is so," he said.

Talking Rain was angry that he could see so deeply into her soul and know that she had feelings for him other than loathing. Even she had not been sure how to react to the sensual feelings he had awakened within her. Momentarily forgetting the pain in her ankle, she leaped to her feet and glared down at him.

"You are wrong about why I chose to steal from you," she said. "I did not plan to fail. I would never purposely allow myself to get caught, especially by you. I wanted to prove my skills, nothing more."

Storm Rider rose to his feet.

He smiled even more devilishly, especially when he saw how her eyes wavered when he took a step closer.

"I believe that you are confused about your motives," he said. "Do you truly not realize that your heart plays more of a role in this than you wish to admit?"

When she said nothing, he shook his head. "No," he said. "You would not admit that you are fighting hard to remain loyal to your side that has always worn a man's moccasins instead of a woman's. Perhaps you have worked too hard at being all things no true woman would ever want to be."

"A true woman?" Talking Rain gasped. "Are you saying that . . . I am not a true woman?"

"Are you, or are you not?" Storm Rider asked more seriously, his eyes searching hers. "Can you answer that? Or are you afraid to?"

"I am afraid of nothing," Talking Rain said in a hiss.

"Then there is your answer," Storm Rider said, idly shrugging. "Nothing more needs to be said. You have proved how you wish men to see you."

Talking Rain felt cornered, and hated that Storm Rider had so unsettled her. She placed her hands on her hips and glared at him.

"Enough of this sort of talk," she said tightly. "It is my captivity that is in question here, nothing else. You will be sorry that you sent my brother away without me. You are foolish if you believe that my father will come now with a mere offering of tobacco to beg for my release, as is the custom between chiefs who wish to remain friends. My father will come like a thief in the night and steal me away; then you will have neither tobacco nor me. And no longer will there be peace between the Assiniboine and Crow. My father will declare war against you for what you have done to me."

She laughed softly. "No, you will not be offered tobacco from my *ahte*, father." Her tone was mocking. "But you might receive something else—a knife in your heart for payment when my *ahte* does come for me."

"You are wrong about so many things, but most of all, about what your father will do when he realizes you are my captive," Storm Rider responded tersely. "Blue Thunder is not your biological father, and you are not so important that he would cause a war between two tribes just to get you back. It is obvious that Blue Thunder needs me and my resources. Since I am so willing to oblige, he will not chance losing the alliance between us."

"No, you are wrong," Talking Rain said hotly. "True, Blue Thunder is not my biological *ahte*, but in both our hearts we are *ahte* and *micinksi*, and I assure you, he will go to whatever lengths he must to get me safely home again."

She laughed humorlessly. "And you are wrong to think of my band of Crow as weak," she taunted. "If you could only have seen them years ago when they saved my life. They were the richest and most powerful band in this region. It is only because disease and raids have taken so much from them that they are not as strong now."

She leaned toward him. "You delude yourself thinking that you are so important to anyone," she spat. "To me you are—"

Tired of bantering with her, and more adamant than ever about taming that wildness in her, Storm

Rider grabbed her wrists. "Enough has been said," he growled out. "Hear me well, woman, when I say that you had best get used to being in my village, for you are here to stay. And you will learn manners as well. You will learn the true meaning of the word *woman.*"

Yes, he would tame that wildness in her; yet if he did, what then?

What would he do with her then?

He did need a woman in his life . . . he needed a wife. *But Talking Rain, his wife?*

That thought made him laugh, for he must be crazy to envision her being anyone's *mitawin,* much less softening enough in her heart to become an *ina,* a mother.

Yet there was a look in her eyes when she momentarily forgot that she was supposed to hate him. Could she . . . ?

Suddenly he yanked her against his hard body and gazed into her lusciously blue eyes. "Yes, you are mine," he said hoarsely. "You are my *winu,* captive, and I cannot help but think it would be interesting to have such a feisty woman in my bed every night. But someone like you, whose behavior is unlike that of any woman I have ever known, would probably not even know how to please a man."

Talking Rain felt the color drain from her face, for his words were like a slap in the face. It was more of an insult than anything he had ever said to her.

And . . . was it true?

She had never considered how men saw her. Oh, but surely they thought of her as undesirable!

Yet she had thought that she had seen a look of appreciation in Storm Rider's eyes when he looked at her. During those brief moments, she felt as though he desired her . . . as though he had looked past her far less than feminine behavior and seen the woman in her.

Had she been wrong? Did he not think of her as anything but a woman who carried the role of warrior too far?

After that first time they had met, she realized he affected her in ways no other man had. She imagined she felt what all women did when they were infatuated with a man. It was a strange yearning . . . a need. It was passion! Had she tried too hard to deny the feelings? If so, would she now regret it for the rest of her life?

Storm Rider was surprised by her reaction. He first saw alarm in her eyes, and then hurt. Had he finally found a way past her defenses?

"In your heart you are all woman, are you not?" he said.

This time she did not lash back at him. Instead she sighed heavily, her eyes steady with his. She said nothing.

When he saw that the fight seemed to have gone

out of her—at least for now—Storm Rider found himself momentarily at a loss.

When she was spiteful, he had found her easier to deal with, because he expected that from her.

But now she seemed somewhat defeated by his questions about her femininity, and he felt a need to reach out for her in a much different manner.

He could think of only one way to fill the empty space left between them by heated words.

"I have something to show you," he said, releasing her wrists. He gave her a soft smile, then nodded toward the pallet of pelts. "Please sit."

He had actually asked her to sit, instead of demanding it of her, and his swift mood change made Talking Rain's own soften. He must have realized how hurtful his words had been, for she *was* a woman, and had a woman's desires.

She could not help but want him, even though she should hate him instead.

Yet there it was, the wild pounding of her heart as he reached out a hand and touched her face so gently, it was as though she were as delicate as a flower.

"I am sorry for saying things I should not have," Storm Rider told her. His eyes met hers. "You *are* a woman. You are a beautiful woman."

His words made her melt inside. "No man has ever called me . . . beautiful, and you have called me that more than once," she said.

"That is because men believed that you did not

wish to hear those words from them," Storm Rider said.

He then stepped away from her.

"I never thought that I would want such a compliment," Talking Rain said. She swallowed hard. "But, Storm Rider, thank you. It *is* special to hear that."

Afraid that feelings between them were changing too quickly, and knowing that she could change her mind in an instant, Storm Rider reached for a buckskin pouch.

"I want to show you something that not many have seen," he said. He slowly opened the bag. "I show only those who I feel will truly appreciate them."

Talking Rain was quiet, awed that he had singled her out to reveal something so special to him, especially after she had been so hateful.

He turned the bag over and shook it. Her eyes widened when she saw what appeared to be beautiful, shiny black rocks falling into the palm of his hand.

"Do you see that scarlet cloth over there?" Storm Rider said, nodding to a cloth that lay folded with his blankets. "Please get it and spread it out between us. What I have will show up much better against it."

Now truly eager to know the mystery behind the

objects in his hand, Talking Rain reached for the cloth, then smoothed it out on the bulrush mats.

"Watch as I spread the glass stones onto the cloth," Storm Rider said. "You will see why they are so special and are kept safely in my bag except for moments like this."

The round black stones rolled onto the cloth, and in the fire's glow Talking Rain could see their loveliness. She sighed. "I have never seen anything quite like them," she murmured. "They are not made of stone, but glass. They must be rare."

"Very," Storm Rider said. He picked one up and held it out for her.

She took it and held it in her palm. She stared at it in wonder.

"Tell me how holding the stone makes you feel," Storm Rider said. He was glad that he had thought of the stones, for they could strengthen the peaceful side of their relationship that was so new to them.

"I feel much spirit and warmth, as though it is actually alive," Talking Rain said, amazed at what seemed to be happening in her heart as she held the glass object.

"Then you are feeling the truth of the glass stone," he said, smiling. "This is a protective stone that shields against harmful forces. It evokes emotional security . . . peace. It calms one's thoughts as it warms the heart. The stone's lifelines actually enter one's soul."

"And you would share such a mystical thing with me, who meant to steal from you, and has spoken so vindictively to you?" Talking Rain asked.

She picked the stone up between two fingers and held it up to the fire's glow. She gasped.

"I can see right through the stone," she exclaimed. "It is translucent. It is more beautiful than words can say."

"The stones are called Apache Tears," Storm Rider said. "It is said that these came from Apache women long ago who were crying for their loved ones lost in battle. When the tears fell to the ground, they turned into these black glass stones."

Talking Rain gazed more intently at the stone. "The story is so sad," she said. "Yet beautiful at the same time."

"As you hold the stone up to the light of the fire, you can see the lifelines in it," Storm Rider said. "They *are* alive and have special healing powers."

"How did you come about having them?" Talking Rain asked, placing the stone with the others on the scarlet cloth. There were all sizes and shapes, yet each was as lovely as the others.

She looked up at Storm Rider. "How did you know their name, their purpose?" she asked.

"They are old, very old," Storm Rider said. He collected the stones and gently put all but one of them back in the buckskin bag.

"How did I find them?" he asked, returning her

gaze. "It happened one day back at our former village, when I was a young brave of twelve winters. We were clearing land for more lodges. The men of my village were having a hard time removing one huge tree trunk. My chieftain father, who was a man of much strength, managed to finally dislodge the roots of the tree, but when he did so, black objects came flying from the ground."

He smiled. "No one knew what they were," he said. "Thinking they might be dangerous bugs, everyone fled inside their lodges until it stopped. When they went back outside, they found the ground covered with these black stones, all sizes and shapes."

He looked down at the bag. "Among them we found a small note written in Apache on buckskin," he said, his gaze returning to Talking Rain. "It told the story of the stones, how as tears they spilled from women's eyes, and falling to the ground, turned into the black glass stones.

"The Apache buried the stones beneath a tree, whose roots then claimed them," he said. "Since my father first uncovered them, he kept them, and then they became mine when he passed on to the other world."

He had kept one stone in his hand. He gazed at it. Then he smiled over at Talking Rain. "Whenever I am feeling restless or worried, I just hold one of my stones in my hand and let the stone's spirit relax me and clear my mind again," he said. "It warms my heart and soul."

"You are so fortunate to have them," Talking Rain replied.

"I had many more, but through the years I have given them, one by one, to those who felt their magic as I have and as you did, as well," Storm Rider said.

He held the stone out to Talking Rain. "This stone is yours, if you wish to have it," he said, smiling.

Talking Rain's eyes widened. She gasped softly. "Truly?" she murmured. "You wish for me to have the stone?"

"Yes, it is yours," Storm Rider said.

He searched her eyes for her true feelings. He could tell that she was deeply touched, and that was good, for he saw this as perhaps the beginning of something more between them.

She took the stone and gazed in awe at it, and then at Storm Rider. "I would love to have it," she said. "*Pila-maye,* thank you. I will always protect it."

"Keep it with you at all times and it will protect *you,*" Storm Rider said. "This stone is your medicine now, and no one else but you should be allowed to touch it."

He got up and went to where he stored his bags. He took from them a small white doeskin bag with a drawstring on it. He handed it to Talking Rain.

"Place your stone in the bag," he said softly.

"Then tie the drawstring to the belt of your dress, and keep it with you at all times."

"I shall, oh, I shall," Talking Rain said as she ever so gently placed the stone in the bag, then tied it to her belt. "Again, thank you."

Pleased with the outcome of the night, Storm Rider said no more to her. He led her to her bed of pelts.

She stretched out onto their plushness, then turned on her side and watched him prepare his lodge fire for the night. She again found herself marveling over his muscles and the sleekness of his copper flesh. She would love to reach out and run a hand across his muscled shoulders. She could even envision herself pressing her lips to his flesh. . . .

When he went to his own bed of blankets and pelts and stretched out on his back, she felt something warm and wonderful go through her, for tonight Storm Rider did not see the need to tie her to him. He trusted her enough to go to sleep without securing her!

She watched him as his eyes closed, then sighed as she found herself more overwhelmed by her feelings for him as the moments passed.

Then she turned on her other side when her eyelids grew too heavy to let her stay awake.

She smiled, clutching the small bag in her fingers. She realized then that for a while she had forgotten the pain in her ankle. Her thoughts had become too involved in a man . . . a man she felt herself being drawn ever closer to.

She went to sleep with him on her mind, and this night, oh, so much in her heart.

Chapter 9

The moon was high in the sky, casting its silver sheen down the smoke hole of Storm Rider's tepee and awakening him.

He opened his eyes and the first thing he saw was Talking Rain, lying there peacefully asleep. He smiled, for he had taken a risk not tying her wrists and ankles again, but she had not taken advantage of it and sought her freedom from him.

Perhaps the special gift had worked its magic on her, and from now on there would be a quiet peace between him and Talking Rain.

Or even more than that, he thought as he rose to a sitting position and continued gazing at her.

There was no denying how attracted he was to her. He wished she would be able to put her wildness behind her and see that a future between them could be possible and good. But could she truly be tamed? Would she ever make a good wife and mother?

He was drawn to her loveliness as she lay quietly

asleep, her thick lashes resting like golden veils against her cheeks. He gently ran his fingers across her cheek, awed by its utter softness against his fingertips. He then leaned low and smelled her flesh. He was so taken by her, he could not help but see her as vulnerable. To him, she was a picture of lovely, sweet innocence. At this moment it was easy to forget the side of her that too often rankled his nerves.

He was so entranced by her he ached, and could not resist brushing a kiss across her closed eyelids.

Then, trembling with want, unable to stand the temptation of his lips so close to hers, he dared to softly kiss her.

His heart leaped when her eyes fluttered open and she wrapped her arms around his neck and willingly returned the kiss. Her sensual moan proved that she found the kiss pleasurable.

Yet did she truly, or had she found a way to fool him into believing she cared? Was he falling victim to an act of seduction, a pretense to achieve, in the end, her goal of freedom? Could she think that he would give her freedom in exchange for sexual favors?

Collecting his senses, he drew away. His eyes were burning with passion as he glared at her accusingly.

Talking Rain was stunned by where her passion for this man had taken her. Then Storm Rider had jerked suddenly away from her, as though she might be poison. Talking Rain scooted away from him, her eyes wide and wondering. He had changed so quickly into her captor.

She had become so lost in passion, she had not realized what her body seemed to do all on its own, as though ruled by its own needs and wants.

"How could you have taken advantage of me while . . . while I slept?" Talking Rain asked angrily, all the while knowing deeply within herself that she had been a willing participant in the kiss.

"Say nothing more," Storm Rider said dryly. He returned to his bed of blankets and pelts. "Just go back to sleep. You can rest assured that I will not do that again."

Her heart pounded. She was confused by how he one moment could treat her so gently, then in the next order her back to sleep callously and unfeelingly. Talking Rain gave him a lengthy stare, then turned her back to him. But she knew now that he had ways to make her forget who she truly was.

She also knew for certain what he meant to her, and saw the danger in it. She had never intended to become enthralled by any man, for marriage was not in her plan.

No! She would not let herself be this man's captive in more ways than one.

She almost hated Storm Rider for causing these

feelings. She loved the life of a woman-warrior too much even to consider doing otherwise.

She was glad when she could feel sleep claiming her again, for she did not want to think any more of tonight. Her feelings were too conflicted.

She had never experienced anything like this before, so how could she know what to do? She felt herself floating into the welcome lethargy of sleep, soon lost again to everything but the peace it brought her.

Storm Rider lay with his back to her, torn by his own feelings about what had happened. He knew now that he must fight with all of his might these feelings for Talking Rain, for he did not see how she could ever abandon the exciting life of a woman-warrior. It was apparent that she did not want anything but that life, despite her response to his kiss.

But she was too stubborn ever to admit to the need that surely ached inside her, as it did so obviously in him.

Yes, he must stop fooling himself into thinking that she could be anything to him. Yet, on the other hand, did he really want to stop pursuing her? Would she not be worth the challenge?

He loved challenges.

And after sharing such a lengthy, deep kiss, he wanted to prove to her how different her life could be.

Yes, he wanted to make her know that she was a

woman. He wanted her to enjoy the wonders of how a man could treat a woman he loved.

Suddenly he heard her sob in her sleep. He turned over on his other side and watched her. He heard the sob again and knew that it was not fake, but coming from deep within her as she slept. He wondered what could cause such emotion. What was she dreaming about that hurt her so much?

Talking Rain stiffened in her sleep and cried out for her mother, caught up in the same dream that plagued her so often . . . of that terrible day when her whole world had changed.

After seeing her mother sink beneath the surface of the water, as she had countless times before in her dream, she was glad when she awakened and could leave it behind again in her subconscious.

She sat up, her eyes wide. She gasped when she saw that Storm Rider was watching her.

Storm Rider leaned up on an elbow. "What saddened you so much in your sleep?" he could not help but ask.

Talking Rain was suddenly aware of the wetness on her cheeks and realized that she had cried in her sleep. She had revealed too much of her weak, feminine side to Storm Rider. Firming her jaw, she gave him an annoyed look, then flopped back down on the bed of blankets and pelts and turned her back to him.

She hated it when a late sob escaped from her lips.

Something made her reach down and circle her fingers around the tiny bag that held the black glass rock. She remembered the gentleness with which it had been presented to her, and the man whose kiss had melted her through and through.

She jerked her hand from the bag and forced her eyes closed, yet sleep eluded her this time. She was too aware of Storm Rider, who was so close that she could hear his even breathing.

She could feel his eyes on her.

She willed herself not to think of him, but instead of how she might find a way to flee this place!

Chapter 10

The sound of horses arriving at his village awakened Storm Rider with a start.

He sat up quickly and glanced over at Talking Rain, who was still soundly asleep. That was good, because he believed those arriving at this early hour had to be Chief Blue Thunder and his warriors.

In case Blue Thunder decided to attack the village in order to get his daughter back, which Storm Rider did not expect, he had made sure that his village was protected. Sentries were in place at strategic points. If they saw the need, they had permission to use whatever means they must to protect their people from arrows or bullets. Thus far, he heard no sounds of fighting.

With only his breechclout on, Storm Rider checked one last time to see if Talking Rain was still soundly asleep. Then he left his lodge and waited for the riders to approach. As they did, he recognized the lead man. As expected, it was Blue Thunder, and he arrived without weapons aimed, which surely meant that this was to be a peaceful council. To be certain, Storm Rider looked past Blue Thunder and saw that none of the ten warriors who accompanied him brought firearms, or had arrows notched to the strings of their bows.

Relieved that Blue Thunder had decided this morning not to kill, or maim, or wrench his daughter from her captivity, Storm Rider nodded at the Crow chief as he finally drew a tight rein directly in front of him.

Then Storm Rider's eyes were averted again beyond Blue Thunder and his warriors. He could still hear more horses arriving.

Alarm shot through Storm Rider as he looked quickly again at Blue Thunder. He was not sure how to interpret the smile on the older chief's face.

Was it a smile of friendship? Or the smile of a man who had chosen to trick Storm Rider today?

Perhaps he had the worst of intentions on his mind, bringing only a few of his warriors with him to call upon Storm Rider at the break of dawn, only to have a much larger force following for a surprise attack.

In a matter of moments Storm Rider saw that his fear was misplaced. The other horses that he had heard carried no men on them. Instead, six warriors led twelve steeds into the village.

Then he saw another steed trailing behind, packed heavily with expensive pelts.

"What is this?" Storm Rider asked, gesturing toward the party. "Why have you come? Why have you brought many horses, and one that is burdened by expensive pelts?"

"I have come for my daughter peacefully," Blue Thunder said, hoping his game would gain him what he wanted in the end. He truly believed that Storm Rider would fall into the trap, a trap that would be in both his and Talking Rain's best interests.

"I will pay well for my daughter's return," Blue Thunder then said. "Chief Storm Rider, do you see the horses? The pelts? They are yours in exchange for my *micinksi*, daughter."

Storm Rider squared his shoulders and tightened his jaw. He had fought and won many battles, yet he knew that taming Talking Rain might prove the hardest of all his challenges, even more difficult than convincing her father to no longer lay claim to his daughter.

But Storm Rider was up to the challenge, and he would win.

"Chief Blue Thunder, I hope you understand when I say that nothing you offer would be enough for me to hand over Talking Rain to you," Storm Rider said stiffly. "You know as well as I that we made a verbal agreement during our council. Should any of our warriors steal from the other tribe, the deed will be punishable by death. Although no Crow warrior came to steal, rather a woman who is your *micinksi,* there is still cause for punishment for the crime."

"Are you saying that you refuse to give my daughter back to me and her mother and her Crow people?" Blue Thunder said just as tensely. "That . . . your plans are to kill her?"

"Your son, Young Elk," Storm Rider began, his eyes narrowing. "Did he come to you saying that I will kill your daughter? If so, he brought home the wrong message. I have no plans to harm your daughter in any respect. But still . . . she is mine, for me to make whatever decision I choose about her. She is my *winu.* But . . ."

"But *what?*" Blue Thunder growled out. "You are planning to keep my daughter, even though you might have just set off the first spark of a fiery conflict between my band of Crow and your band of Assiniboine."

"I would hope that is not the case," Storm Rider replied. "I do not want to war with you, or anyone, except the Snake. And to prove how I wish to prevent the chance of war with you, powerful Crow chief that you are, I am willing to offer you twice as many horses and pelts as you offered me for Talking Rain. Take those you have brought back with you to your village, along with what you choose of my best stock. I will send magnificent pelts to you later."

Blue Thunder's eyes widened.

Then he glowered down at Storm Rider from his saddle. "You would give all this to keep Talking Rain for yourself?" he asked. "You would offer so much?"

"Even more, if required to seal the bargain," Storm Rider said. He took a step closer to Blue Thunder. "And you know that I am being very generous today. You know that I owe you nothing, for your daughter is a thief. But as we are avowed friends, I do this to show how much I appreciate your friendship and want to avoid losing it."

"You will do everything but hand my daughter over to me," Blue Thunder said. He turned away from Storm Rider, straightened his back, then looked again at the young Assiniboine chief.

"Your plan is to marry her?" he asked, smiling to himself at how well this had turned out. His plan had worked. Pretending to be angry had worked. And it was not so much that this agreement would benefit him. He would agree to Storm Rider's offer to benefit Talking Rain.

Although Blue Thunder had met Storm Rider only recently, the tales of his noble, generous, and peace-loving nature made Blue Thunder think that he would make the perfect husband for his daughter. And his daughter was already past the usual age for a woman to marry.

Many of the women of his village wedded when they were mere girls of fourteen winters, the mar-

"As I said, take what you wish of them," he said. "These are my most prized steeds. But if you do not find what you want here, then I will take you to our larger herd. All I want is to know that you are satisfied when you ride from my village."

Blue Thunder stepped into the corral, Storm Rider following him as he and the Crow warriors awaited the chief's choices.

Storm Rider's breathing was shallow as he watched the older chief go from horse to horse, studying them. Blue Thunder tapped one and then another on its flanks, sorting out those he wanted, and his warriors came and separated them from the others.

When Blue Thunder stepped up next to Storm Rider's prized strawberry roan, Storm Rider's heart skipped a beat, for although he had promised Blue Thunder that he could have his pick, he had hoped that his strawberry roan would not be among them. But knowing that no man could turn down such a handsome steed, Storm Rider prepared himself to also lose it to the Crow chief.

Blue Thunder had already chosen a dozen of the special steeds. He stood beside the strawberry roan, stunned by its magnificence. If he got only this one horse in exchange for his daughter, he would walk away content, for never had he seen such a proud steed.

But he did remember seeing Storm Rider riding

this particular horse. That had to mean that he valued it over the rest.

Smiling devilishly, and feeling that he needed to do something to repay Storm Rider's stubbornness about keeping Talking Rain, he tapped a hand on the horse's flanks.

"I have made my choices," Blue Thunder said as he walked back to Storm Rider.

Storm Rider forced himself not to look at his favored steed, knowing that he had no choice but to hand him over in order to finalize the agreement. Stiffly he nodded his approval.

"Round them up and bring them from the corral," Blue Thunder told his warriors. "We will take them to our village."

Storm Rider did not look back as his strawberry roan was led away, knowing that the horse was confused about being taken from the only master he had ever known. But Storm Rider still realized that he had gotten the best bargain, anyhow—Talking Rain.

They went back around to the front of the tepee. When they got there, Talking Rain was standing just outside the entrance of the lodge.

In her eyes was a mixture of emotions—but most of all, hurt. She had overheard everything said between her father and Storm Rider.

For a moment, after she had heard her father agree to let her to stay with Storm Rider in exchange for the horses and a promise of pelts later, she had not been able to move from her bed.

She kept hearing those words over and over again in her mind and could hardly sort through them to make sense of what had happened today.

Her *ahte*, the man she had adored since he had found her alone and brokenhearted by the river those long years ago, had actually given her away? He favored owning horses over having her as a daughter?

Only when they had gone to the back of the tepee to select the horses had she found the strength to get up from her bed to go outside. She exited just in time for her father and Storm Rider to return to the front of the tepee.

She watched, still speechless over her father's behavior, as Blue Thunder mounted his horse, gave Storm Rider a silent nod of thanks, and then—without even glancing at Talking Rain in acknowledgment—rode away with his warriors, the horses trailing behind him.

She gasped when she saw Storm Rider's favored horse among those being led away. Fighting back tears, Talking Rain rushed back inside the tepee.

Storm Rider entered after her and tried to pull her into his embrace. She yanked herself free.

She gave him an angry look, then rushed to her bed and grabbed a blanket. She went as far back as she could in the lodge and sat down, pulling the blanket around her and turning away from Storm Rider.

She fought against the urge to cry, but it was hard. She felt forsaken by the man she had called *ahte*. Since that day she had been orphaned he had become a father to her, and she had loved him devotedly ever since.

She never knew that fathers could give daughters away so callously. Horses were important to all the bands. But this important? Had her father's economic concerns taken precedence over his feelings for her? Had he never truly cared for her as much as she had thought? And what of her *ina*?

For now, Talking Rain was so perplexed she couldn't think, but instead only feel.

She felt betrayed and unloved. But something within her told her that there was more to this than she knew. Therefore, she could not allow herself to fully resent her father. Not yet, anyhow. She would wait and hear his reasoning behind today's actions. For now, all she wanted was to be left alone. She wanted time to think . . . to plan. . . .

Storm Rider understood how she was feeling. Betrayal by a father was the worst kind. He wanted to go to her and soothe her woes, but he knew that was the last thing she wanted at this moment.

He would leave her be. He would let her sort this out by herself, for what could he say to her that would help? Surely she loathed him more than she resented her *ahte*. Yes, for now, at least, he would leave her to her thoughts.

But he knew better than to leave the lodge, for she might be planning to go and question her father about his decision. Storm Rider could not chance that, for Blue Thunder might change his mind and keep her.

He sat down beside his lodge fire and stared into the flames.

Now and then he glanced at the woman he loved, still wrapped in the blanket.

He would occasionally hear a sob, and knew that she was hurting deeply. But something made him stay by the fire.

Eventually, though, he would have to try to make amends with her. But he would wait. He would give her time to face up to her future . . . a future with Storm Rider!

Chapter 11

A maiden brought the morning meal into Storm Rider's lodge, and the smell of food made Talking Rain's stomach growl. She had stayed the entire morning hunkered stubbornly at the back of the lodge, choosing to remain alone, since she was not free to leave the lodge.

But she was weary now of it, as well as hot and hungry. She had wanted to stay there until night came, for that was when she had planned to make her escape. She was going to wait until Storm Rider went to sleep for the night; then she would make her move.

But she needed to eat to have the strength to carry out her plans tonight, which would involve escaping his lodge, then stealing one of Storm Rider's horses.

Yes, she had to go to the Crow village. She must ask Blue Thunder why he had given her up to Storm Rider so easily. Had she not proven her worth time and again to him?

And had he not told her many times how much he loved her?

She wondered also about her mother—if she had argued with him over it, or had accepted his decision since he was not only her husband, but also her chief.

It was because of women like both her mothers—the biological and the adoptive—that Talking Rain grew determined at a young age never to succumb to the weaknesses they did.

The only time she had faltered was of late, and that had been in Storm Rider's arms, or simply in his presence. Then she felt herself succumbing to another sort of weakness—that of fascination with a man, a man she now knew without a doubt she felt more than fascination for.

She realized that she was falling in love with this man, for never in her life had anyone made her feel so sensual. It was as though she were a flower, her heart opening itself to this man, as a flower opens to the warmth of a summer's sun.

Again the scent of the food wafted toward her. She inhaled deeply. Her stomach growled again, and she knew she had to eat some of what Storm Rider was no doubt already enjoying.

But still she paused. She was afraid that Storm Rider might read in her eyes her plans, for, yes, tonight she would flee and get answers from Blue Thunder. She hoped to discover that he had had something else on his mind when he gave her to Storm Rider so easily.

She hoped to learn that Blue Thunder planned to come for her and steal her away, yet keep all of the horses and pelts that he had received from Storm Rider in payment for her. Then she would not have been wrong to give her devotion for so long to Chief Blue Thunder and his wife, whom she loved as much as any daughter could love her parents. If she learned that they had taken her in only to eventually achieve material things, her heart would break and she would never love or trust again.

"The food is good," Storm Rider said.

He was purposely taunting Talking Rain so that she would emerge from her seclusion, still finding it hard to believe that she had stayed there for so long.

He had tried to understand why she chose to behave so strangely, and had concluded that she had felt the need to hide from the reality that her adopted father had given her away to another man.

Yes, it had to have hurt her terribly, especially since Blue Thunder did not tell her why, or even say farewell. Storm Rider had been stunned about that, himself, for how could Blue Thunder have given her up so easily? Did he need this alliance with Storm Rider so badly that he would turn his back on his adopted daughter?

Or . . . was it something else?

Perhaps Blue Thunder thought that he was doing

Talking Rain a favor by giving her to a man he would like to see married to his daughter.

Did he imagine Storm Rider was the man to change her into a woman who wanted the right things in life?

Maybe he had seen how Storm Rider felt about Talking Rain, and guessed that he had not held her captive as punishment, but because he had fallen in love with her and wanted to marry her.

Yes, he understood how Talking Rain could be so confused about what had happened, for he was confused, as well. But he was certain of one thing: He would not disappoint Talking Rain. He would give her a life that she would find far more satisfying than the unconventional one she had grown accustomed to.

Yes, he was going to tame that wild side. He was going to draw from within her the sweetness that he knew was there. He would nourish it so that she would be happier than she could ever imagine.

"The duck tastes of honey today," Storm Rider said, again trying to lure Talking Rain from her blanket. "And the bread? Smell the bread that Summer Stars baked for her chief today. She brought enough for two. But it tastes so good, so sweet, I might eat it all myself."

Her stomach growled unmercifully, and Talking Rain knew that she could not go much longer without enjoying some of what Storm Rider talked about. And she reminded herself that she must keep her strength up for what lay ahead.

She decided to pretend that all was well again between her and Storm Rider. He would trust her enough to go to bed tonight without tying her. Then, she would prove that even he could not stop the confrontation she must have with her father.

Tears sprang to her eyes when she thought of how he had ridden away from her without even looking at her or saying good-bye. It was as though she had never been anything to him—just a pawn to keep peace with a man whose alliance was more important to him than a daughter's devotion and love.

Suddenly she flung the blanket aside and emerged from her hiding place, her hair mussed. By the way Storm Rider gazed at her so incredulously, she must be a sight, and not for "sore eyes," like the phrase her white mother had used so long ago.

Talking Rain knew that she was unkempt in a way she would want no one to see, especially the man who made her heart thunder so wildly.

Talking Rain avoided Storm Rider's eyes, as the food was her objective at this moment. She sat beside him.

Without saying a word, she grabbed a piece of bread in one hand, a portion of baked duck in the other.

She ate ravenously, then gave Storm Rider a glance when she noticed that he was holding out a wooden cup for her. The water was welcome, and she took the cup and gulped it down.

She could see out of the corner of her eye that Storm Rider had risen and gone to the back of his lodge. He came back and held out a hairbrush.

"When you are finished eating, I will leave the lodge so that you can brush your hair," he said. "If you wish, I'll have a clean dress and moccasins brought for you. You are free to go to the river and bathe. No one will accompany you. I trust that you will bathe, then return to my lodge. I would like to talk with you about what transpired today between myself and your *ahte*."

She was touched by his kindness, but still angry that she remained his captive—and not even that any longer. She was his in whatever respect he wished to have or use her. Talking Rain folded her arms stubbornly across her chest and avoided looking at him.

"I can understand your hurt over your father's behavior today," Storm Rider said softly. "I find it hard to understand myself, but the fact is, he did it. He has given you to me. Therefore, you are no longer a captive, but instead, my woman. Talking Rain, there is a part of you, deep in your heart, that knows what has happened between us. You should allow yourself to feel it. When we kissed, your response proved so much to me, and I know it did to you, as well."

He paused. "It is good that you have chosen to accept what Chief Blue Thunder did, and I believe you will even accept your role as a woman, not a warrior, soon," he said. "Your kiss and your eyes have revealed that you are more woman than any I have known. Although I cannot help but admire your fierceness, your difference, I do plan to bring out the woman in you."

Although Talking Rain was still refusing to meet Storm Rider's eyes, there was no escaping how his words were affecting her. It was true that she still felt the wonder of his kiss, and secretly ached for him to kiss her even now. Yet she just could not see herself succumbing to this man—to *any* man.

Yes, more than before, she knew that she must escape . . . and she would.

Tonight!

Chapter 12

The sound of his name spoken in a panicked voice outside his lodge made Storm Rider jump to his feet and hurry to the entrance flap.

He shoved it aside and found himself facing a distressed mother whom he knew well.

It was Yellow Flower. She had been widowed four winters ago, when her husband was mauled by a bear. She had been left with a son of four winters called Little Beaver. The child was now eight and mischievous, and sometimes uncontrollable. Storm Rider had hoped that he would outgrow his bad behavior, yet so far it had only worsened. Little Beaver often ran off, worrying not only his mother almost to her deathbed, but all of the village people, whose hearts went out to the woman.

"Please come quickly, Chief Storm Rider," Yellow Flower pleaded. "It is my son, Little Beaver. He was gone from our lodge when I awakened this morning. I searched for him, but know that he has left the village. I did not want to bring my fears to you as I have so often, so I asked Fast Wolf to go and find him."

"And he has not returned with the child?" Storm Rider asked. "Have you come to me to ask me to join the search? If so, I can gather many warriors. With so many searching, I'm sure your son will be found."

"No, your search is not needed," she cried. She grabbed his hand and pulled on it. "Come. Oh, please come and see. Fast Wolf found Little Beaver. He brought him home to me, but my son is not acting as he should. He is behaving strangely. He . . . he is unconscious. His body was limp as Fast Wolf carried him into my lodge. I fear for him so much, Chief Storm Rider. I feel that I will lose him this time, and I do not believe I can bear the loss. I have already lost too much. I cannot lose Little Beaver."

"Have you summoned the village shaman?" Storm Rider asked. He walked quickly with Yellow Flower toward her tepee, which sat five lodges from his own. "Sharp Eyes will know what to do."

"Sharp Eyes is at my son's side, but I need you there, as well," Yellow Flower said, her eyes still filled with anxiety. "Your presence calms me, my chief. Thank you for caring so much that you would leave your lodge and the woman you hold captive there. You give me strength in my heart. With you there, I will gather the courage to get through these next moments, not knowing whether my son lives or dies."

"I am always here for you," Storm Rider said. His eyes moved quickly to a young brave standing outside Yellow Flower's lodge. He looked afraid and filled with a guilt that he could not hide.

Storm Rider stepped up to the young brave. "Four Wings, I see much in your eyes. Why do you lower them to the ground?" he asked.

He placed a finger beneath the child's chin and lifted it so that the child could no longer avoid his chief's inquisitive gaze.

"He was with Little Beaver," Yellow Flower said, her voice tight with anger. "He is too often a troublemaker with my son. Sometimes I believe he is the cause of most of it."

"Young brave, why did you and Little Beaver leave this morning without permission, and where did you go?" Storm Rider asked, his voice drawn. He placed his hands on the child's bare shoulders. "What made Little Beaver so suddenly ill?"

"We planned to leave this morning to search for rocks that we could carve into arrowheads," Four Wings said. A sob caught in his throat. "We did not ask permission because we planned to return home before our mothers even missed us. It is more exciting to be alone in the forest without adults watching our every move. And it was fun, until . . ."

He stopped and gulped hard, and seemed afraid to continue with his story.

"And . . . ?" Storm Rider prodded. "And then what happened? Why is Little Beaver ill?"

"We found a cave and . . . and we entered it to explore, and then . . ." Four Wings stopped as tears sprang to his eyes.

Then he continued. "We saw eyes glowing at the very back of the cave. We were afraid it was a bear, so we started running, but we weren't quick enough. It was not a bear. It was a wolf. A sick wolf. It bit Little Beaver on the leg, then ran away."

"How did you know it was sick?" Storm Rider asked, almost afraid to hear the answer.

"There was a strange, white foam dripping from the wolf's mouth," Four Wings cried. "After it bit Little Beaver's leg, my friend got sick so quickly. He fell to the ground and his eyes closed. I could not get him to answer me when I called his name."

Talking Rain had followed, and reached Storm Rider just in time to hear the small brave's story and his description of the sick wolf.

It filled her with dread, for she was familiar with the wolf's particular sickness and how ill it could make a person.

Her Indian uncle, a much older brother of her chieftain father, had known all ways of healing people while he was alive.

Talking Rain had adored the old man from the

moment she had met him, and enjoyed hearing his tales of times long past. She had visited him often in his lodge.

And she had not only listened to her uncle's interesting stories. He had taught her much about herbs and medicine, and how to treat numerous illnesses with them. She had been an eager student of her uncle's wisdom, and knew immediately today why this child had grown so ill.

A few years ago a mad wolf had roamed the land near her Crow village. It had bitten five children before it had finally been caught in a trap and killed. But before it died, it spread the deadly disease hydrophobia to victim after victim.

She was almost certain that this child had contracted the dreaded disease. And she knew how to treat it because she had proudly helped her uncle treat the children at her village.

Forgetting her own plight and her plans to flee tonight, she stepped quickly to Storm Rider's side. "I am afraid that the wolf has given this child a terrible disease," she hurried out. At the sound of her voice, Storm Rider turned to her. "I am very acquainted with the disease. Five winters ago, several children of my village were bitten by such a wolf. Like them, this child might have hydrophobia. My uncle, who is now with his ancestors in the sky, was our village shaman. I admired him and learned much from him, including how to treat hydrophobia. I would like to offer the knowledge I gained those five winters ago to help this child. Will you give me permission to treat him?"

Her voice had carried into Yellow Flower's lodge to the shaman's ears. He was quickly at the entrance and glared at Talking Rain with old, faded eyes. His gray hair was so long it touched the ground. He wore a bearskin robe and necklaces of bear's teeth around his neck. His face was wrinkled and gaunt.

When he talked, Talking Rain saw that his front teeth were missing, and that his tongue seemed to get in the way of every word he spoke, especially now, when he was obviously angry.

"You are not needed here," Sharp Eyes said adamantly. "Go. Leave me to care for the ill child. I have never accepted help from anyone when my skills are needed. I especially would not accept help from a woman. Only I have the skill to make this child well."

Talking Rain was not surprised by the medicine man's anger at her request to help, since most shamans did not see a woman as capable of the same medicine as they. She made no reply. She simply hoped that this elderly man knew the skills that her uncle had, for this disease could take a child's life quickly if not treated in the right way.

But in case this shaman did not have the knowledge required to save the child's life, Talking Rain suddenly changed her plans. She could not leave this village without knowing whether the child survived, particularly since her experience with this disease might be useful. Surely if the older shaman did not feel he was using the right medicine, he would value the child's life enough to ask Talking Rain for help.

Word had spread far and wide of her uncle's knowledge of medicine, so many had come from great distances to ask for his help when no one else's medicines worked. But she doubted that word of his expertise had reached as far as Storm Rider's former village.

Yet there was a chance that Sharp Eyes might have heard. If so, he would almost certainly ask Talking Rain to offer her uncle's knowledge of medicine to save the child. When a child's life lay in balance, she hoped pride would be set aside, for the children were the future of all Indian tribes.

Then again, if the elderly shaman did not ask for her help when it was needed, she would have to demand the chance to doctor Little Beaver herself.

Yes, for now, a child's welfare came before Talking Rain and her plans to sneak away. Answers from her father must wait.

She loved children, and there was no doubt that this child's health was very much in jeopardy.

She had to force herself not to battle with this old shaman as he continued to glare at her.

She was relieved when he finally turned and

went back inside the lodge, Yellow Flower following behind.

"I will return to your lodge. Please tell me about the child after seeing for yourself how bad his condition is," Talking Rain said, returning Storm Rider's questioning gaze. "I am so very afraid for the boy."

"I will let you know how he is, and thank you for offering your help," Storm Rider said. He was amazed to discover another side to this woman who already seemed to have so many aspects to her heart and mind.

She took him by a hand and urged him farther from Yellow Feather's lodge so that Sharp Eyes could not hear her. Then she said urgently, "Storm Rider, please promise me that should your shaman not have the skills required to cure this young man, you will allow me to use mine. You see, I learned much from my shaman uncle. I admired him so much. At the time I was thinking of perhaps becoming a shaman myself."

She paused, lowered her eyes, then gazed back at Storm Rider. "But it was the lure of freedom I found on horseback, and in the hunt, that changed my mind. I did not want to be confined to a lodge where only medicine was practiced," she rushed out. "But I still remember all of my uncle's teachings. I can make this child well. If given the chance, I can."

She swallowed hard. "I saw how terribly a person can die from this disease if it is not treated properly," she said. "I would not want this child to die in such a horrible way."

Each moment with Talking Rain made Storm Rider's admiration for her grow. For the first time, he saw her as loving, caring, and not as self-centered as she wanted people to believe.

He was certain at last that beneath her outward toughness, there was much softness and sweetness. Little by little, she was showing to him her true person. Although he could not help but admire that fierceness of her personality, he loved her tender side so much more.

Yes, this new side of her epitomized the qualities he wanted in a wife, and he knew for certain that he had been right to want her in his life, forever.

Something had finally broken down the barrier that hid her womanly side, the side that could even love a man.

It had taken a child to do this. That meant that she cared enough for children to perhaps want little ones of her own one day.

"Yes, I shall come to you soon," Storm Rider said. He looked past her into the forest, where a wolf eerily howled in the distance.

"I will also send warriors out to search for the wolf and kill it before it attacks someone else," Storm Rider said.

When Talking Rain heard the wolf, a new sense of foreboding clutched at her heart.

It was a strange sort of fear, as though the wolf's howl carried a message with it.

She saw it as a possible omen . . . hopefully not a bad one!

Chapter 13

Talking Rain listened to the instruments playing outside Yellow Feather's lodge. Their purpose was to accompany Sharp Eyes as he performed his ritual on Little Beaver. The instruments were a drum, a *chi-chi-quoin*, gourd rattle, and a horn made of the horns from a bull buffalo.

Singing accompanied the music, all of which would continue until the child was recovering. It would get louder should the child's health worsen.

Talking Rain kept watching the entrance flap for Storm Rider's return. She was anxious about the young brave's condition. If the shaman did not know the best ways of dealing with such a wound, the child would die a painful death.

She reached for a blanket, drew it around her shoulders, and scooted closer to the lodge fire. Although the tepee was warm from the burning logs in the firepit, she felt strangely cold. She could not forget that long, mournful howl of the wolf.

Even Storm Rider seemed to have been affected

by it, and not only because it might be the very animal that had bitten the young brave. Just as she was touched by the eerie call, he may have thought it an omen, as well.

She hoped it did not mean that the child would die.

Then she recalled her encounter with the Snake and how she had been left alive by him. She had thought he had done so as a warning of things to come.

A shiver coursed through her when she thought of what his future plans might be. Was the Snake taunting her, only to kill her later? Or did he plan to take his evil to her village?

If that was the omen sent to her today by the wolf, she must return home soon and give them fair warning.

Yet she still felt that the Snake had no one in mind on that day he killed her beloved steed except her. The thought of what he had planned for her made a shiver course through her again.

"I shall place another log on the fire," Storm Rider said as he came into the tepee. He had seen Talking Rain shiver when he entered. "If you wish I will even get you another blanket."

His voice startled Talking Rain out of her troubled thoughts. She turned to him as he knelt beside her and lifted a log onto the flames. She was touched by his concern for her. She wanted to thank him, yet she knew that it would not be fair to show that she cared deeply for this man, only to leave—to escape—at her first opportunity.

Now, though, her departure was delayed, for she could not leave until the child was out of danger.

She should know soon whether Sharp Eyes had the skills to keep the child from entering the treacherous world of hydrophobia. Soon everyone would know, for if the shaman did not stop the progress of the terrible disease before it was too late, the signs would be very visible.

She did not want to ponder that, for she hated to think of an innocent child afflicted so horribly only because of his curiosity, which had led him into a cave where the injured wolf had lain, it seemed, in waiting.

"*Pila-maye*, thank you. I feel somewhat better already," Talking Rain said, letting Storm Rider place the second blanket around her shoulders. "I just can't shake the foreboding that has grabbed hold of me after hearing of the child so ill, and . . . and after hearing the warning in the wolf's cry."

She leaned toward Storm Rider as he sat down beside her, his eyes holding hers. "How is he?" she quickly said. "Is he showing signs of . . . ?"

"He is resting as well as can be expected, and no, thus far there are no real signs of hydrophobia," Storm Rider said. "Whether or not you want to believe it, Little Beaver is in good hands. For many winters and summers, Sharp Eyes has been a very capable shaman for my people."

"Has he treated hydrophobia before?" Talking Rain asked, daring to show that she still did not trust the abilities of the old, frail doctor.

"Not that I know of," Storm Rider said, then gazed into the flames, where the new log crackled and popped. He did not want its sparks to fly onto Talking Rain.

He repositioned the log so that it settled into the original flame, the sparks now consumed by the fire. "Sharp Eyes is our people's physician and sorcerer, and has never let us down when he was needed," he said. "Nor will he now."

"I meant no disrespect for the man, but I do know that sometimes divining men try too hard to prove their great experience, and are artful enough to convince others to believe in this knowledge. They can drum, sing, and act the part well, but are not at all capable of curing some of the worst diseases, like hydrophobia," Talking Rain said.

She winced when her continued doubt of the old man made Storm Rider give her a quick frown.

She reached out and gently touched his arm. "I spoke out of turn again," she said. "It is just that I was taught by the best of divining men, who was an excellent doctor and soothsayer. Can I tell you a story about him?"

"Yes, do. I would like to know of this man who

has made you so untrusting of others of his same practice," Storm Rider said.

He wanted to prove that he could be patient with her, even when he had good cause to be angry with her criticism of his people's shaman. He truly believed in Sharp Eyes and his abilities to heal. But it was true that the shaman had never had experience with hydrophobia. Storm Rider hoped that he had knowledge enough to bring the child back to health, and soon.

When Storm Rider had left the child's bedside, Little Beaver's body was terribly hot with a fever.

Storm Rider had seen many die from such a raging temperature. He prayed that it would not be so for Little Beaver, for although the child had practiced mischief more often than not, he had every mark of being a great leader one day.

"Gray Hawk, my shaman uncle, was the best of teachers, and my respect for him grew even more after he died, then came back again to us to heal and teach," Talking Rain said, picturing in her mind the elderly divining man.

Ah, but he had had the kindest eyes, so knowledgeable, so caring. And his warm smile had reached right into one's soul.

At the end, though, he had suffered as any human being would when his health gave way under the pressure of a terrible coughing disease.

She could still hear that hacking cough when she thought of him.

Although she had hated losing Gray Hawk, it was a relief when he finally took his last, ragged breath, because she knew that he was no longer in pain. Finally he was on his journey into the stars, where he would again be with his loved ones who had passed on before him.

"Did I hear right? Did you say that your shaman uncle died, then came back to life?" Storm Rider asked, raising his eyebrows.

"That is so," Talking Rain affirmed.

In Storm Rider's eyes she saw the same kindness, knowledge, and caring she had seen in Gray Hawk's eyes, and she knew that this man who loved her would be missed, oh, so terribly if something happened to him. So many depended on him.

In a way, Talking Rain depended on him as well, but still had to leave him in order to get answers from her *ahte*.

"How can that be?" Storm Rider asked, trying hard to keep the skepticism out of his voice. What she spoke of happened only in myths, not in real life.

But he cared enough for her not to show his mistrust of her story, for to him it was surely only a story, not truth. Perhaps she had only convinced herself that it was real.

"It did occur," Talking Rain said. She realized that

Storm Rider found what she had said far-fetched, yet was not insulted by this. He was polite enough not to openly deny her story.

"Then tell me how it came to be," Storm Rider said, reaching for and placing a blanket around his own shoulders.

"One day, long ago, Gray Hawk grew ill and died suddenly while traveling with warriors to another village for council," Talking Rain said. "The warriors wrapped him in rawhide and blankets. After crying over him, they placed his body in the fork of a tree, as is the custom of my Crow people, then proceeded on their journey."

She cleared her throat, then said, "Gray Hawk came back to life. After great difficulty he worked himself out of his bonds, then walked until he came upon the night camp of our warriors, some days after they had left him. He told them that during his time in the blankets, he had been in other worlds, seen much, and learned everything past, present, and future. From then until his true death, he was not only considered a great divining man, but also a prophet. He continued to speak to us about his time when his spirit momentarily left his body."

"What else did he tell?" Storm Rider asked, moving closer to Talking Rain.

It was not so much that he believed the tale, but he saw in talking about it, Talking Rain looked more at peace than she had since her abduction.

It also took Storm Rider's mind off the child he worried might be struggling with his last breaths of life. He expected to hear the loud cry of mourning at any moment as his mother learned she had lost the child she adored.

He, too, would join in that despair, for he loved all of the children of his village, and the death of one was like losing a part of his heart.

"Gray Hawk told about paradise, which he found to be in a warm region, not necessarily in the heavens, but in some country not belonging to earth," Talking Rain said. She was glad to have this to talk about, since it helped keep her mind off the child and whether he grew better or worse. "He said that in this place there is perpetual summer, an abundance of game, and handsome women. Every comfort awaited those who go there, as well as the joy of seeing one's friends and relatives. He said that all live there in perfect harmony."

"Yes, this is how we are taught the afterlife should be," Storm Rider said. "So the teachings are correct, according to your shaman uncle?"

"It does seem so," Talking Rain said, nodding. "He also told me that it is true that departed spirits have the power to revisit their native lands and manifest themselves to their friends in dreams. And if their relatives have neglected crying for them in a feast, the spirits can trouble them with whistling sounds and startling apparitions, many of which have been seen and heard, and therefore are most religiously believed in by all."

"Yes, that is our people's belief, as well," Storm Rider said. "That is why the dead are feasted in a long ceremony, sacrificed to, and invoked, besides being cried for for years after they are gone, often as long as their relatives are left living."

"Then your people and mine are much alike, more than I would have guessed them to be," Talking Rain said. "It is good that my Crow people have become friends with your people, rather than enemies."

Then she turned from him, for talking of such things made her relive all over again that moment when her father forsook her as he rode away without an explanation or even a good-bye.

She could not help it when a sob arose from the depths of her throat, where her heart seemed momentarily centered.

Then she was aware of something—someone— else when she felt strong hands reach out for her and hold her. Her blankets fell away from her shoulders.

Stunned by Storm Rider's embrace, Talking Rain felt a warmth fill her soul. She badly wished not to disrupt this precious moment, for it was so sweetly delicious to be held by this man who had brought life into that part of her that had lain dormant until now.

She could feel it—how she ached inside for him, how she hungered for his kiss again, how her body seemed to scream for something even more than this.

And when his lips did claim hers in a wondrous kiss, she momentarily returned the kiss because it was too wonderful to say no to. She found herself melting sensuously, her heart thundering inside her chest.

Then she realized what she was allowing to happen, and knew that she shouldn't, since her plans were to leave him as soon as she learned the child's fate. She wrenched herself free.

She gave him a look of wonder, then, sobbing almost uncontrollably, leaped to her feet and left his lodge. She struggled as she ran, her ankle paining her so much that she almost gave in and went back into the lodge.

But she needed time away from him.

She was so confused, so . . . so in love.

She managed to get to the darker depths of the forest, where no one could see the torment she felt over wanting a man so much, yet not wanting to want him.

Stunned for a moment, Storm Rider watched the swaying of the entrance flap after Talking Rain rushed through it. He was torn over what to do, since he had felt Talking Rain's response, only to have her flee from him. Then Storm Rider jumped to his feet and ran from the tepee. He looked in all directions and saw her nowhere! He gazed at the ground and saw her moccasined footprints in the dust. They led into the forest.

Not knowing where she might go, perhaps even as far as her own village, Storm Rider broke into a hard run. He stopped when he saw her sitting beneath a tree, her head hanging, her face resting in her hands.

He did not approach her just yet. He was not sure how to, or what to say. He knew that she had wanted the kiss, yet still would not admit it to herself. She was certainly a mystery, the sort of woman he had never encountered before. That made him even more determined that she one day realize her attraction to him, and her need to be a woman in all respects. It was obvious that she had a woman's desires and wanted them fed; yet she was afraid to allow it to happen.

When Talking Rain raised her eyes, she found him standing there, watching her. She felt a strange fluttering in the pit of her stomach that only one thing would cause. Oh, but she wanted him so badly she could hardly bear not admitting it to him.

She said nothing when he approached, bent down before her, and took her wrists to gently pull her to her feet. He drew her against his hard body.

"Please do not kiss me again," she murmured,

her eyes wavering as she looked up into his. "Please . . . let me go."

"I cannot let you go, and it is hard not to kiss you when I know that you want it as much as I," Storm Rider said. "Why do you fight these feelings? It is right, you know, to feel the way you do. You are all woman, Talking Rain, with the desires of a woman. And you are a woman who cares for this Assiniboine chief."

"I do not want to care for *any* man," she said softly. "Damn my body. It has betrayed me worse than Chief Blue Thunder did by selling me as though I am no more than a pelt to be bargained over."

A sudden outcry of despair drew them apart. They gazed at each other.

"Yellow Flower," they said in almost the same breath when they recognized the grief-filled voice.

Storm Rider took Talking Rain by a hand, and together they ran back to the village. When they reached Little Beaver's tepee, they saw that his mother had collapsed outside the lodge.

"Little Beaver has worsened," a maiden said as she sat beside Yellow Flower and brought her head onto her lap. "Little Beaver is having one fit after another. He is foaming at his mouth!"

Having heard enough and knowing what must be done, Talking Rain ran determined into the lodge and pushed her way to the child's bedside.

Sharp Eyes gave her a glare, then stepped aside. "Do what you must to save the child, if he can be saved," he said dryly.

Storm Rider entered the lodge just as Sharp Eyes brushed past him. He gazed at Talking Rain, who knelt beside Little Beaver's bed.

Talking Rain turned quickly to Storm Rider. "I need a rawhide from a fresh buffalo kill," she said. "Please hurry, Storm Rider. It may already be too late."

He nodded, then left.

Talking Rain softly caressed Little Beaver's brow. "Please do not leave us," she whispered. "Please give me a chance."

She glanced over when the child's mother came back into the lodge, tears still streaming from her eyes.

Yellow Flower went and knelt on the other side of the bed and gave Talking Rain a look that let her know this child's mother trusted her . . . and depended on her.

"I shall make him well," Talking Rain said, truly believing that she could.

She could feel the spirit of her old shaman uncle with her, as though he were standing beside her, showing her the way to heal the young brave.

Chapter 14

Talking Rain had sat for three days and nights with Little Beaver while caring for him, getting bits and pieces of sleep herself, and eating only what she must to keep her strength up.

She had seen the dread on Little Beaver's mother's face when Talking Rain had explained the treatment she must use to rid the child of the dreaded disease.

At first Yellow Flower had not agreed to it. But after a very frail, worsening Little Beaver had two more fits and the foam at his mouth increased, she gave Talking Rain permission to do whatever she thought best.

The whole village had grown quiet with worry as Talking Rain had proceeded with the treatment.

First she had applied a concoction of cattail root directly on the wound on his leg.

Then came the part of the cure that made everyone grimace as they silently witnessed it being done outside of Yellow Flower's lodge.

First Little Beaver was sewn up in a fresh buffalo rawhide. With two cords attached to the head and foot of the bale, he was swung back and forth above the outdoor hot fire until he began sweating profusely. Then he was plunged into cold water.

Again he was swung over the fire, and again plunged into cold water.

The final time he was plunged into the cold water, the wet rawhide had been taken from him, and he was then wrapped in soft, warm blankets and carried inside to his own bed.

And then the waiting began, to see if he survived not only the dreadful disease, but also the drastic treatment, which many questioned.

One day had passed.

The child slept somewhat fitfully, yet he no longer foamed at his mouth.

Two days had passed.

Little Beaver's color started to return, and he slept with much more ease. But he had not yet opened his eyes.

It was now the third day.

Exhausted, Talking Rain lay on a pallet to one side of the child's bed of blankets, asleep. His mother sat on the other, steadily watching her son.

That was how it was now that he was better. While one slept, the other kept watch for Little Beaver to show signs of awakening.

"Talking Rain, he is waking up," Yellow Flower

said, her voice filled with joy. "My son. His eyes. They are fluttering as he tries to open them."

Talking Rain awakened with a start.

She sat up quickly, then knelt beside the child's bed. She smiled with relief when Little Beaver opened his eyes all the way, gave Talking Rain a look of wonder, and then turned to his mother and held a shaky hand out for her.

"My son, my son," Yellow Flower cried, taking his hand and kissing its palm. Then she drew him into her arms. "I was afraid for you."

"What happened?" he asked, clinging to his mother.

She leaned away from him and their eyes locked. "You do not remember?" she asked, her voice breaking.

"I remember a wolf, then nothing more," Little Beaver gulped out. He turned his gaze to Talking Rain. "Why are you here?"

"She has good medicine," Yellow Flower said, smiling warmly over at Talking Rain. "Son, if not for her, you—"

She stopped short of telling her son that most had not expected him to live.

"Hello, Little Beaver," Talking Rain said, reaching a soft hand to his cheek. "I'm so glad to see that you are feeling better."

She turned her eyes to Yellow Flower. "His fever

is gone, and his true color has returned, especially in his lips," she said. "He is going to be all right."

"How can I thank you enough for what you have done for my son?" Yellow Flower asked, her voice filled with emotion.

"It is enough to know that he is going to be fine and will soon join the other young braves in games and pretend hunts," Talking Rain said softly. "But to be sure there will be no setback in his health, I have one more thing I must do."

"What is that?" Yellow Flower asked, eyes wide.

"I want to make something special for him to drink," Talking Rain said. She rose to her feet. She felt her knees almost give way from lack of food and sleep these past three days.

But she still would not think of herself—not yet, anyhow. She had to make certain that the child received this one last medicine, and then she would go to Storm Rider's lodge and catch up on her sleep.

And then she would return home to get the answers she needed. She had purposely delayed going because of the child, who came before anything else at the moment—or anyone.

"Where is Sharp Eyes?" Little Beaver asked. He looked past Talking Rain at the closed entrance flap, then gazed questioningly at her again. "He is our people's shaman. Not you. Why are you here, and not Sharp Eyes?"

"Son, Sharp Eyes cared for you first, but it was

not enough to make you well, so we, he and I, agreed to allow Talking Rain to see if she could do something for you. She has learned much from her shaman uncle," Yellow Flower said. She smiled up at Talking Rain. "I am so glad that she listened to his teachings carefully."

"He was a very intelligent divining man, and I, too, am glad that I found what he did so interesting," Talking Rain replied. "Now I must go and gather supplies to make the medicine that I feel will finalize your son's recovery."

"Thank you again," Yellow Flower said. She reached a hand out for Talking Rain.

Talking Rain took it, squeezed it affectionately, then stepped out of the tepee and found herself facing practically everyone of the village, who had stood vigil over Little Beaver.

The music had stopped long ago, as well as the singing. All that remained was a hush as everyone's faces showed their deep concern for a young brave whose future was in question.

She looked quickly over when Storm Rider came to her side. "He is all but well," she said, smiling at him. She turned to the people and shouted the same to them.

"Little Beaver is all but well," she said, smiling proudly. "Soon he will be out of his bed and playing and laughing along with the other children."

Shouts of happiness erupted; then she became

lost in the crowd of people taking turns hugging her. Storm Rider stood back and watched, a wide smile on his lips, a brightness in his eyes.

Laughing softly after the last of the people stepped away from her, Talking Rain ran her hands through her hair, which she knew was tangled from having not brushed it for three days and nights. It was in bad need of a washing, as was she.

She smelled the stench of sickness on her doeskin dress and was anxious to remove it, and take a bath. Then how wonderful it would be to go to bed and sleep, knowing that the child was in no more danger.

"I shall walk you to my lodge," Storm Rider said. "I know how much you need to sleep."

He wanted to place his arms around her waist and draw her closer. But he did not dare to, for that would be showing to his people too much affection for a woman he had not yet totally won.

Should he not succeed at gaining Talking Rain's love, he did not want his people to see him as weak.

This could turn the tide against him. They might begin watching him for further weaknesses, and in the end call for a different chief.

"I need more than just sleep," Talking Rain said, laughing softly. "You surely can tell how much I am in need of a bath."

"You still smell like forest flowers to me," he said. Even complimenting her in such a way was a dangerous thing to do, even in the eyes of only himself. He did not want to be made a fool of.

"Come," he said. "I shall see that you get all that you wish—a bath, clean clothes, food, and then much-needed sleep."

"Those must all be delayed for a while longer," she told him. "I still have something to do to help strengthen Little Beaver and speed his recovery."

"What else needs to be done?" Storm Rider asked, perplexed. "Is he not past the crisis?"

"He is, but again, one more thing will reassure me that I have done all I can for the child," Talking Rain said.

"Tell me and I will do it for you, because, Talking Rain, the weariness you are feeling is not only in your voice, but also your eyes," Storm Rider said. "Let me do at least this, since I was not able to do anything else for the child."

"Your presence was felt throughout the ordeal," Talking Rain murmured. "That was enough."

"Tell me what I can do *now*," Storm Rider said, placing his hands on her shoulders.

"What I need might take some time," Talking Rain said. She sighed. "So yes, I would appreciate your doing it, for I am so tired my legs will hardly hold me up any longer."

She proceeded to tell him the ingredients required for a drink that would be given to the child. It was to be concocted from powder made from pulverized roots that she described, the rattle of a rattlesnake, and calcified buffalo bones.

"When this is all gathered and boiled in water, give it to Little Beaver to drink," Talking Rain said. "He will not enjoy it, but please assure him that it will finalize his cure."

She slid free of his hands. Avoiding his eyes, she walked again toward his lodge.

"This I will do for both you and Little Beaver," Storm Rider said, walking beside her. "But first I will escort you to my lodge. From there you do as you wish and get the rest you need. Sleep for as long as you like. From here on, others will see to the child's welfare."

"I think I will sleep some first, and then take a bath, eat some nourishing food, and sleep again," Talking Rain said as they reached Storm Rider's tepee.

She turned to him and smiled into his eyes.

"I am so glad that I was here for Little Beaver," she said. "It makes one feel good to give life when it was surely going to be taken."

"Perhaps you missed your calling," Storm Rider said. "Perhaps you now will think more about the life you have led and reconsider another way, which would still include Little Beaver, if you stay willingly among my people, and not as a *winu*, captive, but instead as my wife."

Talking Rain could feel the heat of a blush rush to her cheeks, and there was no denying how his words affected her. Although she knew that she must leave as soon as she had her full strength back, a big part of her wanted to stay forever with this man.

She was touched knowing how deeply he felt for her; yet, again, she had more than being a wife on her mind at this moment.

She had a father to confront!

And when she got answers that she understood, only then would she consider what else she wanted of life.

She did know that being near Storm Rider made her insides feel deliciously warm. She did feel deeply for him, yet could not help but still be afraid to give up everything she had ever known—and loved—just for him.

No, she was not certain yet what she would do after she got answers from her father.

For now, the best thing for her was to get some badly needed rest. Then, only then, would she make any decisions about the rest of her life.

"I will go now and gather what I must for the drink," Storm Rider said quietly.

He knew by her silence that Talking Rain still did not know that it was he she truly wanted in life. He would not press her for any decisions, or answers. In time she would know, and then they would become as one heartbeat, husband and wife.

"Tell Little Beaver that although the drink will taste bad, it will hasten his recovery so that he can join his friends sooner and laugh and run with them again," Talking Rain instructed.

Without further thought, she stood on tiptoe, twined her arms around Storm Rider's neck, and gave him a soft hug.

She could feel his heartbeats hasten as her chest pressed against his, and knew that it was because of his deep feelings for her. She wondered if he could feel how her heart reacted to him. It was thudding within her chest so hard that she felt somewhat dizzy.

Not ready to give in to those feelings yet, if ever, she rushed from his arms and into his tepee.

Storm Rider watched Talking Rain's quick departure into the tepee. Although she was still fighting her feelings, he was certain that her resolve was weakening.

Smiling, he went into the forest for the supplies that he needed for the drink for Little Beaver.

After that was done, and the child had drunk the last drop, he would go to his secret praying place and give thanks to *Wah-con-tun-ga*, the Great Medicine, that the child had lived through the ordeal, and that Talking Rain had shown many good sides of herself these past days. It made it so easy for him to love her.

The mood in his village no longer somber, but filled with laughter and hope again, Storm Rider found himself humming as he dug up one root, and then another. He even hummed as he found and cornered a rattlesnake and killed it for its rattle.

Soon he was sitting beside Little Beaver's bed, glad that the child gulped down the concoction without even blinking his eyes.

"You are more warrior now than child," Storm Rider said.

He took the empty cup and patted the child on his bare shoulder.

"It is good to have you back, young brave," he said softly.

"It is good to be back," Little Beaver said. He sighed and lay back down on his plush blankets and pelts. "And I will always remember why that is. The woman. She will always be special to me."

Storm Rider nodded and smiled, then left the lodge and went to his own. Talking Rain still slept soundly beside his lodge fire.

He then ran into the forest, and soon was saying his prayers of thanks to *Wah-con-tun-ga*. His world was a much brighter place now because of Talking Rain.

He would not give up on having her as his.

Ever!

Chapter 15

Talking Rain had slept soundly for two days and nights, awakening only long enough to eat, bathe, and check on Little Beaver.

It was now early into the third night. The sky still held a lovely blush of pink along the horizon, where the sun was making its last farewell for another day. Elsewhere, the moon was already rising in its own sort of glory, the stars like sparkling sequins in the darkening heavens.

A voice coming from somewhere close by outside awakened Talking Rain. She leaned up on an elbow and gazed around her. Storm Rider wasn't there, but he had left the fire burning slowly and a pot of delicious-smelling stew hanging to warm over the flames.

She yawned and stretched her arms above her head. At last she was thoroughly rested enough to proceed with her plans. She would go to her father and finally get the answers she sorely wanted from him.

The same questions that had plagued her since that day her adopted father had left her without giving her a reason, or even so much as a farewell, came to her now. They made her head almost swim, there were so many.

Had Blue Thunder never loved her?

Had she been kept, even treated grandly, only to have her to use as a pawn when the need arose?

The fact that he had so brazenly given her up without even so much as a nod in her direction, much less a warm hug and word of farewell, was something she just still could not accept without knowing why.

"And I will. Tonight," she whispered to herself.

She determinedly rose from the warm bed of blankets and pelts.

"Yes, I will, tonight," she affirmed again to herself.

She looked toward the entrance flap when she heard the voice once more.

It was deep and resonant, kind and warm. It was Storm Rider's. She could hear what he was saying.

It was obviously myth-telling time at his village, and Storm Rider had been the one to volunteer for tonight's gathering. In her village, the elders usually drew children around them so that they could tell tales of long ago. But here, it was the chief who had the children gathered around him by a large outdoor fire.

Talking Rain smiled when she saw Little Beaver listening raptly to the tales. He lay on a thick cushion of pelts, his mother sitting next to him. His eyes were wide with wonder at the myth that his chief had chosen to tell tonight.

It was wonderful to see the child being able to enjoy the evening, since only a few days ago his life was uncertain.

Talking Rain felt a deep pride for her role in saving the child's life. It made her appreciate life more, herself, and only increased her determination to discover why hers had changed, why her father had turned his back on her as though she were a worthless stray puppy.

She looked at Storm Rider. Watching him telling stories to the children made her truly not want to leave him, but rather stay and profess her love. She ached to have his arms around her again, and to have him kiss her as though she were the only woman on earth.

A sensual thrill swam through her as she recalled their last kiss and embrace. Though short-lived, it had been enough to make her hunger for more.

Even though she knew that precious moments were passing by when she should be preparing herself for her escape tonight, she stood awhile longer listening to Storm Rider, and looking at the children who were leaning forward to eagerly listen.

Talking Rain was thrown back in time to her

home in the Crow village, when at night, once all work was over, a large pot would be put over the large outdoor fire. Some nights it would be a choice meat steaming in a rich broth. Other times it might be a hearty stew made from fat, vegetables, and chunks of buffalo meat. Sometimes it would be of a more frivolous nature to please mainly the children. They loved popped corn. On those nights when popped corn was the favored food, they would make huge pots of it, the wondrous fragrance wafting through the air and tempting even the oldest of the elders to take part in eating it.

Even those elders whose teeth were mostly gone and had to gum the corn to finally chew it, enjoyed the special treat.

Tobacco mixed with other plants was always prepared for the storyteller chosen to share his interesting tales with the Crow people. He often prolonged his narrations the greater part of the night.

Sometimes there was a private storytelling time in her father's lodge, where the stories would be only for Talking Rain to enjoy. She had enjoyed those moments so much, and had hated when the storyteller told his last story and left.

She could smile now at how some of the more frightening tales had left a long-lasting impression on her youthful mind. They contributed to her fear of ghost monsters and other imaginary supernatural powers when she was alone in her bed and could not sleep. When she grew older and looked back to those nights, she could laugh and know they were only stories, not fact.

Yes, at her village there was always a very old *we-chah-chape*, man, who was talented in reciting fables and creating mirth for the rest, and who would also sing for the doctors and cry for the dead when paid. He would never sit in council, but would stay at home, making pipes, smoking, and eating, and was ready at all times to offer services when something was to be gained.

But tonight, at this Assiniboine village, the story-teller was a young chief whose story was not one of alarm or fear.

Talking Rain listened a moment longer and got caught up in the myth that Storm Rider was telling. She had never heard this one before and felt for a moment as though she were a mere child again, hoping the story would not end.

Storm Rider gathered a child closer on each side of him, his arms warmly around their waists.

He looked toward his lodge and saw Talking Rain standing at the entrance, watching and listening.

He was glad to know that she was awake and rested. He planned to go to her after the stories were over and talk of a future—theirs.

He had felt her growing closer to him and had seen the look in her eyes when they talked. There was no longer any resentment in their depths, only a quiet peace.

And he knew why.

Helping the child had brought this peace, and had drawn her closer to his people, which he hoped would one day be her people as well, in all ways that he had prayed for.

Marrying her would ease the torment in his heart and soul. He ached unbearably with need of her.

He had waited for the perfect time to choose a woman, and for that perfect woman to cross his path.

It seemed to him now that his need to travel here was not so much to finally have his vengeance on the Snake. Instead, it was because his heart knew he was being led by *Wah-con-tun-ga* to the woman he had waited all of his life for. That woman was Talking Rain.

Yes, he would not let her slip away from him. He would marry her.

As he saw her still watching and listening, Storm Rider continued the tale that the children of his village were so hungrily listening to. . . .

"Long ago, an old woman lived in a lodge with her children," Storm Rider said. He looked from child to child. He always enjoyed their awed expressions when he told a story they enjoyed hearing. Tonight they all seemed eager to hear everything he had to say. That was good. When the children listened, they learned.

"This woman raised corn in a garden," he said as he proceeded with the story. "One day, when the sun was bright and the sky was a clear, beautiful blue overhead, one of this woman's little boys, called Eagle Wing, was shooting birds with arrows in the garden. He was trying to keep them from eating the food that was meant for him, his brothers and sisters, and his mother. Suddenly a sackful of rice appeared before Eagle Wing. It was dancing up and down before the young brave. The sack of rice sang out to the child, 'Eagle Wing, shoot me and eat me.' Eagle Wing shot an arrow into the sack and all of the rice spilled onto the ground. The voice had stopped. Eagle Wing stood back, afraid. But being the smart young brave that he was, he had listened closely to things his mother taught him. Suddenly he realized why the rice had appeared. It was to feed the birds, so that they would no longer eat his mother's corn, and Eagle Wing would no longer need to shoot them. Birds soon flocked around the spilled rice, devouring it instead of the corn. Loving animals and birds so much and glad that he did not have to shoot any more, Eagle Wing went home to his mother, content."

As the children applauded and laughed, Talking Rain slipped back into Storm Rider's lodge.

After a few brief moments, Talking Rain could

hear the children quiet again. Storm Rider was telling them another tale.

"I must leave now while Storm Rider is occupied," Talking Rain said to herself anxiously.

She reached for her moccasins and slipped into them. Then her stomach growled. She realized that she must stop long enough to get some nourishment, for it had been many hours since she had eaten.

She hurriedly ladled some stew into a wooden bowl, gulped down several bites, then stopped again and listened guardedly to see if Storm Rider was still speaking.

He was, and she knew that the moment had come for her escape. Earlier, she had noticed that no one was standing guard outside the lodge. That meant that Storm Rider trusted her.

A tinge of guilt made her sigh heavily, because Storm Rider had been so good to her. Yet she knew what must be done, and it must be done now or never.

And when she got answers from her father, she hoped that she could forgive him enough to stay if her mother wanted her to. She simply could not believe that her mother had a role in trading her off so heartlessly.

And she wanted time to test herself while she was away from Storm Rider. She had to be certain about her feelings for him: whether she wanted a future with him, or would rather continue to live as she always had. If she chose the former, she knew that her future would change entirely from the one she had always dreamed of.

She would be giving in to her womanly desires, not the part of her that enjoyed hunting and stealing horses.

Her stomach comfortably full, and afraid that time was running out, she rose to leave.

Then she stopped.

She gazed down at the tiny doeskin bag tied to her belt, which held the beautiful glass stone inside it. It had been given to her by Storm Rider, a gift from his heart. She just did not feel it was right to keep it any longer, not with her leaving him in such a way.

She realized her fingers were trembling as she untied the tiny bag, then laid it and the special black stone beside the fire for Storm Rider to find. Surely that would be message enough that she did not want him to follow her. He would realize that she was doing what she wanted. And if he truly cared for her as much as he professed to, he would not come for her.

He would allow her her own choices in life.

Although she was his by trade, and even worse, by stealing his horse, he would not likely come for her and demand her return.

She only hoped that he would not be so angry

that he would send out warriors and treat her like an escaped captive. That would break her heart.

It came to her suddenly that by leaving the special stone for him to find, she had just made her decision about the rest of her life. Subconsciously, she had made the choice. But she was torn with how to feel. Could she live without him and those wonderful feelings that he aroused in her? Was her life as she had previously known it truly enough to fulfill her now?

After having been held in this man's arms, after being kissed by him, it was one of the hardest things she had ever done to walk away, knowing that she could have had a lifetime of such hugs and kisses . . . of such wondrous passion.

Firming her jaw, she took one last, lingering look around the tepee. Somehow she did not feel as though she had ever been a captive. There had been too many other emotions that had entered into her time there.

"I must stop this," she whispered harshly to herself.

Yes, she must leave.

She only hoped that she could find a moment when Storm Rider wasn't watching the lodge, and that she could get back to his horses without being detected by anyone else, either.

Sentries were posted in strategic places to keep the village safe. But if she could get away from

Storm Rider's corral and into the darker shadows of the forest, the rest of the way could be traveled easily.

She knew the lay of this land better than did the Assiniboine warriors, for she had walked and ridden upon it since she was five. She knew every nook and cranny, and could elude anyone who might be appointed to watch for intruders in the night.

Her pulse racing, Talking Rain crept to the entrance flap. Slowly she drew it aside and gazed cautiously toward Storm Rider. Luck was with her. He had changed positions.

Storm Rider sat on the other side of the circle of children, his back now to his lodge.

Looking at his powerful back, sleek, copper skin, beautiful, long hair that reached to his waist made so much of Talking Rain regret what she had chosen to do.

But she must flee this man. The closeness she felt for Storm Rider frightened her.

She was afraid to explore those unfamiliar emotions, almost certain where they would lead her— down the road to marriage, and then to motherhood.

Ah, how she did love children, proved even more to her by how it felt to have helped save Little Beaver's life.

But to have her own? To be responsible for them

day in and day out? She had not paid any heed to lessons on mothering or on being a wife when other girls her age had hungered for such teachings. She knew absolutely nothing about any of it, especially how to totally please a man in bed.

But now was not the time to be thinking about anything except for going home and getting answers from her father!

Her knees felt weak, and her stomach felt as though the bottom were ready to drop from it. Talking Rain looked over her shoulder one last time at the tiny bag she had left for Storm Rider to find, then crept stealthily from the tepee.

She hunkered down to keep in the shadows of the lodge as much as possible. The moon's brilliance was hindered, luckily, by clouds that had rolled over it.

When she did not think anyone could see her, Talking Rain hurried into Storm Rider's corral.

She chose a dark brown mare, one that would blend into the darkness of night. She readied it for riding. Then, holding its reins, she quietly led the mare free of the corral.

After successfully reaching the deepest shadows of the forest, Talking Rain still did not mount the steed, but instead led it hurriedly onward until she felt the sound of the hoofbeats would no longer be heard.

Talking Rain was finally far from the village, and

could no longer hear Storm Rider's wonderfully masculine voice. She mounted the steed, grabbed its reins, and rode hard farther into the night.

Suddenly she thought of something that made her blood flow cold through her veins: In her haste to get away, she had not thought to bring a weapon for protection.

If the Snake found her riding alone in the night, he might not stop this time at killing only the horse she was riding.

This time he might kill her, too.

"Or he might . . . rape me, then kill me," she whispered to herself, a sense of dread making her feel almost ill.

She forced such thoughts from her mind. She set her jaw and rode onward into the night. She focused only on arriving at her village, and stepping up to her father to demand answers.

"Finally I will know why," she said.

She inhaled a quavering, nervous breath, for did she truly want to know?

Might knowing hurt too badly? If so, would she hurry back to Storm Rider? Would he then even want her? She might find herself lost to both worlds!

Chapter 16

Talking Rain reached the summit of a hill where she had sat often on horseback and gazed down at her village, so proud of being a part of the Crow people, so grateful to them for having taken her in after the most horrendous tragedy of her life. She drew a sudden tight rein, gasped, and felt the blood drain from her face at what she saw down below, in the darkness.

The moon was bright again, the clouds having floated past it, and its light revealed something happening at her village that made Talking Rain's blood run cold. It was so horrible a sight, she was too frozen to move. Her eyes remained locked on the massacre and bloodshed below as a group killed and maimed her beloved Crow people. The tallest of them rode away from the others, and sat laughing at the mayhem he had caused. Talking Rain knew who it was. She could tell by the maniacal laugh and his thin, straight figure in the saddle.

The terrible laughter was familiar—she had

heard the same after her horse was struck with an arrow. Yes, the man who had come to destroy and kill tonight was none other than . . . the Snake!

"The wolf's howl . . . the omen," Talking Rain whispered, her voice breaking. It *was* a bad omen. It meant her to see into the future and know what the evil man was planning. It had foretold this tragedy for the Crow people, surely planned on that very same day that the Snake had spared Talking Rain's life.

"You villainous snake!" she screamed, the urge to kill so hot in her veins that she forgot that she did not have a weapon to defend any of her people, much less herself.

She sank her heels hard into the flanks of the brown mare and rode down the steep slope, the screams and cries of her people cutting a deep, hurtful path into her heart.

The closer she came to her village, the more distinct were the wails of mourning and the cries of death.

And then she heard the loud crashing of horses' hooves as the Snake and his renegade cohorts rode off in the opposite direction from Talking Rain, having apparently not seen her. If they had, they would have waited and taken her life, as well.

She watched them flee into the night and badly wanted to pursue them, to chance dying herself in order to kill the renegade leader. But a thought came to her suddenly, one that turned her heart cold. She had no weapon! Even if she did chase them, she had no way to kill any of them.

And had the Snake and his men not left when they did, she would have ridden defenseless into the midst of what she knew was a terrible massacre, and would have soon been among the dead herself.

The wails strengthened, and she could envision the horror within the perimeters of the village. Tears sprang to her eyes.

Her *ahte?* Her *ina?* Were they still alive, or had they been unmercifully killed?

What, also, of her younger brother and sister? Were they among the dead or wounded? Or . . . might they have been taken captive?

Pulling from deep within her the strength that had gotten her through the worst day of her life, when she had lost her true parents in the river, Talking Rain continued onward until she finally reached the village.

Then she drew a tight rein and looked disbelievingly around her.

Her heart sank.

Her courage almost failed her when she saw how many lay on the ground, dead or wounded, while others ran frantically from one fallen person to another to see what might be done to help or save them, if anything at all could be done.

Many of the lodge coverings had been slashed

from their poles. The barren poles now stood tall in the moonlight, resembling skeletons. Others had been dragged down by the raiders and burned in the huge outdoor fire in the center of the village.

Then it hit her—her parents' lodge was completely gone and surely among those burning in the great, leaping flames.

She almost fainted when she saw two bodies lying where her parents' home had stood so tall and proud. She knew whose they were.

One was her mother.

The other was her father.

Her mother was lying totally still. Her father seemed to be struggling to crawl over to her. He stopped and lay flat on his back, his chest heaving.

Talking Rain leaped from her steed and ran to her parents. She knelt first beside her mother.

A choking sound came from within her when she saw the death stare of her beloved mother. And then she saw the reason why: An arrow had entered her right side. Blood still streamed from the wound, making a pool of red on the ground.

"*Ina*, Mother," Talking Rain cried. "Oh, Mother, why you?"

She gently, lovingly, closed her mother's eyes.

She then crawled over to her father, who was watching her, tears rolling down his face, a face that she had adored for oh, so long.

"Talking . . . Rain . . . *micinksi*, daughter . . ." Blue

Thunder said in a voice unlike his at all, but instead a gasping sort of grunt.

He reached a slow, trembling hand out for her.

She took his hand and held it to her heart as she gazed down at him. "Oh, *ahte*, Father, why would the Snake do this?" she said between deep, gulping sobs. "*Ina*, she . . . is dead. And you? Oh, *ahte*, where are you wounded? Is it severe?"

"The back of my head," he said between gasps of breath. "It . . . it . . . was . . ."

Talking Rain almost fainted when she saw the blood pooling where her father's head rested. She knew then that a hatchet had taken its toll. But she was thankful his scalp had not been taken. The hair that was not soaked in blood beneath him lay proudly around his shoulders, loosed of its usual braids.

Blue Thunder tightened his hold on Talking Rain's hand. "Listen to me . . . while . . . I have the breath left to talk to you," he said. His eyelids now drooped, as he fought to stay awake. "*Micinksi*, daughter, I apologize . . . for . . . what I did. Will you forgive me? I could . . . not . . . enter . . . the after-life . . . if you did not forgive me."

"You know that I would forgive you anything," Talking Rain said. She placed her free hand gently to his cheek. "*Ahte*, oh, *ahte*, I have loved you more than I could have ever even loved my true father.

You *were* my father. I am a daughter so very proud of her *ahte.*"

"Let me explain, while . . . I . . . can," Blue Thunder said, his eyes searching hers.

She heard the mourning around her, and she ached to have been able to tell her mother that she loved her one more time. She listened to her father explain why he had turned his back on her and left her at Storm Rider's village.

She discovered that he had acted out of love, not callousness.

Tears came to her eyes as he poured his heart out to her, but she was afraid, for she could see him struggling to stay conscious.

His every breath was labored.

His eyes grew anxious and wide as he continued talking to her, each word now a labor of love.

"I am so sorry for causing you pain by leaving you with Storm Rider instead of taking you home with me," Blue Thunder said now between short, gasping breaths.

Talking Rain had to strain her ears to hear him, his words now so faint.

"My daughter, everything I have done for you since that day I found you alone and afraid has been in your best interest and out of love for you," he said. "Daughter, I decided to leave you behind as I rode from Chief Storm Rider's village because you were past the marrying age. I truly felt that if I did not do something to change your course in life, to see that you got married, you would never realize that you are a woman and filled with love that would sustain marriage and any children you gave birth to. I saw Storm Rider as the likely choice for a husband, especially since he is admired by all who know him and would make any woman a good husband."

He paused, coughing.

He then continued. "I . . . I . . . gave you away the way I did, for I knew that you might never leave your Crow people and choose a man yourself. And it is time for you to stop riding with men, behaving like them. In my dreams I have seen you as a mother and myself as a grandfather. Now it seems I will see neither, for my days are over."

"*Ahte*, oh, *ahte*, I will make you well," Talking Rain cried. She leaned down and gave him a soft kiss. "I will use your shaman brother's skills. I will make you well again."

"It is too late for me, but not for you, my *micinksi*, daughter," Blue Thunder said. He reached a trembling hand to her shoulder. Again their eyes met and held. "Please marry Storm Rider, Talking Rain. Have children. I can at least watch them grow from the heavens, where I will be forevermore with my ancestors."

He gripped her shoulder as tightly as possible. "Promise me, Talking Rain," he said almost desperately. "Promise that you will marry . . . and . . . have children."

Talking Rain heard the desperation in his voice, as though he knew that he was close to never saying words ever again to his daughter.

Talking Rain could hardly stand her remorse at knowing that the time was short with this man she had adored for so long.

How could she stand life without him? Yet she had to . . . for he was dying before her very eyes.

"*Ahte*, yes, I promise you that I will do both things, but you will not be watching from the heavens; you will be here with me," Talking Rain said, a sob catching in her throat as she said what she knew was not true.

Yes, she understood that he was dying . . . that she was spending her last, precious moments with him.

"My children will sit on your lap, *ahte*," Talking Rain said, forcing herself to be strong to get through these moments. She could hardly stand the thought of watching him take his last breath.

Oh, but if it were only her. She would trade places with him in an instant if she could. But as it was, she was destined to live . . . he to die. It had been written in the stars long ago which of them would go first.

"*Ahte*, you will tell my children, your grandchildren, the same tales that you told me," Talking Rain said, her eyes wild now as she saw him struggling so hard to stay with her.

"No, that will not be, but you can keep the stories alive for me by telling them to my grandchildren yourself," he said. A smile quivered across his lips, which had grown strangely bluish purple in color. "*Micinksi, micinksi,* daughter . . . daughter . . . *techila,* I love you so. . . ."

Talking Rain's heart sank when she saw him take one last, deep gasp, then go silent, the words *I love you* the last he would ever say, and the most important words he could have ever said to her, for she had hated thinking that he had never truly cared for her.

Now she knew that he had, and had done everything for her benefit, not his.

She slowly closed his eyes, then leaned down and pressed her cheek against his chest. She broke into deep, hard sobs. His hand had fallen away from her shoulder and now lay limply against her arm.

"How could I have lost you also?" she cried, remembering the day her mother took her last breath and sank into the river. Talking Rain had cried out for her mother and her father, over and over again, never seeing either of them again.

"*Ahte,* I shall never forget your kindness, nor Mother's," Talking Rain whispered.

She was then aware again of the other mourning cries around her. She suddenly felt selfish thinking only of herself and her own hurts, while so many of the people she loved had also lost those they loved.

"*Ahte,* I must go and see to others," she whispered as she rose to take one last look at his face.

She gently touched it, wondering at how his copper flesh was still warm to her touch, for she knew that in a matter of moments his skin would be cold forever.

Suddenly she felt a heavy hand on her shoulder.

She turned, looked up, and found Brave Shield there. For a long time now, he had been the next in line for chief of their people should Chief Blue Thunder die. She saw the choice as good. He was a kind, caring man, who had always put his people's interests first in his heart. Yes, he would be a good chief, and would one day be as revered as her chieftain father.

"Talking Rain, your brother and sister are missing," he said, his voice drawn. "They were almost certainly abducted by the renegades, for they have not been seen since the renegades rode from our village."

"No." Talking Rain gasped.

She rose shakily to her feet and looked desperately around her.

She had been so lost in despair over her mother's death, and knowing that her father followed soon behind her, she had forgotten everyone else, even her brother and sister. She grew cold inside when she realized the extent of the death and destruction that lay around her. The Crow village had been all but wiped out, with only a few warriors, women, and children left alive.

She could see how the elderly sat in a tight cluster together, having not been touched by the enemy at all, most likely because the renegades knew of their uselessness and had purposely left them alive as a way to mock the deaths of the vital ones of their village.

"My brother and sister," she said, her voice breaking. "Are they . . . the only two who are missing—I mean, actually missing?"

"It seems so," Brave Shield said, gazing at the ruined village. All around them, the loud wails vibrated into the heavens.

He looked at Talking Rain again and placed a gentle hand on her shoulder. "I am so sorry that I could not have done more for your father and mother . . . for our people," he said. "It all happened so quickly. Those of us who could ready our weapons brought down as many of the renegades as we could."

He gazed past her, up at the bluffs overlooking the village on one side. "The sentries must have been murdered, or they would have sounded an alarm that the renegades were near," he observed.

"How many able-bodied warriors are left?" Talking Rain asked.

"Very few," Brave Shield said. "I have already sent two out to follow the path of the renegades. If they can find the renegades' camp, they will try to recapture your brother and sister while the evil ones sleep. That is all that I can promise you, Talking Rain, that at least their rescue will be attempted."

"Thank you," Talking Rain said.

She sighed heavily.

She knew that she must be strong now in the eyes of her people. Although Brave Shield was the acting chief now, she was still the late chief's daughter, and more would be expected of her than mere tears and wails of mourning.

She turned from Brave Shield. She bent to her knees beside her father again and gave him a soft kiss, then turned to her mother and gave her the same. Then, with courage she was finding from deep within herself, she bravely and determinedly went among the people and began caring for the wounded and preparing the dead for burial.

The wails continued. One by one the heavens received them, as it did the spirits that were rising into the sky, their long path to the afterlife having already begun.

Talking Rain tried to put her concern for her brother and sister behind her. She just had to believe that the *Wah-con-tun-ga,* Great Medicine, would not also take them from her; that they were being watched out for, and were safe.

As Talking Rain assisted in every way possible, she mulled over what her father had said to her. She was so glad that she knew why he had given her away, and to whom. It had lifted such a burden from her heart when she discovered that her father had not left her at the Assiniboine village for monetary purposes. She knew that he had been right to think that she might never alter the course of her life, to what was truly best for her. If it hadn't been for Storm Rider forcing her hand in his own way, awakening her to how life could be for her now, she might never have stopped riding with the warriors, considering herself, in a sense, one of them.

She might have lived on and on and become a lonesome old lady in her later years, a spinster whose only memories were those of stealing horses and hunting buffalo, not of children or grandchildren, or a husband who adored her and made her older life more bearable.

She knew that her promise to her father about marrying and having children had been from the heart. It had not been said only out of loyalty to him during his last moments of life.

She did love Storm Rider.

She stopped when she thought of having left Storm Rider's gift, the black stone, for him to find with the silent message that by giving it back to him, she did not want him to come for her.

Now she regretted that with all of her heart. Having experienced so many losses tonight, and learning how short one's life could be, she knew what she wanted for the rest of her life—Storm Rider!

But what about Storm Rider?

Would he still care for her, or would he hate her for her having left him?

She hoped that he would think it through and understand a woman who was torn with hurt. She hoped that he would know that this caused her to do things that might not be rational at that moment of escape. She had to believe that as compassionate as Storm Rider had been about everything else, he would be about this, as well.

She hoped that when he saw that she was gone, he would soon follow, for she needed him now more than she ever thought that she would need a man.

She silently thanked her father for being so caring. He would suffer losing a daughter, and perhaps her love and devotion, in order to assure her the right sort of life—and especially the right man!

She turned and looked in the direction of Storm Rider's village. "Please come," she whispered. "Please, oh, please do come. I need you so badly." She had never thought that she would ever utter those words, or that she would need any man, but she did. Oh, how she did need Storm Rider.

But did he now still need—want—her?

Chapter 17

Storm Rider felt at peace with himself. He was relieved that Little Beaver was well on the road to recovery having enjoyed the special stories tonight. Storm Rider had picked ones he knew Little Beaver especially liked.

Now he was anxious to get to his lodge. He knew that Talking Rain must at last be rested. He had seen her standing at the entranceway watching him and listening to the stories. When he had no longer seen her there, he had to believe that she had gone to sit beside his lodge fire and wait for him, possibly eating a bowl of the stew that had been there for her for when she awakened.

He had much to say to her tonight. It was time they talked seriously of their future together.

It did seem that she was trying to get past her hurt over having been left there by her adopted father. Though Storm Rider knew that such a hurt could possibly last a lifetime. But he was going to make it better for her. He was going to make her so happy, she would even thank her *ahte* for choosing this future for her.

If Blue Thunder hadn't, Storm Rider was not sure he could have ever made Talking Rain realize the strength of her love for him. And she might even still hunger too much for that side of her life that she had known for so long. She would not want to give it up so easily.

Yes, it was up to him now to make her know where her true happiness lay—with him.

Walking faster now, he approached his lodge. The reflection of the fire within shimmered along the walls of skins that covered his lodge poles. He searched for Talking Rain's shadow, as she might be moving about inside his tepee.

But when he did not see anything of her, he smiled. She must be enjoying waiting for him by the fire.

Perhaps she was still eating, or was contentedly full and as anxious to see him as he was her.

"My woman," he whispered.

He smiled at how that sounded on his lips, how certainly it belonged there.

"My wife . . ." he then whispered.

He liked the sound of that even better, for he did intend to make her his wife before many more moons rose into the heavens.

He gazed up at the stars and the moon.

The sky was a beautiful place tonight, so peaceful . . . so right for a night on which he planned to request this woman's hand in marriage.

"It is so right," he whispered, stepping up to the entrance flap.

He hesitated, sucked in an anxious breath, then placed a hand at the buckskin flap and slowly shoved it aside.

His eyes shining with excitement, he stepped into the tepee.

But that excitement soon faded into a sudden foreboding, which swept through him with the coldness of a surprise early snowstorm. His lodge was empty.

Then he heaved in another breath and smiled, for surely he was wrong to think anything amiss just because he did not see Talking Rain in his lodge.

The night *was* beautiful. While he had his back turned to his tepee, she must have stepped outside to take a walk and enjoy the wonders of the evening. She was free to do so, for she was no longer a captive. But the memory of her behavior after her father had left her made him think that maybe he had been a bit premature in allowing her her freedom.

Had she just been waiting for an opportunity to flee? Had she not done so earlier only because she had been devoted to caring for the child? Then had she slept away the days and nights, needing the rest so that she was strong enough to flee into the dark shadows of the night at her first opportunity?

"No, she would not do that," he said aloud.

He frustratedly raked his fingers through his hair.

She *knew* the dangers of being alone, especially during the wicked hours of night, when renegades roamed the land in search of someone to loot or kill. She knew that the Snake was a clever, elusive man, who could have been waiting for an opportunity to seize her and do with her what he had not before.

"No . . ." he said in a groan of despair. He took a step farther into the tepee, and then stopped.

His heart skipped a beat when he stared disbelievingly at what he saw lying on the bulrush mats beside the fire, beside the blankets upon which she had slept, beside an empty bowl that proved that she had eaten the food left for her—food that she had eaten, he now believed, to gain the strength to get to her Crow people's village.

He was torn by anger, hurt, and the fear that she might not live through the night, since she had apparently, unthinkingly, left the safety of not only his lodge, but also his village. His heart pounding, he knelt and plucked up the tiny doeskin bag.

Its weight, and the defining shape of what lay inside the bag, proved that Talking Rain had chosen to leave behind the black glass stone that he had given to her.

That tore at Storm Rider's heart for more than one reason. Leaving the special stone was surely a message that she was leaving him forever. She did not care for him enough to stay with him.

Apparently she had forgotten the true importance of carrying this stone with her at all times. It was not only a token of his love for her—it was also for protection. He had explained to her that this stone had a special purpose: Whoever wore it would be kept safe from all dangers that they might face.

It might have helped save her from the Snake!

"The Snake," Storm Rider said in a low growl.

His heart thudded like many horses' hooves thundering across the land. He tied the small bag to the waist of his breechclout, then hurried to the back of his lodge.

There he sheathed his sharpest, deadliest knife at his side. He grabbed up his quiver of arrows and positioned them on his back. Then he yanked up his most powerful bow and ran in his moccasined feet from the lodge.

When he reached his corral at the back of his tepee, he realized in one sweep of his eyes which horse was missing.

It was the brown mare that was one of his favored steeds, second to his strawberry roan and the magnificent black stallion that was watching him even now in the moonlight with eyes that seemed to know Storm Rider's dark mood.

The steed dug at the ground with its thick hoof, shook its heavy mane and whinnied, then came to Storm Rider and sniffed at his bare chest.

"Yes, you are the chosen one tonight, Midnight," Storm Rider said. "You seem to know my needs and my fears."

He readied the horse quickly for riding, led him from the corral and mounted in one quick movement.

He did not need to follow tracks left by the brown mare, since he knew in which direction Talking Rain would ride her. Storm Rider slapped his reins and rode off in a hard gallop beneath the moonlight, the happiness of his people, their soft songs as they had came together beside the fire after the stories to the children were over, quickly left behind.

The feel of the tiny bag against his flesh made Storm Rider's heart ache.

Yet its presence made him even more determined to find Talking Rain, hopefully before anything happened to her.

She was so vulnerable at night, especially with the moon so bright and revealing. If renegades had seen her alone, especially the Snake, it might already be too late.

If he lost her in such a way, he would forever

blame himself for having not realized that she would never be able to accept what her father had done.

She would never rest until she knew the reasons why.

Yes, he should have known. And since he was so full of himself and thinking that she would forget everything else but him, she might even now be . . .

He shook his head in an effort to erase all bad thoughts from his mind.

No, he would not give up hope, either for finding her safe, or for still believing that he could make her understand her own heart.

Yes, he would find her.

Hopefully she had made it safely to the Crow village and already had answers to the questions that had plagued her.

By now she must know that her father had left her behind for her own good, not his.

He drew a tight rein and halted his stallion when a noise in the air came to him like a cold wind seeping into his very soul.

It was wailing!

It was the mournful cries of grieving, of despair, of such an unhappiness it made him wince to think of what might have caused such emotion. And it made his heart skip several beats, as utter fear coursed through him. He realized from which direction these sounds came.

They were from the Crow village!

And if so, it meant only one thing: They had fallen victim to an ambush. Surely many had died.

"Talking Rain . . ." he whispered.

He shivered uncontrollably at the thought of her reaching the village just in time to fall victim to something infinitely worse than a father's rejection.

"Let it not be so," he cried to the heavens. "Please let her not have entered my life only to be taken so soon from me!"

Fighting his emotions and summoning his strength for whatever he found when he arrived at the Crow village, Storm Rider slapped his reins and sent Midnight into another hard gallop. He came to the summit of a hill that looked down over the Crow village. The moon's glow revealed to him a place of havoc, destruction, and devastation.

He stopped long enough to take a longer, harder look and see if he could make out in the moonlight who was left alive.

All that he could see were shadows moving about . . . and many lifeless bodies lying prone on the ground, loved ones kneeling beside them.

The central fire leaped higher into the sky than usual, and he knew why: Many of the lodge coverings had been removed and were a part of the fire. He strained his neck forward to see if he could see whether the chief's larger lodge still stood. When he saw that it had also been razed, he knew then that most likely the Crow chief and his wife were among the dead, and possibly their children as well.

His despair so intense he could hardly bear to see if the woman he loved had died tonight so needlessly, he sat there a moment longer.

Then, needing to know, and wanting to offer whatever help he could to those who had survived the ordeal, he sank his heels into the flanks of his steed and rode onward.

Endless questions raced through his mind. Had Talking Rain been at the village when it had been attacked? Was she dead? Had she been raped, or even scalped?

The thought of any of the horrors happening to Talking Rain made him almost physically ill. He realized just how much he did love her and wanted to care for her. . . .

And as he came to the very edge of what was left of the village, he could make out someone standing there, watching his approach. His heart filled with such relief that tears sprang to his eyes, for it was Talking Rain!

She must've heard the approach of a horse and had come to see who it was.

It was obvious that she was ready to stand her ground against an enemy should they be arriving again, for she had a rifle aimed straight ahead, poised for firing, as did several warriors. They were on each side of her, ready to fire, but stopped when they saw that the lone rider was anything but an enemy.

He was their new friend—Chief Storm Rider!

Realizing that it was Storm Rider, Talking Rain dropped the rifle and broke into a mad run toward his horse, her arms outstretched. Her tears were hot against her cheeks as they streamed endlessly from her eyes.

"Storm Rider!" she cried. He leaped from his steed and grabbed her to him and held her close. She melted into his embrace.

She clung to him, her cheek pressed against his powerful, bare chest, her tears wetting his flesh. If ever before she thought never to need a man, this moment in time proved her wrong. She needed Storm Rider's strength, his courage, his love!

"Oh, Storm Rider, it is so terrible," she said, sobbing. "The Snake and his renegades came and did this. My parents . . . they . . . they are dead. My brother and sister are missing. The Snake took them away, for no one has found them anywhere."

She leaned away from him and gazed up into his eyes. "Storm Rider, I have lost two sets of parents in my lifetime, and now maybe even my brother and sister." She sobbed. "How can life be so cruel to me? How?"

She turned and looked toward the village at those who sat crying beside their loved ones who had died.

"My people, they have lost so much," she said, a sob catching in her throat. She turned tearful eyes up at him again. "Even their chief, my father," she said. "I feel so alone, oh, so very alone. My people do, as well."

He placed gentle hands on her shoulders. "No, neither you nor your people are alone," he said. "I am here for you. I will help you. My people will open their hearts and homes to your people. Your people can place their full trust in me. I will do what I can to right these wrongs."

Brave Shield approached and stepped up next to Talking Rain.

He held out a friendly hand toward Storm Rider. "It is good that you are here offering assistance," he said, his voice drawn from weariness. "I am Brave Shield. I am now acting chief for my Crow people. Chief Blue Thunder appointed me not long ago to take his place were he to decide to step down, or . . . die."

"It is good to make your acquaintance again," Storm Rider said, accepting the handshake of friendship. "I remember you from the council between our warriors, although you were not introduced at that time as the next chief in line."

"No one would have thought it would happen so quickly, so there was no need," Brave Shield said humbly. He gazed down at Talking Rain. "My people have lost so much tonight, but Talking Rain has lost the most."

Fresh tears sprang from her eyes.

Storm Rider lovingly reached a hand and smoothed her tears away with a thumb, then drew her to his side and placed an arm around her waist, which proved two things to Brave Shield—that this woman was his, and that he would take over for her.

She gazed up at Storm Rider, so glad that he had come, and that he had obviously forgiven her for departing without even a word of good-bye and leaving behind the bag he had given her.

But now everything had changed. She knew just how much she needed and loved him. Nothing would ever change her mind again. She would take from him whatever he gave to her willingly.

"Do you want to say a final good-bye to my mother and father before they are put in their burial wrappings?" she asked, her voice breaking.

"Yes, I would like to do that," Storm Rider said tightly, for although he had seen many deaths in his lifetime, even of those he loved very much, it was never a task he was prepared for. To him, Chief Blue Thunder was a friend, even if only for a short while. It would be hard to look down at his face and see no more life in his eyes. He had had such a friendly smile, such a gentle laugh.

Brave Shield stayed behind as Talking Rain took

Storm Rider to her parents, who now lay side by side, their hands touching.

"I already miss them so much," Talking Rain said, a sob lodging in the depths of her throat. "Life will be so empty without their smiles, laughter, and warm hugs."

"They are smiling even now, Talking Rain, as they gaze at you from the stars," Storm Rider said.

He reached for one of her hands and held it lovingly.

He gazed at her parents for a moment longer, then led Talking Rain from them when she broke down into hard, body-racking sobs.

Brave Shield came to them again. "Talking Rain, those warriors whom I have assigned to search for your brother and sister are ready to leave now," he said. "You said that you wished to accompany us on the search. Do you still wish to? Are you strong enough? The pain I see in your eyes and hear in your voice has surely weakened you."

"I am strong enough, yes, to search for my loved ones," Talking Rain said.

She turned to Brave Shield and forced herself not to cry anymore. She lifted her chin proudly.

"I must help," she said with determination. "I must do all that I can to find them. Then when I return, I must see to the burial of my parents."

Storm Rider had looked past Brave Shield and saw just how few warriors were left to go on the search. Their departure then would leave too few at the village to protect against the possible return of the Snake.

He turned his eyes back to Brave Shield. "May I suggest leaving as many as you feel are necessary to protect those who have survived tonight's ambush, and bring other warriors with me to my village," Storm Rider said. "There we will add to the number searching tonight for the two children. With greater numbers, there is much more hope of a successful search."

"Yes, that is good, and thank you for your kindness," Brave Shield said. He reached a hand over to Storm Rider and placed it on his shoulder. "I was not certain before that it was wise to make your friendship so quickly without knowing you better, but now I see that it was very wise of my chief to have chosen an alliance with you. I hope to continue the alliance and together build a bond that will last an eternity."

"From now on we are brothers in all ways," Storm Rider said, clasping hands with Brave Shield for a long moment.

Then Brave Shield went and instructed his warriors, and Storm Rider led Talking Rain to a steed that was very familiar to him—his brown mare she had taken tonight.

He stopped, placed his hands on her shoulders,

and turned her toward him. "Did you and your *ahte* talk before . . ."

It was hard to speak the words that he knew pained her, so he did not complete his question. She knew without his even doing so what he wanted to know.

"Yes, he explained everything to me," she said, her voice breaking. "And it was all done for love, not for material gain. He wanted you and me to be together . . . to marry. He wanted grandchildren from our union."

Storm Rider smiled. He placed a hand to her cheek. "And?" he said. "What did you tell him?"

"I assured him that I would fulfill this last wish for his daughter," she said, again ready to cry as she recalled those precious moments with her father.

That response made Storm Rider's heart leap with as much joy as he could feel in the face of such a disaster as tonight's.

Knowing that Talking Rain had all but promised herself to him at this moment was enough to make his heart sing, and helped somewhat with the sad feelings.

He didn't get the chance to outwardly respond to what she said. Brave Shield had ridden up with his warriors. They were equipped with what weapons had not been destroyed tonight; mostly bows and arrows.

"Let us ride!" Storm Rider said, running to his

steed and mounting it in one leap. "We will go to my village and get warriors and then end our search with success!"

Feeling love, gratitude, and pride for Storm Rider, Talking Rain rode at the lead with him and Brave Shield, each chief on either side of her.

Then she felt something else: guilt. Guilt for having not been with her people when they were attacked so that she could have fought hard defending them.

Instead she had stayed at Storm Rider's village, sleeping her days away after having made the young brave well.

She could not help but feel cowardly to have taken the time to rest instead of fleeing to her adopted father. Had she gone sooner, she would have been there to help defend her people. Most certainly her brother and sister would never have been abducted. Not while she was alive, anyway. She would have died defending them.

Now?

Her heart ached to know that they may both have been defiled, which was a fate nearly worse than death. It would leave a scar on their souls forever, and would never allow them to feel innocent again. They might never want to take a husband or wife into their lives. Tears filled Talking Rain's eyes again as she rode onward.

Storm Rider felt Talking Rain try to stifle a sob

and glanced over at her. In the moonlight he saw that she was being tortured inside by guilt, and he wished that he could do something to lessen her pain.

He also felt guilty for not having helped her understand why her father had turned his back on her.

But that was then. This was now. And nothing could change how it had been.

He just couldn't help but be thankful that he hadn't let Talking Rain return with Chief Blue Thunder, or she would have either died tonight, or been abducted and possibly raped.

And he was so afraid for the twins. The mindless, heartless renegades did not always stop at raping young girls, but also sometimes raped their boy captives. It removed all spirit from the young brave, so that he would be ashamed for having been defiled in such a way, and would never grow up to feel worthy of being called a warrior.

Yes, he did worry that both children would be raped, but hoped that the renegades first toyed with them, making them dread the moment they knew would occur. This might give him time to find them.

The agony of waiting for a terrible fate was the sort of thing the renegades were expert in prolonging.

It was just another way to use fear to, in the end, totally demolish the pride of their captives. Were they ever released, the captives would be left with only memories they could never forget, or live with. Children who had been held captive then released often died at their own hand. They could not live with the knowledge that their young bodies had been violated in such a way.

Storm Rider was glad when his village came into view a short distance away. Soon he could gather together his most able-bodied warriors for the search.

He must find the children before it was too late. And then the Snake would die!

He reached down and untied the tiny doeskin pouch that held the black stone. He rode closer to Talking Rain and offered the bag out toward her. She smiled, reached out, and took it.

"I should have never left it behind," she said, circling her fingers tightly around the bag. "I shall never again."

They exchanged smiles, then rode into the village together. Shortly after, they left again with twenty of Storm Rider's warriors.

Talking Rain felt hope for the first time that her brother and sister would be found.

Chapter 18

Talking Rain sat beside a campfire, a blanket draped around her shoulders. Her spirits were as low as her gaze locked on the flames. She now doubted that she would ever see her brother and sister again. Several days had stretched into a week of searching for the twins without any sign of either of them.

Talking Rain had stayed with the search except for one day, when she had returned to her village to see to the proper burial of her parents.

Those of her Crow warriors who searched with her and Storm Rider had taken turns, as well, returning home to bury their loved ones, then rejoining the search.

Every nook and cranny, bluff, cave, and valley had been gone over so carefully, and everyone but Talking Rain and Storm Rider had returned to their villages.

Downhearted and distraught, Talking Rain had not wanted to return yet to the problems at her village, where she faced decisions about her people's future.

And she trusted that Brave Shield was capable of doing what was needed for their Crow people. He had been taught by the best, most skilled, and most adored leader—her *ahte*.

She guessed that Brave Shield was torn by pondering whether to make a new village elsewhere, or rebuild close to the graves of those loved ones who had not lived through the ambush.

Tomorrow Talking Rain would ride to her village and take part in the council, as final decisions would be made.

Storm Rider had volunteered to go with her and sit among her people as well. He would not offer advice unless asked, but would be there as moral support for Talking Rain.

These past days, Storm Rider and Talking Rain had grown closer than she had ever thought possible with a man. But these past days had also taught her a lot about life—how a person could awaken one morning with dreams of a wonderful, bright future alive in her heart, only to have life whisked away in the next heartbeat by a madman's thirst for blood.

Talking Rain knew now that she did not want to be alone as she walked into the future days of her life. She wanted to be with Storm Rider, even though giving her heart to him was the same as turning her back on all that had previously made her feel alive, that had made her leap from her bed each morning with eagerness for what the day ahead held for her—the excitement of the hunt, or the challenge of horse-stealing raids with the warriors of her village.

Yes, all of that had changed, but not necessarily because of the ambush on her people.

She had to confess that the change had begun that first time she had seen Storm Rider and experienced so many strange, yet delicious feelings in her heart.

Although she had tried to fight these feelings with every fiber of her being, she knew that particular battle had been lost.

And now, yes, now she no longer fought the feelings that lay claim to her heart. Tonight she knew what would transpire between herself and Storm Rider.

That was the main reason they had fallen back from the others and had chosen to spend a night alone beneath the stars.

She glanced quickly to her left when she heard the crackling sound of a snapped twig.

She relaxed when she saw that the person responsible for that sound was Storm Rider. He walked toward her with an armload of broken tree limbs that he had gathered to feed the fire for the rest of the night.

It was autumn now in these hills and valleys, and the nights sometimes turned so cold the water froze at the very edges of the rivers and streams.

But Talking Rain did not expect to be cold even if the fire did go out, for she intended to spend the night in the arms of the man she was going to marry.

Yes, marriage was something that she truly wanted. And as her father had so hoped for, she would have children.

She smiled when she realized how he had said that he would be watching from the heavens as his grandchildren grew up. And she believed that he would. She even felt his presence now and knew that he would be happy that she had followed the part of her heart tonight that belonged always and forever to Storm Rider.

Thinking of Storm Rider made a strange sort of heat rush to that private place between her thighs, where no man's hands had ever touched.

She had never had these sensations, which made her somewhat dizzy with pleasure, until she saw Storm Rider. He was causing her body to react in such a foreign way to her.

If just looking at him made her feel so deliciously wonderful, his touches and caresses would be infinitely more arousing. She could hardly wait to be taken away on clouds of rapture with him. For those moments she would be able to forget the heartache of having lost so much at the hands of the Snake.

One thing did concern her, though: The fire that would keep her and Storm Rider warm through the night might be a beacon, luring unsavory characters to their campsite, like the very man they hunted.

But she reassured herself that no land for miles and miles around had been left untouched by the Crow and Assiniboine warriors as they searched for the elusive killer. They had not only gone over this area once, but three times, until they knew that the Snake could not possibly be anywhere near.

"I did not mean to frighten you," Storm Rider said, approaching her. He knelt on one knee and let the wood roll from his arms.

He turned to Talking Rain. "Are you warm yet after your bath in the river?" he asked. His hair was still wet from his own bath.

While swimming together in the river he had reached out and touched her breasts, causing her to moan sensually. Then he had drawn her against his hard body and kissed her.

In the way her slim, silken body had strained against his, yielding to his caress, he knew that she was ready to surrender to him, as he was to her.

He could have had her in the river, but knew the dangers to staying in the water for that long. It was not the chance of people coming upon them, but the coldness that presented the true danger. After just a short while, the chill had sunk clean into his bones. He had been glad to leave the water and return to the warmth of the blankets and the fire.

He knew that he could have approached Talking Rain even then for lovemaking, since her eyes had shone with passion, but finding enough firewood for the entire night came first.

Now that was done, and he saw that Talking Rain still looked seductively at him in a way that would make any man's heart stop. He could not delay any longer what he had hungered for since that first time he saw her. She had been riding her steed, her golden hair flying in the breeze, her beautiful face marred only by streaks of paint. He had never seen such strength and pride in a woman before.

Intrigue had quickly turned into a need that only now would be fed. And she, too, had fought hard not to give into her needs.

Even that had made her more attractive to him.

"I am warm enough," Talking Rain murmured, her pulse racing at what she saw in his eyes. His hunger for her was stronger than ever before. There was a definite passion there, smoldering.

He came to her and smoothed her long, damp locks back from her shoulders, then gently lifted the blanket away and let it fall down around her. Her nude body was now fully revealed to him. She felt herself trembling, but not from the cold. Her own passion was fed by his gaze, his touch, his kiss, as he filled his arms with her. He kissed her heatedly, long and hard.

"My woman," he whispered against her lips as he lowered her to the blankets. "I have waited for so long. Are you truly here? Are you truly willing?"

"I am here, and, ah, yes, my love, I am willing," she whispered.

She trembled with ecstasy as he set her completely down on the blankets and ran his hands slowly, searchingly, down her body.

Then, as her breathing quickened, she watched him lower his breechclout, so that he was completely nude. Seeing his magnificent manhood made her gasp, partially with desire, and partially with fear of the unknown: she had never made love before, but sensed that *Wah-con-tun-ga*, the Great Medicine, had been very generous to this man as far as his anatomy was concerned.

She had traveled with the warriors of her village, which often took them from their homes for more than one night, but she had never seen any of the men unclothed. They had treated her with the utmost respect and made certain they were far from her for their baths.

She was glad of this now, having never seen a man unclothed before only enhanced the moment when the man she loved revealed himself to her.

"Touch me," Storm Rider said softly. He saw her eyes transfixed on the part of him that was hard and ready for lovemaking. He reached for one of her hands. "Feel its strength before I place it inside of you."

"I have never before . . ." Talking Rain started. "You are so . . ."

She trembled when he placed her hand on his warm manhood, and then purposefully closed her fingers around it.

"Move your hand on me," Storm Rider said.

She did, and his jaw tightened when the pleasure rushed through him, hot and pulsing. He gritted his teeth and held his head back as she continued moving her hand, the sensation rising, spreading. And fearing that he was too near to the ultimate passion, he pulled her hand away from him. He wanted to reach that height only with her.

But where he then placed it made her gasp, her eyes widening. He had actually guided her hand to her own private place, which seemed tonight to have a heartbeat all its own. It throbbed strangely and made an ache begin within her.

"What are you doing?" she gasped.

She tried to yank her hand away, but he held it in place.

"Move your hand on yourself as you moved it on me," Storm Rider said huskily. "It is all right to do this. We are together learning each other's bodies."

When she still did not move her hand on herself, he showed her how it was done.

It felt so blissful she thought she might faint dead away with the pleasure.

Then suddenly it was not her hand, but his caressing her there. Moaning, she closed her eyes and slowly tossed her head back and forth.

"It feels so good," she whispered.

She licked her lips and ran her fingers through her hair. Then she gazed down with wide-open eyes when she felt something warm and wet on the place on her body that was so alive.

She looked in wonder at Storm Rider and saw that his tongue was flicking along the swollen nub. When his teeth nipped her there gently, she cried out with an ecstasy she had never known before.

"What are you doing?" she asked, her heart throbbing.

He gazed up at her, his eyes filled with dark, hot passion. "What I am doing is preparing you for the ultimate pleasure," he said huskily. "Do not be afraid of the feelings you are experiencing. Relax. Enjoy. From now on, you will never again be without the lovemaking I will give you tonight, for, my woman, you will be mine in every way possible."

She swallowed hard, closed her eyes, then let herself enjoy.

Her whole body seemed to be floating. She was so lost in passion she hardly noticed that he had moved on top of her, blanketing her with his body.

He was probing with his manhood where his caresses had felt so warmly delicious.

His lips came down hard upon hers, and one of his knees spread her legs farther apart. She noticed that his manhood rested against the hot flesh of her womanhood, its heat pressing slowly inside her warm, wet place.

His kiss deepened as he held her closer in his arms and made the last plunge that broke through the thin barrier that had kept her virginally pure.

For a moment she felt a sharp pain, but his lips on hers, his arms holding her so wonderfully against him, made her soon forget the discomfort. She experienced the wonders of his body as it aroused even more rapture within her. She clung to him, meeting each of his thrusts with abandon as her body became a river of sensations.

He drove into her, the yielding silk of her flesh setting him afire with pleasure. He felt the heat growing, spreading, the fires leaping within him, and he knew that he could not hold off for much longer. Breathing hard, he paused. He gazed lovingly into her eyes. A soft smile fluttered across his lips.

"Tonight was worth the wait," he said. "You have awakened in me so much that I did not know was even there."

"As you have within me," Talking Rain murmured.

She sucked in a wild breath of ecstasy when he bent low and flicked his tongue across one of her nipples, then sucked it between his teeth.

She drew another ragged breath and gasped with rapture, then ran her fingers through his hair and down to the tight muscles of his hips.

She splayed her hands there and gave a light press, with him following her lead as he pushed himself more deeply within her, and began his rhythmic thrusts again.

"I feel a hunger so new to me, and wonderful," she whispered against his lips as he laid his cheek against hers.

"I am feeding that hunger," Storm Rider said.

He again kissed her passionately, his whole body fluid with desire.

He sculpted himself to her moist body. She wrapped her legs around him and met each of his thrusts with her own.

He pressed endlessly deeper, then held his head back away from her, groaned, and gave one last thrust that brought them both over the edge of a tremendous ecstasy.

They clung and kissed; then his body subsided exhaustedly against hers.

As a loon echoed its eerie cry over the river a short distance away and an owl answered with its own strange call, Storm Rider and Talking Rain lay enjoying the bliss that still encompassed them both.

She gently stroked his back, damp with perspiration.

He kissed her softly on the beautiful column of her throat, then lowered his lips and kissed first one breast and then the other.

"I do love you so," Talking Rain said.

He slowly rolled away from her, then lay beside her, one hand sweetly stroking one of her breasts. "*Tecihila*, I love you," he said, smiling at her. "With all of my heart and soul, I love you."

He touched her cheek. "My woman, I vow to you now that I will never allow anything to happen to you," he said. "I also vow that I shall never give up searching for your brother and sister. Tomorrow, after the council at your village, I will send out warriors again to search for the twins. I just cannot believe the renegades have gone so far with the twins that we cannot find them. The Snake lives for terrorizing this area. He would not give it up now, when he has not before."

"I, too, do not think that he has given up his desire to harm my people and yours," Talking Rain responded. "And I appreciate so much your commitment not only to finding my brother and sister, but also to helping my people as a whole."

"It is so terrible, what happened to your people," Storm Rider said. "It could have happened as easily to my own. So whatever I can do to help, I shall do."

"For tonight, let us just think of us," Talking Rain

said. "I had never known it could be like this between a man and a woman. I feel so foolish for thinking I did not need such attention from a man." She smiled over at him, placing a finger to his lips. "But you are not just any man. You are so . . . so—"

He didn't let her finish. He rose above her again and covered her with his body, his lips now speaking everything to her that his heart and soul felt.

Again they made maddening love, then fell asleep in each other's arms, the fire burning softly nearby.

Far away from where Talking Rain and Storm Rider had found such sweet passion, Dancing Wings and Young Elk sat trembling as they watched the Snake and his renegade friends laugh and drink beside a campfire.

"Brother, what do you think comes next?" Dancing Wings asked, tears filling her eyes. "Do you think the firewater tonight will cause them to . . . to . . . ?"

"It seems they do not have us on their mind in that way," Young Elk said, stiffening when the Snake gave him a strange sort of gaze. "But soon we shall discover their purpose in stealing us away. And when that happens, sister, I will protect you. I will fight to my death before I allow any of those madmen to touch you."

"So shall I protect you," Dancing Wings whispered. "I shall grab the evil one's knife and kill him. . . ."

They both grew quiet again, then sighed with relief when the renegades all went to their beds of blankets and fell into a drunken sleep.

Young Elk's eyes never left their captors as again he tried to work loose the ropes at his wrists, which were tied behind him. His ankles were tied to stakes in the ground, as were his sister's.

"Try harder, brother," Dancing Wings said, swallowing hard. "Please try harder. My courage gets less and less each day. . . ."

Chapter 19

It had not been a kiss on her lips from her loved one that woke Talking Rain. Instead, it had been the cold sting of several snowflakes on her cheeks.

As the wolf's howl was a bad omen, she could not help but feel that this early snowfall was just as bad a sign of the approaching winter—it might be one of the worst in history.

She had awakened Storm Rider and they gathered up their belongings and hurried to her Crow village to sit in council for the decision of the Red Root band's future.

They sat now in a circle around a huge outdoor fire. The snow had stopped after having dropped only a few snowflakes from the sky. But it had been enough to frighten the Crow into a quick decision.

Talking Rain sat on a thick pallet of pelts between Storm Rider and Brave Shield, a warm blanket around her shoulders. All of the remaining Crow people huddled beneath blankets as they awaited their band's fate.

"Since all of our lodges were destroyed in the ambush, today we were forced to awaken with snow
on our faces," Brave Shield said, his jaw tight with
an angry determination to do what was right for his
people.

"Either we stay and hurriedly rebuild, or move
on and find a home elsewhere," he then said. "If this
place, which has been our home for many winters,
harbors too many sad feelings, then we will move
onward. If you feel that you cannot withstand the
painful memories as you look around you at land
upon which many of our loved ones died, then I
would say we must leave now, or be forced to wait
until spring. Please voice your feelings about what
we should do. Stay? Or leave?"

Talking Rain looked around her and saw on the
faces of her people that most were torn. She knew
that many would not want to leave the graves of
their loved ones, most of which were new.

Yet was not what Brave Shield said true? Could
the memories of land bloodied by their relatives and
friends be too much to bear in their village each day
and night? Even now the stains were there, even
though attempts had been made to brush them
away, or cover them with fresh dirt, which was
pounded down tight by moccasined feet.

Storm Rider wanted to offer a suggestion—that
they all come to his village for the duration of the
autumn and the approaching winter. He was afraid

that they could not get where they intended to go before winter struck in its fury.

If they accepted his offer to stay, they could move on to a new land, a new home, when spring breezes warmed their faces, not when snows and cold winds bit almost right into one's soul.

After he and Talking Rain left their campsite where they had made love for the first time and were on their way to her village on their steeds, he had offered the suggestion to her.

It was up to her now whether she presented it to her people, for Storm Rider had told her that he would sit in her people's council, not participate verbally. He did not want to belittle Brave Shield's new position of leadership by making suggestions. It was Brave Shield's place to make the proper decision for his people. But Talking Rain could speak up and all would understand why.

She was her father's daughter. Her *ahte* had led the Crow with much love, care, and devotion. Talking Rain had sat in council with him, and learned leadership from him. Had she been a man, she would be chief now, not Brave Shield.

As though Talking Rain sensed what Storm Rider had been thinking, she suddenly stood up. She fought back the urge to cry, since this was her first council without her *ahte* at the lead. He had been appointed the Crow's chief even before Talking Rain had joined their people.

There was a void today not only because of her father's death, but because of all of those who had died with him.

Her mother was among them. Whenever her mother's beautiful, sweet face came to Talking Rain's mind, she had to brush it aside quickly or cave in to her feelings of remorse that tore her heart to shreds.

Instead, clutching the blanket around her shoulders, she forced herself to stand straight and tall.

She tightened her jaw as she looked from face to face.

"I have been a part of your lives now for thirteen winters, and I have shared many wonderful and difficult times with you, but the ambush was the worst we have had to face in my time with you," she said.

She smiled down at Brave Shield. "We now have a new chief, an *otancan,* a new principal leader, one that my *ahte* personally picked to be your *otancan* should my father die," she said. "Brave Shield is a *wicasa-iyotanyapi,* man of honor, a man of *woksapa,* wisdom."

She looked again into the faces of her people.

"I do not want to take away from his leadership by making suggestions today myself," she said, her voice drawn. "But he has asked for suggestions, and since none of you have offered any, might I say how I feel?"

Again everyone sat quiet. None had responded. And Talking Rain understood. Her people hesitated at speaking up to say, Yes, do please speak your mind. She knew they wished so from the looks in their faces. After all, she was the daughter of her father.

But they did not want to take away from the leadership of their new chief. They did not want to make him think they did not trust his judgment. Therefore, they stayed silent.

"Yes, Talking Rain, do speak your mind," Brave Shield said, breaking the tension, since he, too, understood his people's silence. "Do you not know that when you speak, it is your *ahte* whose words our people will hear? *Ho*, do tell us all your opinion. All will listen."

Their prized council house lay behind them in a pile of ashes, and the smoke still rising from it resembled the ghosts of all their lost relatives. Talking Rain could feel her father's presence and drew from that the courage to continue saying what she felt was right for the people her father had loved.

She gave Storm Rider a quick glance and a smile, then turned again and faced her people. "I truly believe that staying here would be too hurtful," she said, her voice cracking. "The blood spilled on this ground will not wash away until spring, when the rains come, and no matter how much you try to cover it or brush it further into the dirt of the ground, it is there, a reminder of the deaths that came at the hand of the Snake and his renegade warriors. I would suggest to you something other than what has been discussed today."

Again she glanced down at Storm Rider. He nodded and smiled. She glanced at Brave Shield, who also nodded and smiled.

Feeling that Brave Shield would honor anything she said, she then turned to face her people again.

"As you know, Chief Storm Rider sat in council with my father and our new chief, Brave Shield, shortly before my father's death," she said.

Talking Rain inhaled a quavering breath, for just speaking the word *father* brought to her mind those last precious moments with him, and their final farewell.

That pained her heart so much, she had to keep brushing it from her mind.

Her *ahte* was gone.

So many of his people were gone, as well.

But there were those who still lived, and she wanted to be certain the decision made today was the right one for them. She did not want the winter to claim any of those who had lived through the horrendous ambush.

Again she felt her father's presence. It was as though his arm was around her waist, comforting her, as she again found the courage to continue speaking.

"Chief Storm Rider, my father, Brave Shield, and other warriors sat together in council and came together as friends. Their futures were joined in the hunt for the Snake," she said. "Oh, my father wished so much to be shared between our Crow people and Chief Storm Rider's Assiniboine people, and I know that he would approve of my suggestion."

She glanced at Brave Shield. His nod and smile of reassurance proved that he still wanted her to continue. He respected her as much as he had respected her father.

She looked at her people again. "I believe that it would be in our people's best interest if we move into Chief Storm Rider's village, to live with his people during the long *wah-nee-e-too*, winter," she said.

Her eyes moved slowly over the crowd as she tried to read their reaction to her suggestion. She could see them leaning on her each and every word, and that made her proud. She realized that they were feeling her father's presence the same as she.

"And then when *wai-too*, spring, comes, if you then wish to search for a new home for our people, that would be a better time to go than now," she continued.

She studied the faces of her people as she finished her speech. She saw a quiet peace come over them. They had dreaded traveling when their burdens were so heavy. With the cold winter winds soon upon them, searching for a new home would be even more difficult.

Chief Brave Shield rose and stood beside Talking Rain. He looked down at Storm Rider and motioned with a hand for him to stand on Talking Rain's other side.

Storm Rider returned Brave Shield's nod and moved up to stand beside Talking Rain. He was truly no intrusion today on these people's council, and he felt as though he belonged there among them. He was especially proud to stand at his woman's side after she had spoken with such deep feeling to her people.

Talking Rain was aware of warm hands sliding into hers at each side. One was Storm Rider's. The other was Brave Shield's. She felt a bond flowing from Brave Shield to Storm Rider. She knew that Storm Rider's band and hers had just made a pact that would last forever.

"I agree with Talking Rain's suggestion," Brave Shield said, smiling at his people. He looked over and smiled again at Storm Rider. "I feel a deep gratitude to Chief Storm Rider for his offer to assist us at this time, when our hearts, but never our spirits, have been broken. *Pila-maye,* thank you, Storm Rider, from the bottom of my heart, and my people's, as well."

He then smiled at Talking Rain. "And *pila-maye,* Talking Rain. The courage your father instilled in you is strong," he said. "Your *ahte* is with you now, proud."

Tears flooded Talking Rain's eyes, but she forced them back.

"*Pila-maye,*" she murmured.

Brave Shield again focused on his people. "Let us vote to see how many of you wish to join Chief Storm Rider's people," he said. "Raise your hands if you wish to accept Chief Storm Rider's offer."

Everyone's hands were raised all at one time. The decision was unanimous.

Brave Shield then gazed solemnly at Talking Rain. "And know this, Talking Rain: The hunt will never end until we have found your brother and sister," he said.

"*Pila-maye,* thank you. That is another reason why I felt it was best for our people not to move to a new home, a new land, just yet," Talking Rain said, again feeling the heat of tears in her eyes. "Should my brother and sister manage to flee the wrath of the Snake and get home, they will not have far to go to find us. We will be only a short distance away at Storm Rider's village."

She gave Storm Rider a warm smile. "Young Elk and Dancing Wings know of the bond of our bands," she said. "They will know where to come for answers."

She felt Storm Rider's hand gently squeeze hers. Even the small gesture sent rapture spiraling through her heart. She could hardly believe what had transpired between them last night, and not so much what had happened, but her feelings toward it. Everything within her now felt feminine, and she wanted nothing more now than to be this man's wife.

After sharing such wondrous lovemaking with Storm Rider, after that sensual passion within her heart had been awakened, she knew what she wanted out of life. Of course, she would always silently wish to join the hunting and horse-stealing expeditions. But she wanted something even more now—to be with Storm Rider forever. She wanted to marry him and share every living moment with him, since life was precious and could be snuffed out so quickly and unmercifully.

She turned to her people again and smiled widely. Her eyes twinkled.

"There is something I would like to share with you," she said, returning the curious gazes. "There has been so much sadness in our lives these past days, I would like to share some sunshine that has been awakened in my heart. I hope that you will find a measure of happiness from my own."

She paused, gave Storm Rider a sheepish glance, then smiled at her people again. "I would like to share with you the news that I will soon wed Chief Storm Rider," she hurried out.

Their gasp of wonder made her know that the

news was a shock, and not only because she was getting married. They had begun to think that she would never take any man seriously. Just as her mother had all but given up on her getting married, so had her people.

So had her father, until he had chosen to push the issue by leaving her with Storm Rider.

"It was my father's last wish that I should marry and have children," she said, swallowing hard. She gave Storm Rider a gentle, sweet smile. "It was my father's last wish that I put my *ie-wakan-lake*, precocious, ways behind me . . . and marry Chief Storm Rider. I promised that I would."

Then she realized how that might sound not only to Storm Rider, but also to her people.

"But do not think for one minute that I am marrying this handsome chief only because my father asked it of me," she hurried out. "I love Storm Rider with all of my heart. It is *my* wish to marry him, as well as my father's."

Storm Rider was stunned that Talking Rain had chosen to announce today that she would marry him. He had thought that telling her people would be a hard thing to do.

Yet it had come so easily for her. That proved to him just how much she did love him.

He was so glad that her father had chosen to leave her that day and take horses instead. If he had not done so, Talking Rain might not have allowed herself to love, but rather indulged the wild side of herself that loved things meant only for men.

He turned to her and drew her into his embrace. "I am proud to have this woman as my wife," he said with emotion. "We will wait an appropriate time, as it is a time of mourning, and then we will have the celebration of celebrations on the day of our marriage."

Talking Rain felt warm inside as she smiled into Storm Rider's eyes.

Again she felt her father's presence, as though he had lain a hand on her shoulder and said *"Anhe,"* that he was satisfied with what had happened between his daughter and Storm Rider . . . as well as with the decision to join the Assiniboine camp until the Crow could make a final decision for their future.

Chapter 20

Another week and numerous searches had passed without any signs of the twins, or of the Snake and his renegade warriors.

It was as though they had dropped off the face of the earth. Nothing was left of the renegades, not even prints of their horses. When horses' hooves had been found in the dust or wet earth, they would suddenly disappear again, as though some magical wand had been waved over them, willing them to be gone. Filled with despair over not knowing the fate of her brother and sister, Talking Rain had found their disappearance hard to accept. She just could not see how this had happened . . . that she would lose all of her family in one day at the hands of her enemy the Snake.

Recognizing her sadness by her solemn mood, Storm Rider had made plans that he hoped would help lift his woman's spirits. He wanted her to enter into the marriage with a much lighter heart . . . with the burden of despair lifted somewhat from her shoulders.

The marriage ceremony was to be in two days.

That left Storm Rider two nights and two days to make Talking Rain smile again.

One thing especially he knew would help her in these moments of heartache. He knew her love of horse-stealing expeditions. He also knew that after she became his wife, those sorts of pastimes that Talking Rain had enjoyed with the warriors of her village would be behind her. She had promised that she would be a proper woman now, especially once her vows with Storm Rider were final.

But Storm Rider knew how she would miss those horse-stealing expeditions, and he had decided that there would be one more for her to enjoy before becoming a wife.

That was his plan—to take her on one last horse-stealing expedition!

As he had traveled to this land, he had passed by a village whose chief was one of his sparring enemies and had also moved to this same area.

Although they labeled one another enemies, their only battle was performed beneath the dark skies of night. It was a game that he and this young Crow chief, Dark Horse, played, as they tried to outdo each other at the game of horse stealing. Never had this game gone deadly between them.

Storm Rider found humor in this particular

horse-stealing expedition against Dark Horse tonight. As far as Storm Rider knew, Dark Horse had no idea that Storm Rider lived within a short distance from his village. Storm Rider learned that Dark Horse had moved there only because he and his people had passed by grazing steeds that Storm Rider had recognized as Dark Horse's. They were among those Dark Horse had stolen from Storm Rider just prior to Storm Rider's uprooting his people.

Storm Rider had not taken the time to steal them back, hoping to one day go back and then remove the horses from Dark Horse's possession.

Tomorrow, after Dark Horse and his warriors found their most prized steeds missing, the Crow chief would come searching and discover that the games continued between him and Storm Rider.

Storm Rider knew to expect some of his own horses, and probably most of Dark Horse's stolen steeds, to come up missing sometime soon after. The game would then continue as it had back when their villages had sat two hillsides from each other.

Only because he knew the chief he was stealing from tonight, and none of his warriors had ever been injured in a stealing expedition from Dark Horse, did Storm Rider include his woman in it.

And he remembered very well that she knew the art of stealing perhaps as well as any man. That, as well, assured him they would arrive home with no casualties, only horses.

The horse stealing now behind them, they rode back to their village with some of the most beautiful steeds he had stolen in some time herded ahead of them.

Storm Rider gazed over at Talking Rain. Beneath the soft glow of the moon, he saw the contentment on her face and knew that tonight's plan had worked. At least for now, she seemed to have placed her sadness behind her and was possibly even thinking of the marriage ceremony, which was not long off.

When the moonlight revealed a soft smile on her lips, Storm Rider sidled his steed closer to hers. He reached out and took one of her hands in his.

"My *mitawin*, what were you just thinking that made you smile?" he asked. He brought her hand to his lips and kissed the palm, then released it again.

"What made me smile?" Talking Rain murmured. She smiled again and she looked over at Storm Rider. "You, Storm Rider. You. And what you did for me tonight. I saw right through the ploy. I knew why you included me in the horse-stealing expedition."

She sighed contentedly.

"And Storm Rider, it worked," she said. "I feel now that I can accept that I will not see my brother and sister again. The hurt is still inside my heart, but I am able now to feel other things that for a while were gone knowing that the latest search for my brother and sister was our final one."

"You know that although there will be no more searches, we will still hope that somehow your brother and sister are alive and can find their way home to us," Storm Rider said.

"Yes, I know, but what you did tonight for me is something I shall never forget," Talking Rain said. "You are so good to me. Your planning a horse-stealing expedition and including me in it to help me get past my grieving is so thoughtful and sweet."

"I did this tonight only for you," Storm Rider said. "I know you hesitated at first to accept your love for me because of such things as stealing horses. I am touched that you are now giving up so much to marry me. So I thought that I would give something back to you. Tonight was a gift, my *mitawin*. I am glad that it put laughter in your eyes once again."

"Yes, I feel much more at peace now, and I promise that I shall not expect you to do this for me again," Talking Rain said. "From this moment on I shall concentrate on being your wife and learning all the things wives should know and making our lodge what it should be for you and me."

"Just you being there with me is all that I need to make our lodge what it should be," Storm Rider said. "You will bring much sunshine into our home. I shall soak it up every day and night and enjoy it."

Talking Rain laughed softly. "Tonight was such fun," she said, again forcing aside her troubled thoughts about the fate of her brother and sister.

She truly did not expect to see them ever again.

"*Pila-maye*, thank you, Storm Rider," she murmured. "*Pila-maye* so much for being you."

She looked ahead at the beautiful steeds they had stolen. She was riding the one of her choice, as was Storm Rider. She got lost in thought, recalling how they had first left the village to steal the horses. Singing the wolf song, their war party had gone on foot. Horse-stealing expeditions were called warring, for there was a chance that if the horse stealing was not done cleverly enough, the warriors doing the stealing would more than likely have to fight to fully claim the stolen horses as theirs.

But most times, if those stealing were skilled at it, no fighting was necessary.

Talking Rain knew that was the only reason that Storm Rider had felt at ease about her going with him and his men.

She thought back to those moments when they had first left their village for the exciting expedition. Each had carried spare pairs of good, strong-soled moccasins in a bag slung across their shoulders.

Some had brought bows and arrows. Some carried guns. And some had deadly lances and war clubs.

A battle was definitely not expected; therefore a profusion of arms had not been necessary and would have proved cumbersome. And they had not planned to be gone for any longer than this one night, and so brought no provisions.

Also in their bags were the warriors' fetish wolf skins, the entire skin of a wolf with the head, ears, and legs intact. If they thought it was necessary, they could wear the disguise and quickly and easily be passed off as a wolf by any person within a short distance of where they chose to steal their horses.

They were not going far tonight, so they rode no horses. Also, by traveling on foot, no horses' hooves would warn that thieves were approaching.

Talking Rain was glad that her ankle had healed enough that walking on foot was no problem for her. She smiled as she continued thinking about the excitement of the night. When they grew closer to the enemy's village, they proceeded slowly. They had seen the shine of the village's outdoor central fire in the dark heavens, and had known they were almost to the horse corral.

Then, in case sentries were posted, they had scattered and hidden themselves at various points behind a hill, lying motionless for a while as they watched in every direction for signs of their enemy.

Seeing none, they gave their signal—the howling

of a wolf—which wafted through the air to each of the Assiniboine warriors, a signal to now approach the camp.

They all came together again, and when they got close enough to the horses, they had stopped and judged their options for getting them unobserved.

They discovered that most horses, even the most valuable ones, were in corrals some distance from the tepees.

The excitement of the moment had lit a fire in Talking Rain's belly. She would never forget how her heart had pounded as she had crawled next to Storm Rider, and then helped him capture more than one horse. How rewarding it had felt to work the stolen steeds gradually into the darkness, until all of the warriors came together some distance away from the village, the stolen horses tied and ready to take back to their Assiniboine village.

Only after they had gotten far enough away from the village so that the hoofbeats would not be heard had they all chosen one steed apiece to ride.

They were growing close to the Assiniboine village now. Talking Rain hated to see the night end, for it had been wonderful to share in such excitement with the man she loved.

She glanced over at him. He seemed lost in his own thoughts. She thought she might know whom he was thinking about—Dark Horse. He had explained to her before they left that he and Dark

Horse loved these sorts of challenges, and that none
of their warriors had ever been harmed while stealing from the other tribe. Surely he was filled with
pride at having bested Dark Horse again.

She knew that Indians could not live well without horses and would risk anything to obtain them.
Horses were looked upon as a measure of public
standing. In the old days, nations that had few
steeds thought they had the right to take them from
those who had many. Whether it was right or not,
now or then, the Indians stole horses.

She remembered Blue Thunder telling her about
the days when he was a child and his father was a
warring chief. In horse-stealing expeditions in
which men were killed on both sides, it produced an
obligation on the part of the relatives of the de-
ceased to revenge their deaths, and war continued,
with various successes on both sides.

During the time of Blue Thunder's father, war
was the most honorable occupation an Indian could
follow. The young men were not noticed, nor could
they aspire to the hand of a respectable young
woman, without having distinguished themselves
in war excursions.

They were taught this when they were young.

She had heard her adopted father quoting to her
what his father had said to him: "There is always an
opening to the heart of the Indian through his love

of gain. The object of war is gain, and dangers attending it make it honorable."

She was so glad that her adopted father had not lived for warring; nor did her future husband.

"We will be home soon," Storm Rider said. He smiled over at Talking Rain. "Was tonight what you wished it to be?"

"And more," Talking Rain said. She laughed softly. "And when do you think these horses will be stolen back?"

"Soon . . ." Storm Rider said, also chuckling. "And I shall allow it. It is just a part of the game that began long ago between myself and Dark Horse."

"How will he know that it was you who stole tonight when he does not know you live close to him?" Talking Rain asked, forking an eyebrow.

"He will know," Storm Rider said, laughing. "He will know.

"*Hakamya-upo*, come," Storm Rider then said. "Let us take a ride alone before going on to my village. The night is beautiful. I am too restless to go to bed just yet."

"I, too, am restless," Talking Rain said. "Yes. Let's take a ride alone, away from the others."

Talking Rain drew a tight rein as Storm Rider went to tell his warriors of his and Talking Rain's plan, and then came back to her. Then together they rode off in a different direction.

The moon made shadows along the land. A

breeze blew lightly, the air no longer as brisk as the day before. There was even a touch of warmth in it.

"Tonight worked miracles for me, Storm Rider," Talking Rain said. "Now I truly am ready to become a wife and accept the sad part of my past."

"And I shall make it so," Storm Rider said, riding alongside her in the moonlight. A loon's song echoed through the night, proving they were near a stream.

"Let us find the stream and stop for a while and . . . well, you shall see what I have in mind," Storm Rider said, chuckling.

"I think I might know," Talking Rain said, laughing softly.

They rode onward, the shine of the water only a short distance away, but something else was there, as well—the glow of a campfire.

Storm Rider and Talking Rain halted almost at the exact same time.

"Who can that be?" Talking Rain asked. She trained her eyes to see if she could make out who might be sitting around the fire, but it was still too far away to tell.

"Dismount," Storm Rider said quietly. "We had best go the rest of the way on foot."

Talking Rain nodded.

They dismounted and secured their horses' reins on a low tree limb.

Carrying his rifle, Storm Rider moved stealthily

forward beside Talking Rain, their eyes never leaving the flames of the fire. It was a beacon in the night, leading them onward, but to whom? To what?

Chapter 21

A few more footsteps was all that it took for them to see who was around the campfire.

Talking Rain's brother and sister were tied and gagged on the ground away from the fire, while the Snake and his warriors sat around it, drinking and laughing. Her breath caught in her throat.

Could it be true?

Just when she had given up on ever seeing her brother and sister again, they were there? Alive?

It took all of the willpower she had not to run to them and cut their bonds and lead them to safety, but she knew that she couldn't. She would have to wait until plans were made to safely rescue them.

She gave Storm Rider a quick glance. She saw that he was stunned, as well, by the discovery. She saw even more than that: His jaw tightened and his eyes filled with an angry fire. She knew just how long he had been searching for this madman and his renegade friends—perhaps even longer than her own Crow warriors had been searching for them.

And Storm Rider loathed the evil man even more now for having taken two innocent children hostages!

She looked again at the renegade warriors, then at the Snake, who seemed full of himself tonight as he sat straight-backed and smug, the flames casting dancing shadows on his evil, thin, pockmarked face. His hair hung in two long black braids down his bare back. His bow and quiver of arrows lay behind him. His rifle lay close at his side, surely primed and ready for firing.

With an aching heart, yet so happy to have finally found her brother and sister very much alive, Talking Rain gazed at them again.

She did so badly want to rush to them and gather them safely in her arms. It was hard to be there, so close, and not let them know that she was near, and that she and Storm Rider would soon set them free.

She was afraid to think about what they had endured at the hands of these evil, vile men. But at least they were alive!

They kept watching the Snake. She could see more anger than fear in their eyes.

Then she noticed something else: Her brother was working with the ropes at his wrist behind him. She could tell that he had tried hard to get himself free, surely more to help his sister than himself. He was a valiant young man, with the spirit and courage of his father.

Storm Rider edged over closer to Talking Rain. "Do not fret. We will release your brother and sister soon," he said loud enough for only her to hear.

"And Talking Rain, even more than that, this is the moment that I have waited for, oh, so long," he said tightly, his eyes still on the Snake. "I want him dead."

"But what can we do to get my brother and sister away from the Snake first?" Talking Rain asked. Her eyes wavered as she gazed into Storm Rider's. "There are only the two of us."

She turned and looked at the men again. She could count twenty of them. She looked guardedly past them, and then up at the bluff that loomed overhead. Would there be sentries posted who could kill her and Storm Rider at any moment? Or were the renegades smug enough to feel they did not need to leave anyone guarding them? Had they not traveled far and wide without being stopped?

Yes, they had to feel smug enough not to concern themselves about sentries, or else she and Storm Rider would already be dead.

They would have been spotted much sooner than now, as they had ridden trustingly and happily before having seen the glow of the fire in the distance.

"You go and catch up with our warriors while I stay here and keep an eye on your brother and sister," Storm Rider said. "Return as quickly as possible with several warriors. Then we shall show those renegades what an ambush truly is and how the outcome should be. The Snake will wish he had never planted the seed of vengeance in my heart."

"But what if the renegades decide to move tonight before I can return with help?" Talking Rain asked, her voice anxious.

"They are settled in for the night," Storm Rider said. He slid his eyes past the renegades to the tethered horses a short distance away. They were unsaddled. Some were grazing and others were sleeping.

"Yes, we have time, but waste not a minute of it, Talking Rain," he said. "Hurry. Get as many warriors as can be spared, leaving only enough to take the stolen horses to the village. Return as soon as possible."

"My brother and sister," she said, her voice breaking. "I wish that I could rush in right now and rescue them."

"We will soon enough," Storm Rider reassured her. "But if I see that they are in more danger before you return with help, I shall do what I can to protect them."

"But you would place yourself in mortal danger by doing that," Talking Rain said. She reached a loving hand to his cheek. "Please wait. Surely nothing more will be done tonight."

Storm Rider drew her into his embrace. He gave her a quick kiss, then watched her run toward their tethered steeds. Holding fast to his rifle, he knelt on his haunches and kept watch, each and every minute seeming an eternity.

He gazed at Young Elk and Dancing Wings. He did not want to think of what they had endured, yet he knew that it had not been good. As evil as the Snake and his men were, how could they not mistreat their captives? Yet by the light of the fire, Storm Rider did not see any bruises or ripped clothing on either child. And in their eyes he did not see fear—only a determined anger.

By the way Young Elk kept working with the ropes at his wrists, he just might manage to get free. But then what was his plan? He had to know that if he got free of his bonds, without more help from his sister, neither of them could escape.

Unless . . .

Storm Rider looked at the renegades again. He saw how they passed a jug around to one another. He could tell by the way their speech became slurred and their voices grew louder that they were becoming intoxicated. That could go either of two ways: It might work in favor of the children, should the men become so drunk they could not think logically or keep from falling to sleep. Or it might put the hunger of the flesh into their wicked minds, and they might want those hungers fed. . . .

He turned his eyes away. He did not want to

think the children might be defiled, or possibly already had been.

If he discovered that they had been raped, the pleasure of avenging himself on these evil men would be twofold for Storm Rider. He would make each man pay for his crimes, individually, in a most painful way. Being a man of peace, it was never Storm Rider's way to harm anyone. But these men were different. As far as Storm Rider was concerned, they were not even human: they were animals.

He could hardly keep himself from going to save the children, yet he knew that he must wait. He was only one man. It would be a while, but Talking Rain would return with help.

But the longer it took, the harder it would be just to sit there and not do something about the Snake. It had been such a long wait already. Even one moment longer was almost unbearable.

Yet he did wait.

He watched the sky, how the clouds would shift and cover the moon, and then slide away again to reveal a moon so bright the whole world was white with it.

He shifted his weight restlessly.

He kept looking over his shoulder to see if Talking Rain and the warriors had arrived yet, but there was still no sign of them. Then he began worrying about Talking Rain. What if something happened to her while she was going for help? Could there have been renegade sentries after all, and they found Talking Rain, yet missed seeing him? Now he felt that he should have gone with her.

Yet there were the children. As long as he was at least near, he felt that they were safe. If their lives were threatened, he would not hesitate to fire into the renegades and kill those he could before being discovered and stopped.

The important thing was to be brave and courageous if needed, not to stay hidden like a mouse.

His shoulder muscles tightened when he heard a sound behind him. He made a sharp turn, his rifle poised and ready to fire.

But relief washed through him when he saw Talking Rain coming on foot with many warriors alongside her. He watched as Talking Rain stopped and directed the warriors in several directions. He smiled. He knew that she was taking it upon herself to issue orders to the men—orders that would leave the renegades surrounded.

Talking Rain moved stealthily forward and stopped beside Storm Rider. "We can attack now," she whispered, the flush of her cheeks proof of her excitement. "We can save my brother and sister now."

"We must be sure everyone rushes them at the same time, or your brother and sister will be killed by cross fire," Storm Rider said.

"Yes, I know," Talking Rain said. She swallowed hard as she peered through the darkness at them.

"I shall go and get them just as the warriors attack," Storm Rider said. He shoved the rifle into Talking Rain's hands. "You keep watch. Shoot anyone who becomes a threat."

Talking Rain nodded.

Her pulse raced as she watched Storm Rider make a wide circle until he was directly behind the children. Suddenly she considered the true dangers of what he was doing. There was no way he could assist the two children at once, because they were both tied and gagged. He wouldn't have time to untie them. That meant that he could carry only one off, leaving the other one to wait.

No.

She just could not take that chance. She had to go and help. Carrying the rifle, and keeping her eyes on the drunken renegades who were not yet aware of what was about to happen, Talking Rain caught up with Storm Rider.

He stopped and gave her a frustrated glare, then turned abruptly when firing began. War cries erupted into the night air as the warriors made their quick rush toward the renegades.

The renegades were so distracted by what was happening, some scurrying for cover, others too drunk to even stand, they did not take notice of the children.

Her heart pounding, Talking Rain grabbed her sister up into her arms and began carrying her toward the trees for cover. Storm Rider lifted her brother and followed behind.

Well hidden in the shadows of the forest, Talking Rain removed Dancing Wings's ropes, and then her gag.

Her sister flung herself into her arms, her body shaking with sobs. Storm Rider released Young Elk of his bonds.

Young Elk rubbed his raw wrists. "*Pila-maye,* thank you," he gulped out. "I was afraid of what the firewater might make the renegades do tonight. Until now, we have been untouched."

Talking Rain stroked her fingers through Dancing Wings's long black hair. "You were not raped?" she asked, her voice drawn.

"No, nothing like that." Dancing Wings sobbed. "We . . . we were on our way to being sold for auction. That is why we were left untouched. The purer we were, the more the Snake would get for us at the auction block."

"Auction . . . ?" Talking Rain gasped, paling. "They were actually going to auction you off as though you were nothing more than animals?"

She suddenly became aware of complete silence. She turned and looked toward the campsite. Some renegades were dead; others were sitting with their hands tied behind their backs.

Her heart sank when she realized that one renegade was missing. The Snake was nowhere to be seen!

Brave Shield approached Storm Rider and Talking Rain. The look on his face said it all: The one man they wanted most of all had managed to escape through gunfire as well as volley after volley of arrows.

Just as the warriors attacked the renegades, the clouds hid the moon again. The campfire had burned down too low to let off enough light to see by. It was under this cover of darkness that the evil man had made his escape.

"Send men out for him," Storm Rider shouted. "He cannot get far!"

"I have sent four warriors to search for him, but as elusive as he is, I doubt that he will be found," Brave Shield said, his voice solemn and angry. "I thought I had him in my sights, but when I reached him, I discovered it was someone else."

"We were so close," Talking Rain said, sighing.

Then she turned to her sister and brother again. She reached her arms out and brought them into her embrace. "But *you* are safe," she murmured. "That's all that matters now."

Storm Rider knelt before them. "Do you know where you have been kept up until tonight?" he asked. "The Snake must have a permanent camp. Could you lead us back there?"

"While we were held hostage at the stronghold, we were blindfolded," Dancing Wings said softly. "The blindfolds were removed tonight only because we were taken from there."

"Can you calculate how far you have traveled from the stronghold?" Storm Rider asked, gently placing his hands on Young Elk's thin, bare shoulders.

"I am not certain, because sometimes it seemed we were traveling in circles. I think they were trying to confuse me and my sister so that when we were sold into slavery we would not be able to take anyone back to the renegades' hideout," Young Elk said somberly. He hung his head. "I am sorry I cannot be of more help, for I, too, wish to end the Snake's days of killing and murdering . . . and selling children into slavery."

"For now, let's get the children home," Talking Rain said. She drew Dancing Wings close again and hugged her. "They have been through such an ordeal. They need to be where they know they are safe . . . and loved."

"Yes, that is what is important now," Storm Rider said, nodding.

And then it came to Talking Rain that her brother and sister did not know the fate of their parents—or their village as a whole. They did not know that when she spoke of taking them "home," that it did not mean their own lodge at the Crow village.

She hated that they still had more trauma to endure, yet there was no way around the ugly truth . . . their beloved parents had died during the ambush.

Talking Rain gazed into Storm Rider's eyes. "There is something they must know before . . . before we go home," she said quietly.

She knew that he understood. He nodded.

"Do you want me to stay?" he asked.

"Please do," Talking Rain said, swallowing hard. "I need your courage for what must be said."

"What are you talking about?" Young Elk asked, looking from Talking Rain to Storm Rider.

"Yes, what *are* you talking about?" Dancing Wings asked as she leaned away from Talking Rain.

"Come to me, Young Elk," Talking Rain said, reaching her arms out for him. "Come and let me hug you while I tell you something."

He went to her. He sat on one side of her lap while Dancing Wings sat on the other.

Talking Rain began, her each and every word causing pain in her heart, especially when it was all said and the children understood their losses.

She clung to them as they both cried out for their mother and father, their sobs all that were left to fill the night air.

Storm Rider's determination to find the Snake was even stronger. He would find him. Some day . . . somehow . . . he would find the man.

Chapter 22

Several days had passed. The sun was lowering in the heavens behind the distant mountains.

A coolness was sharper in the air than the day before, as the scent of snow wafted down from the highest bluffs of the already white-capped mountains.

There were many new lodges in the Assiniboine village, the Crow having settled into a daily routine with Storm Rider's people.

Today Talking Rain and Storm Rider were helping to put the final touches on the last tepee to be erected.

Dancing Wings and Young Elk had also assisted, their eyes still sad at knowing they would never see their parents again.

Talking Rain had encouraged them to help with building the new homes for their people, hoping that the activity would occupy their minds with something other than their sorrow.

Before they had been carried off by the renegades, Dancing Wings and Young Elk had already seen the death and destruction in their village. But they had not thought that they would lose both parents on that hideous day.

After learning this Dancing Wings had cried until no more tears would come. Little Elk had shown his bravery by not crying as much as his sister, but his hurt, his lonesomeness for his parents, showed in his eyes.

"The last lodge is now completed," Storm Rider said, breaking through Talking Rain's deep, troubled thoughts. "Now, Talking Rain, we can return to our lodge and talk of tomorrow and what it brings into our lives."

"Our marriage," Talking Rain murmured, a blissful feeling now taking the place of the sadness she had moments ago been experiencing.

She smiled over at Dancing Wings. She reached out and took one of her hands. "And sweet little sister, do you like your and your brother's new home?" she asked, nodding toward the tepee that stood before them, the last one to be built.

"I do love it," Dancing Wings said, clasping her hands before her as she gazed at the tepee that was now finished and ready to live in.

Talking Rain silently admired the lodge as well, and was glad that the children understood that it was theirs alone.

Talking Rain and Storm Rider had discussed

where the children would live and decided that Dancing Wings and Young Elk should have their own lodge. That way Talking Rain and Storm Rider could have their privacy as newlyweds.

But Talking Rain and Storm Rider had made certain the children's tepee was erected close to their own, so that they would be there should either child need them.

The thought of having their own private lodge had helped to take some of the sadness from the children's hearts, for their tepee made them feel older and more mature; very independent.

Having learned the skills from her mother, Dancing Wings knew well the art of cooking, keeping house, and sewing. Young Elk knew how to hunt and fish, which would keep food on their plates, and provide hides for their clothes and moccasins.

But Talking Rain had assured them that she would be inviting them to her and Storm Rider's home for most of the meals, if Dancing Wings would teach her what she knew about cooking, since Talking Rain had not taken any time to learn such things from their mother.

That, as well, had made Dancing Wings feel important, in that her older sister needed to be taught things that Dancing Wings already knew.

And Young Elk looked forward to going on the hunt with Storm Rider. Young Elk admired him so much, and was so grateful for how he had taken in his Crow people. In the short time he had known Storm Rider, Young Elk felt a bond, a keen fondness and love for him.

Dancing Wings reached up and pushed back a fallen lock of hair from her brow. "Yes, I love our home," she said, still looking at the newly made tepee. "Soon we shall have a fire in our fire pit. I look forward to our first full night beside our very own lodge fire."

"You did a good job helping build the tepee," Storm Rider said, fondly swinging an arm around Young Elk's shoulder. "It is strong and should stand up against the cold, blustery winter winds and the heavy snows."

"I enjoyed building a lodge that is mine and my sister's," Young Elk said, his chest swelling with pride.

He studied his lodge of buffalo skins. The hair had been shaved off and dressed, then sewed together in such a manner that when placed upright on poles, it presented the form of an inverted funnel.

He and his sister would enjoy painting designs on both the inside and outside of the lodge, which would help make it individual to them. He remembered well the artwork of his parents' lodge, which had been painted mainly by his father.

Young Elk would try his best to duplicate what his father had painted: the stories told in pictures of his father's life as a chief, hunter, and husband and father. Then, when Young Elk married one day and had a lodge to share with his bride, he would paint the story of his *own* exploits.

But for now, using his father's designs would keep his father close to him, at least in some small way.

His mother was there with him when he looked at his sister, for Dancing Wings was their mother's exact image, only younger.

"Brother, let's go inside and build our first fire," Dancing Wings said, smiling broadly at Young Elk. "Yellow Flower has promised us a pot of freshly made stew to hang over the fire for our evening meal."

She turned to Talking Rain. "Will you and Storm Rider come share the first meal in our new lodge with me and Young Elk?" she rushed out, her dark eyes wide and excited.

Talking Rain glanced over at Storm Rider. They had looked forward to being alone in their lodge tonight so that they could discuss tomorrow . . . the day of their wedding.

But her sister had asked her so eagerly. By the look in her eyes, Dancing Wings truly wished to share the first evening with not only her brother, but also her sister and the man she would marry tomorrow.

Realizing the pride that Dancing Wings and

Young Elk felt in helping build such a nice, substantial lodge, Storm Rider smiled over at Talking Rain.

"It would be good to share the first meal, fire, and evening in your sister and brother's new lodge, don't you think?" he said.

"It would be a wonderful way to celebrate their new home," Talking Rain agreed. "Together."

"Then, yes, Dancing Wings, your sister and I will spend part of the evening with you," he said. "And then Talking Rain and I must return to our own lodge and finalize plans for our special day tomorrow."

"A wedding," Dancing Wings said, smiling sweetly at her sister. "It is good, Talking Rain, that you have met such a wonderful man as Storm Rider. I hope that one day I shall find and marry a man just as fine and good."

"And you will, Dancing Wings," Talking Rain said. "I now know that there is that perfect man for each woman to find." She gave Storm Rider a soft smile. "And to cherish, for I shall cherish you, Storm Rider, always."

"A man has to be very special to have taken my sister away from her love of horse stealing . . ." Little Elk said, then stopped and glanced quickly over at Storm Rider. "It is good that you forgave her the crime she committed against you. That day, when I came and found my sister captive here at your village, I would have never thought that your feelings would come to this."

"*Ahte* helped bring this about," Talking Rain said, unsure of whether her brother and sister knew the details of their father's schemes—how he had given Talking Rain up only for her sake, so that she would marry Storm Rider and forget her tomboyish ways.

"I know some of what he did, and why, but not all," Dancing Wings said. She raised her eyebrows. "Would you please share it with us?"

"Tonight, after we have eaten, I shall tell you all that *ahte* said just before . . . just before . . . he died," Talking Rain promised, her voice breaking.

"Were you with Father when he took his last breath?" Dancing Wings asked, her voice also filled with emotion.

"Yes, and he died with grace and in peace," Talking Rain said. She knew what the next question would be, and dreaded it.

"And, *ina,* Mother?" Dancing Wings asked, a sob lodging in her throat. "Were you able to say good-bye to her, as well?"

Talking Rain's eyes lowered. She went to Dancing Wings and drew her gently into her arms. "No, her last good-bye was to our *ahte,*" she murmured. She wasn't certain whether her mother had been given a chance to say a good-bye to her beloved husband. It was a comforting thought, though, and that was what she would hold in her heart, not the fear that her mother might have taken her last breath alone.

"And is the lodge fire ready for the pot of stew that I have made for you?" Yellow Flower asked as she came carrying the stew that she had prepared for the children's evening meal.

Talking Rain was glad that Yellow Flower had chosen this moment to arrive, for the talk had turned to sad subjects, and such sadness was best left behind. The children, as well as Storm Rider and Talking Rain, were beginning a new chapter in their lives. It was best that they enter it feeling hopeful, not despairing.

"It smells delicious," Talking Rain said, turning toward Yellow Flower. "I hadn't realized I was hungry until now."

"Let me take it for you," Storm Rider said. He grabbed the handle of the pot from Yellow Flower. "You are so kind to do this for the children."

"Kindnesses are always returned," Yellow Flower said, looking at Talking Rain. She still held such love for her for having helped heal Little Beaver. She smiled and looked over her shoulder at her own lodge, where the evening meal waited to be eaten with her son. She gave Talking Rain a hug.

"Come someday soon with your new husband and share a meal with me and my son," she offered. She stepped back from Talking Rain. "It would please me so to have you spend an evening with me and Little Beaver."

"We would love to," Talking Rain said. She smiled over at Storm Rider. "Wouldn't we?"

"Yes, we will come after a few days have passed once our marriage vows are shared," he said, nodding.

"*Pila-maye,* thank you," Yellow Flower said, then turned with a swish of her doeskin skirt and walked away, her face bright with a smile.

"Now all we need is a fire," Storm Rider said, chuckling as he held the pot of steaming stew at his left side.

"I shall get it started faster than you can wink an eye," Young Elk said, using a slang phrase that he had learned from his older sister, who had learned it while living in the white community. "The wood is already in the fire pit." He hurried inside.

Soon smoke spiraled upward from the smoke hole. Wooden bowls were filled with the stew as Talking Rain and her brother and sister and Storm Rider sat on blankets around the fire, enjoying the rich, hearty meal.

"Yellow Flower is such a good cook," Young Elk said, licking the wooden spoon after finishing off his third bowl of stew.

"As good as your sister?" Dancing Wings teased, pretending to pout.

"No, not as good as my sister," Young Elk said,

chuckling. He rubbed his belly. "And absolutely better than what those criminals fed us. They exist mainly on rabbit cooked over an open flame. Never any vegetables or rich stew meat."

"I'm just glad they fed you at all," Talking Rain said dryly. "I'm so glad they didn't—"

She stopped before saying what she was thinking. She didn't think it was good to even mention the fact that the children could have been so brutally injured. To have been left untouched for the slave trade had been a blessing. But the thought of having not found them before they had been sold made her grow sick to her stomach every time it came to her mind.

"We are both safe and healthy, and I do not want to ever again think of those days and nights with those evil men," Dancing Wings said, visibly shuddering. "We are no longer with those criminals. We are . . . home." She lowered her eyes. "I mean we are at our *new* home, since our true home is gone, along with so many others, with so many lives."

"Think about the good that has come into your life, not the bad that has been left behind you," Talking Rain said. She went and sat beside her sister. She drew her into her arms. Dancing Wings clung to her.

"Sweet Dancing Wings, you have so many who love you," Talking Rain said. "Please try to put what happened behind you. It is always best to look forward, not backward. And you have much to live for, to look forward to. One day you will find a man. You will fall in love. You will marry. You will have children."

Dancing Wings pulled quickly away from Talking Rain. She gazed in wonder into her sister's eyes. "Are you going to have children soon?" she blurted out. "It would be so wonderful to help you take care of a baby. I would adore it."

Talking Rain reached a loving hand to her sister's cheek. She glanced over at Storm Rider, then gazed into her sister's eyes. "I hope to have many children for you to help me with," she said, laughing softly. "You might regret having offered."

"Never." Dancing Wings squealed. "Oh, how I shall love being an aunt."

"As I would enjoy being an uncle," Young Elk said, smiling widely. "Why, I shall show my nephew how *ahte* taught me to make a bow, and how to hunt, and—"

"Whoa, there," Talking Rain said, again laughing. "You had best leave something for the child's father to do, don't you think?"

Young Elk laughed, then smiled over at Storm Rider. "Yes, but I do hope to be able to help," he said. "May I, Storm Rider? May I help teach my nephew how to hunt and make bows and arrows?"

"You can have a big role in everything that your sister and I do, before we have children and after," Storm Rider said. "We are family. Families share."

Talking Rain's heart soared. She could hardly believe her luck—that she could have met such a man as this, who loved her so much and was willing to share all aspects of her life with her, especially her brother and sister. They had lost so much, but, oh, had not they gained much too, in having this man in their lives?

Tomorrow.

Was tomorrow real? Was she truly going to marry this wonderful man? Was she truly going to be a wife? Was she truly saying a final good-bye to all that she had enjoyed doing before she met and fell in love with the young, handsome Assiniboine chief?

Yes . . . yes . . . yes . . . to all of that, she thought laughingly to herself.

Chapter 23

Had Talking Rain known how the ecstasy of being in love felt when she was trying to prove herself anything but a woman, she would never have gone on that first hunt, or stolen that first horse. She would not have pursued anything that she had lived for before she cast her eyes that first time upon Storm Rider's handsome, noble face.

Today she felt so feminine in her wedding attire, her golden hair hanging in long, lustrous waves down her back and her face flushed with the excitement of having just exchanged vows with the man she adored.

She would never forget what Storm Rider had said as he had gazed lovingly into her eyes, "I take this woman for my wife," which had sealed their hearts forevermore.

It still seemed so unreal . . . a dream that had come beautifully true!

And she felt beautiful. Yellow Flower had made her a special, lovely fringed dress of the whitest doeskin. Small, round beads of varied colors adorned every portion of the dress. Yellow Flower had also made moccasins from the same doeskin, and had sewn matching beads across the top.

Storm Rider had presented Talking Rain with beautiful jewelry to wear, which had been his precious mother's. The necklace and matching bracelet were made from shells called *Ioquois*, which were eagerly sought after by the Indians. These special shells had been brought from the Pacific coast. They were about two inches long, pure white, and about the size of a raven's feather at the larger end. Being curved, tapered, and hollow, they were easily strung and used for necklaces and bracelets.

Talking Rain wore a crown of late-autumn flowers, which had not yet been destroyed by frost. The blooms looked like white daisies, but had the aroma of gardenias.

She sat now beside her new husband on a thick pallet of white furs inside the village council house. This lodge was used for such special occasions instead of the larger soldiers' council house, which was used mainly by the warriors and their chief.

At the back of the council house, several warriors beat drums in a low, rhythmic manner, while others stood behind the drummers, playing softly on flutes.

There was a cozy fire in the center of the lodge. Sitting back from it were as many Crow and Assiniboine people as could be crowded into the large room for the special wedding ceremony of their Assiniboine chief and his woman.

The celebration would have been held outside so that everyone could attend except that the blustery north winds had come suddenly upon them, bringing with them snow from the low-hanging gray clouds. Even now the winds whistled down the smoke hole and around the corners of the council house.

But all that Talking Rain could think of was her beloved husband sitting at her side in an outfit made of the same white doeskin as her dress and adorned by the very same beads as had been sewn onto hers, all by the deft, skilled fingers of Yellow Flower.

Talking Rain gave Storm Rider a soft smile when she felt him looking at her, then melted inside when he leaned over and gave her a kiss. Everyone witnessed it, as they had also listened to him speak the words that had made them husband and wife.

"Tecihila, I love you," she whispered, reaching over and taking one of his hands. "I have never been so happy. Thank you, my husband, for bringing so much into my life that I never imagined could exist."

"And you have given me a contentment that I never knew existed until you," he whispered back. "Just looking at you fulfills me."

She started to tell him more of her feelings, but loud whistling sounds and the harder thumping of the drums drew her eyes quickly away. She realized that she was just about to see one of the Fox band's most favored dances, which was only performed during their more important celebrations.

A larger space in the council house had been left for these dancers so that they could have the room and freedom to do the dance with abandon.

Talking Rain had never seen this particular dance. It was performed only by those who belonged to the Fox band of the Assiniboine people, just as her own people's special dance was done only by them.

She brushed aside thoughts about her people's dance, for she had last seen it while sitting with her mother and father. The memories were still too raw to revisit today. They might ruin her special moments with Storm Rider.

Today she was just going to think of herself and the man she had married and the life that lay ahead of them, not behind. Their future held the promise of happiness and children.

Yes, she did want to have children born of her and Storm Rider's love. The thought of carrying his child within her womb made her so happy she thought she might be glowing were someone to look at her at this moment.

She smiled and settled in closer to Storm Rider.

His arm slid around her waist and drew her closer to his side.

She was aware of eyes on her and Storm Rider. She looked to her left, where her brother and sister sat beaming, their faces filled with the wonder of the day.

Was this wedding helping to lift the burdens they were carrying over the loss of their mother and father?

Talking Rain smiled at her brother and sister, then looked ahead again as the warriors performing the main part of the dance made a wide circle around the lodge fire.

Talking Rain was instantly awed by the warriors' attire. Their costumes consisted of deer skins, shirts, and leggings painted a bright yellow. Their faces were painted with yellow stripes. A dressed fox skin was spread out on each of their shoulders, the heads of which lay on their breasts. The tails hung down their backs, and the whole skin was fringed with colored porcupine quills and bells. Polished buttons were placed in the eyeholes.

The dancers each wore a headdress of fox teeth, bored and strung, and stretched across the middle of the head from ear to ear. A lock of their hair was tied in front, projecting out several inches. The rest was combed straight down behind, and decorated with four eagle feathers.

Their lances were wrapped with fox skins cut in

strips, and the tails of that animal were sewn onto the handle every twelve inches or so.

Some of the warriors also would carry their bows and quivers of arrows at their sides during the performance.

Talking Rain saw several women go stand behind the drummers. They began singing along with the drumming, and whistling as the warriors lined up for their special dance in front of the fire.

They began at a swift pace, moving in a circle that resembled the coiling of a snake.

After winding up in this form, they all commenced jumping up and down, striking one foot after the other on the ground as they kept exact time with the music. Suddenly a flourish on the drums and a shout from the dancers concluded that round. Their places in a straight line were resumed and they stopped. A warrior stepped forward and pretended that he was counting coup with his lance, then spoke for a while of his exploits as a warrior.

This was followed by more dancing, which was again followed by another warrior speaking. All who wished to spoke, the drum denoting by taps the value and number of coups counted by each.

And then it was over, the feasting done, and Talking Rain and Storm Rider were finally alone in their lodge.

As they stepped through the entrance flap, Talking Rain gasped at what she found. The floor was covered with soft, white feathers and the same sort of flowers she wore on her head.

Numerous candles splashed a warm, shadowy glow along the inside wall of the dwelling. A low fire in the fire pit also cast its soft figures everywhere.

"It's so beautiful," Talking Rain murmured, slipping off her moccasins and walking amidst the flowers and feathers. "And so many candles?"

She spun around and rushed into Storm Rider's arms. "My darling husband," she said, "you have made our home a paradise."

"No, wife, *you* are the one who has brought paradise into my home, my heart . . . my life," Storm Rider said huskily.

He bent and softly kissed her lips, then pulled her more closely against his hard body and gave her a deep, passionate kiss that made Talking Rain's knees almost buckle, the desire was so swift and overwhelming.

She put her arms around his neck and pressed her body into his, then gasped when he reached his hands down and cupped her buttocks in his palms, his body gyrating into hers.

"I am breathless with desire," Talking Rain whispered against his lips. "Husband, I want you so much. Please take me to our bed. Let us make passionate love."

Storm Rider's muscled arms lifted her. He carried

her to their bed, which he had prepared while she had been at Yellow Flower's lodge getting ready for the wedding.

He had made certain she would be resting against the softest of pelts as he made love with her. The flowers he had scattered lay all around the bed.

He kissed her, bending down to put her on the plush pelts. Then his hands went to the hem of her dress and he lifted it above her knees.

Both hands went up inside her skirt, the fingers of one finding her soft, wet place. He began stroking her pink, swollen mound, eliciting moans of pleasure from her.

Lost heart and soul to this moment, Talking Rain sucked in a wild breath when she felt one of his fingers enter her. She ached to have all of him there.

She wrapped her fingers through his hair as pleasure spread through her with a tremor.

She smiled into his eyes when he rose and stood over her. He slowly undressed, and she stood up before him and undressed as well, a piece of clothing at a time, to match what he discarded from his own ready body.

When they were both naked, Talking Rain reached out to him and ran her fingers down and across his muscled chest, then lower, across his belly.

She smiled at how her touch made him quiver.

Then her smile turned more seductive when she

sent her hands lower and clasped his manhood, which was throbbing and ready for her.

He closed his eyes and threw back his head when she began moving her hand on him oh, so very slowly. The muscles of his legs corded as he spread his legs farther apart.

She sensed what else he might desire as she bent to her knees before him and pleasured him in a way that he had pleasured her the first time they made love. His hands went to her shoulders and he held on to her as his body tensed and swayed with pleasure. She continued giving him what she knew he was enjoying until he opened his eyes and stepped away from her.

Words were not needed between them now. Their bodies moved together. He held her against him as he gently lowered her onto her back. Then he spread himself over her and with one push was inside her.

Their lips came together in a frenzy of kisses. He kneaded her breasts, then tongued them. His body moved, heat spreading through him like wildfire.

And then he kissed her again. She clung to him.

They rocked and moaned. Their bodies were afire with ecstasy.

And then they both soared to the purest rapture, until their bodies subsided into a soft, sweet bliss.

Storm Rider brushed locks of hair back from Talking Rain's damp brow, then kissed her there.

She reached up and pushed some of his hair back as well, then smiled as he rolled away and lay close beside her.

"I am truly in paradise," Talking Rain said. She reached away from the bed and ran her fingers through the soft feathers and flowers. "I don't want anything to change from how it is for us tonight."

"Nor do I," Storm Rider said. He leaned up on one side, resting his face in a hand as he gazed at his wife. "Let us make this night go on and on and on."

"Until we are old and gray?" Talking Rain said, laughing softly.

"Yes, until we are old and gray," Storm Rider said. He leaned over and kissed her cheek. "But tonight, *mitawin*, I feel so very, very young and ready to make love again."

"Then, my love, I am ready as well," Talking Rain said, her voice filled with the passion she was already feeling. As Storm Rider's hands roamed across her body, she closed her eyes and let nothing else enter her thoughts but her husband—and his skill at making her forget that she had been anything, ever, but a woman!

Chapter 24

The fire had burned down to soft, glowing embers as Talking Rain sat before it on the bed of luscious pelts.

Still filled with the ecstasy of the evening, Talking Rain had found it impossible to fall asleep. She had lain beside Storm Rider, held close at his side, and watched him fall into a sweet slumber, a smile on his face.

But she was just not ready yet to go to sleep.

She kept remembering how her body had reacted so sensually to her husband's, and how wonderful it sounded to call him her husband when only a few months ago she would have laughed at anyone who suggested such an idea.

But how glad she was that she had been proved wrong. She cherished these precious moments with the man she loved, even now, as he slept and she watched.

It was like a miracle that this day had happened in her life.

She looked slowly around at the white feathers and flowers and could imagine Storm Rider spreading them for her to find after the wedding celebration was over.

It had been done with much love and care. He had made certain that almost every inch of the floor had been prepared for his wife's feet to step upon.

"You are so sweet and thoughtful," she whispered.

She reached a hand gently to his chest and slowly roamed her fingers downward, then followed this same path with soft kisses.

"*Mihigna*, my husband, *mihigna*..." she then whispered, sitting up again and gazing in wonder at his sculpted, noble features. Never had she seen such a handsome man... and he was hers.

The cry of a loon came from somewhere far away, followed by another loon, perhaps its mate, returning the call. The soft spiraling of the moon's glow down the smoke hole gave Talking Rain the sudden urge to step outside and admire the magic of nature. Then she would return and finally give in to her need for sleep. She wanted to awaken fresh tomorrow so that she could begin her first day of marriage performing the duties that came with being a wife.

Although she knew little of how to do these things, Yellow Flower was going to come to Talking Rain's lodge and teach her one important thing at a time.

Talking Rain had always been an astute student to her father's and mother's teachings. So would she be to Yellow Flower's—especially Yellow Flower's, because Talking Rain wanted to be the best wife that she could be for the best husband that a woman could ever have.

Smiling, she rose quietly from the bed. She held the entrance flap aside and saw that snow had fallen while she and her husband had made love. But that would not dissuade her from going outside. It made her even more eager, for she loved a first snowfall. She loved walking through it.

She dropped the flap and dressed warmly in a buckskin dress, knee-high moccasins, and a warm cape made of many white rabbit pelts.

She stopped and took one last look at her husband, then went outside into the moon-splashed night.

She stopped and gazed heavenward.

Earlier the sky had been dark with clouds that had brought the snow. Now it was radiant with a full, white moon and twinkling stars.

Hugging the cape more closely to her body, Talking Rain looked suddenly toward the river when once again she heard the sound of the loons calling to one another. How sweet was that sound, for the birds were voicing their love for one another, as had Talking Rain and Storm Rider only moments ago after making love for the third time tonight.

"Sweet, sweet love . . ." Talking Rain whispered. She gazed up at the bluff overhead.

When she saw no sentry there she wondered about it, then shrugged. Surely Two Leaves had slipped off for a moment but would soon return and be as vigilant as always at keeping his eye on the village.

Talking Rain heaved a sigh when she thought of how cleverly the Snake had escaped capture. His warriors now sat as prisoners in a lodge at the far side of the village. They were bound and gagged and guarded by a sentry on each side of the entranceway.

Her eyes wavered when she thought of how she had been kept captive and guarded by the very same two warriors. Had she not attempted to steal Storm Rider's horse, what then would her future have held? Having been caught and held captive by such a handsome man was surely the only way that she would have ever discovered that her heart beat soundly for a man, not for the adventurous life she had lived until she knew Storm Rider.

And her father's scheme had helped her know for certain that she wanted Storm Rider, not stolen moments with warriors on horse-stealing expeditions.

It now seemed so long ago that she had ridden valiantly with the warriors, laughing and sparring with them as though she were one of them. In truth, it had been only a few short weeks ago.

Talking Rain still did not want to give in to sleep, and the loons were making their calls into the night, which might prevent her from sleeping should she even try. More restless than she had first guessed, Talking Rain began slowly walking toward the river, where she might by chance see one or both of the loons. Although they gave off an eerie sort of cry, they were lovely birds. She had watched loons many times at a stream by her Crow village. They had not known she was there.

She stopped and listened when she realized that much time had elapsed now since she had heard the birds. Had her presence scared them away?

Or might it be something else? Or . . . someone?

Talking Rain again shrugged, wanting to stand by the river and watch the stars for a while before going back to her husband's side. She gathered the cloak more closely around her and continued to the river and stood in the snow gazing at it.

Ah, it was such a peaceful night. She was scarcely aware of the nip in the air, for her body was still warm, even throbbing almost from the lovemaking tonight. She had never known that love could be so intense, and so sweet.

But she had never known anyone like Storm Rider before, either. Only he could have awakened all of these sensual feelings within her. Only he.

She knew that was true, for she had ridden with many a handsome warrior, and none of them had caused her heart to pitter-patter so erratically as Storm Rider had that first time she had looked upon his face.

Again wondering why the loons had become so suddenly quiet, Talking Rain began walking slowly beside the river, her eyes watching for a loon to take flight from the trees.

Then she became aware of something else. She found herself gazing at a lone canoe that was beached only a short distance away.

It was not usual for her or Storm Rider's people to beach their canoes away from everyone else's, especially this far from the village. There was always a chance of theft.

This made her suddenly aware of how far she had walked from the village. She turned quickly and could only scarcely see the reflective glow in the sky that came from the outdoor fire. It was left burning all night to frighten stray animals that might come snooping too close to the village.

She could not even see the tepees, though the moon's glow was bright.

"I must hurry back," Talking Rain said, suddenly feeling eerily alone.

Her thoughts went quickly to the Snake. She eyed the lone canoe again.

Then she gasped and the breath was robbed from

her lungs when a strong arm from behind her went suddenly around her chest, then threw her down onto the snow-laden ground. She was gagged, and her wrists were bound behind her with a rope.

Able to breathe again, Talking Rain gazed, her eyes wide over the gag, at the very man she loathed. He had flipped her over onto her back, straddled her, and held her down. His dark eyes gleamed in the moonlight, and his lips in his thin, pocked face lifted into a smug, menacing smile.

"You were foolish to stray from your lover's side," the Snake said, chuckling throatily. "I have been waiting for the opportunity to seize you. I was hiding in the shadows of the aspen trees. When I saw you leave the chief's lodge, I went to the bluff and killed Two Leaves. Two Leaves so carelessly did not see my canoe as I came down the river and beached it."

Her heart thumping, Talking Rain glared up at him. The hate she felt for this man was more pronounced than her fear.

"And why would I risk being caught just to have you?" the Snake said. He leaned down so that his foul breath warmed Talking Rain's face.

She turned her face away, but he just as quickly placed a hand at her chin and turned her face back around so that her eyes were forced to look into his.

"Yes, why would I take you captive now when I

had a better chance before without having to kill someone?" the Snake said in a snarl.

His eyes narrowed as he glared into hers. "Long ago, your father sent me from the village in disgrace and banished me forever from our band of Crow because I was caught stealing weapons from another warrior of our band. I vowed vengeance against a people who were no longer mine," he said in a growl. "I came and killed and maimed those of my band who laughed at me when I was forced to walk away in shame. But my vengeance would not be complete unless I had you, the light of your chieftain father's eyes."

He stood up. Then he grabbed Talking Rain by the waist and yanked her to her feet. He shoved her until they reached the beached canoe, then lifted her and placed her on her back on the floor. He arranged her cloak over her in place of using a blanket to keep her warm.

Unable to respond because of her gag, Talking Rain lay there watching him as he walked the canoe into deeper water. Then he boarded it and began taking the vessel upriver in the opposite direction of where her husband lay peacefully asleep, thinking that she was asleep beside him.

Suddenly she heard the loons again, singing their songs back and forth across the water. Their calls became fainter and fainter the farther away she was taken from her home. She wrestled with the ropes at her wrists, succeeding only at making her flesh raw and sore by trying. She tried to sit up, but the Snake kicked her down again.

"You are going only where I am taking you," the Snake said, chuckling. "And then you shall see what my plans are for you."

As he continued to pull his paddle through the water, his eyes never left Talking Rain. "I remember very well the day you were brought into our village," he said. "You were such a tiny thing, but unafraid. I knew then that you would be a strong woman as well."

He chuckled.

"But who would have believed that you would turn into more of a man than a woman?" he said. "Such a beautiful, golden-haired woman as you was born to be a wife, not a woman-warrior, and that is exactly what you are going to be. You are going to be my woman, my wife. We will stay at my stronghold for the duration of the winter, and then I will take you far from here so that we can live a normal life as man and wife. My renegade days are behind me. I only want to live as all warriors live—in peace and with a devoted woman at my side."

He laughed. "Yes, your eyes tell me that you will fight this decision I have made for us," he said. "But you will learn to accept me as your husband, for you will have no other choice. If you do not cooperate, I will be forced to teach you how. And my ways of taming you will not be pleasant."

He chuckled. "But then again, if you do become too hard to tame, I will be forced to take you and sell you to someone as their slave," he said. "Yes, that might be the answer anyway. What a price I could get for you!"

He smiled smugly at her, then concentrated only on traversing the river.

Talking Rain could not believe that this was happening, that she had become so careless that it could, and that this evil man had killed someone else in order to have her.

What was most incredible was that he had actually fooled himself into believing that he could have her as his woman.

He must know her reputation well enough to realize that she would not allow him to get away with this . . . that she would kill him at her first opportunity.

Then her eyes wavered when she recalled what he had said about having ways of taming her. He was surely speaking of torture. If someone was tortured enough, would not they give in to the one who inflicted it to have it stopped?

She firmed her jaw. Her eyes became lit with fire.

There was no way this man would get away with this. When Storm Rider discovered that she was gone and found the dead sentry, he would stop at nothing to find her. And when he did, then this evil man would finally get his comeuppance.

But she knew that there was a chance that neither she nor the Snake would ever be found.

He had been so elusive that no one had found his stronghold yet. So why would they now?

And there were no horse's hoofprints to follow tonight. The Snake had cleverly taken her away in the water!

Strangely enough, as much as she did not want to sleep now, she could not fight it any longer. She felt herself drifting, and then fell into a deep sleep, where dreams joined her again with her husband.

When strong arms lifted her from the canoe, she awoke with a start. She looked quickly around her as the Snake set her on the ground, then hid his canoe amidst a thick stand of brush.

Dawn was just breaking along the horizon, giving Talking Rain enough light to see the lay of the land. And she did not see anything familiar about it.

She concluded from that, as well as the hour of the day, that the Snake had traveled far to get her where they were . . . or that he had cleverly made it look that way, when he might be closer to the village than she would have imagined.

Perhaps he delayed taking her from the canoe, even beaching it for some time so that when she awakened she would think he had traveled far.

She stiffened when he forced her to her feet,

grabbed her by an arm, and walked her away from the river.

She looked again for something familiar, but still she saw nothing.

She continued to walk with the Snake for some time; then she stopped when she heard the distinct howling of wolves.

She could not help but recall the wolf that had bitten Little Beaver. Could that hydrophobic wolf have been a part of this pack she was hearing now? Were others ill now with the same disease?

Suddenly she saw six wolves running toward her and the Snake. She could tell that they were friendly with the Snake by how they approached him, then began following behind.

The Snake did not acknowledge the wolves, but instead kept walking onward with Talking Rain. Suddenly he stopped.

Talking Rain watched him shove loose limbs and brush aside, soon revealing the entrance of a cave. She recalled how Little Beaver and Four Winds had said they had found a cave. When they had entered, the shine of eyes inside the cave had frightened them away, but not in time, for the sick wolf came out and bit Little Beaver.

Was this the same cave? Was that ill wolf still there?

Her heart raced as the Snake shoved her into the cave, the wolves following.

The Snake then stopped. "Wait here," he said, turning toward the entrance of the cave.

She watched as he repositioned the loose branches and brush back at the entrance of the cave, obviously disguising the entrance so that no one could find it.

"Stay close beside me," the Snake said, grabbing her by an arm.

Her eyes were wide as she followed the Snake farther into the cave. It was so dark now, she couldn't see anything before her, behind her, or on either side of her.

But the Snake obviously knew where he was going.

Then, after being taken far into the dark, dank place, she saw the light of a fire up ahead. Her breath was stolen away when she saw what looked like a place of luxury. Surely this was the Snake's home.

"And so you now know why I have been so hard to find," the Snake said, placing her on a blanket spread beside the fire. "This has been my home for years. I shared it with my men until they were downed during the last ambush or taken captive. Now I am alone . . . except for you."

He bent low and removed her gag, but still left her wrists tied behind her.

He stood up and gestured with a hand. "Come and let me show you around," he said. "There is enough food, wood, water, and comforts here to last the duration of the long winter."

The wolves had left again. Talking Rain looked carefully around for them. "Where are the wolves?" she asked.

"They have returned to their post," the Snake said, idly shrugging. "I trained them well. The only time they leave their assigned post is when they sense me approaching. They always come to me. Otherwise, they stand guard a few feet inside the entrance of my cave."

"Have any ever become hydrophobic?" Talking Rain asked guardedly.

"Yes," he said, raising an eyebrow. "Why would you ask that? I buried a hydrophobic wolf only a few weeks ago."

Talking Rain was afraid that she had said too much. He might know that the children had been there. If that was true, she was not all that far from the Assiniboine village. She tightened her jaw.

"I'm afraid of wolves, especially because they are known to carry hydrophobia, that's all," she blurted out.

"My remaining wolves are well enough," he said. He lit a torch. "Come. See your new home. I think you will be impressed. I have quite a collection of things that I have gathered through my many years of raiding and murdering."

She was so awed by what she was seeing that

whatever he was saying was lost in the wonder of the many different passages in the cave, all of which were filled with goods he had stolen and brought to his stronghold.

And when he took her to one of the rooms, the amount of firearms and weapons was particularly alarming. There were enough weapons to supply a cavalry!

"And so now you see what I have accumulated through the years," he said. "Should I have wished to, I could have succeeded up against the most skilled warriors or cavalry."

He shrugged. "I am getting older now and tiring of all that," he said. "And I am weary of hiding out. I wish to move to a new land and make a fresh start." He reached a hand out to her face. "That is where you come into the picture. You will go with me."

He frowned. "But should you prove to be too much of a challenge or a bother, I will get what I can for you at the slave auction, then go by myself to a new land," he said in a growl. "It's up to you." He chuckled. "You have plenty of time to decide. We are in my stronghold for the duration of the winter."

"Not if Storm Rider has anything to say about it," Talking Rain said in a low hiss. "Your days are numbered."

His only response was to chuckle, then to give her a shove back toward the campfire.

Talking Rain would not let herself lose hope of being found, yet as tricky as the Snake had always been, there was a chance that she would never see her husband again. Or anyone, for that matter, should the Snake tire of battling with her, for she would battle him to the very end.

Now she was glad that she had been a strong-willed, independent woman who knew the art of survival well before she became caught up in the love of a man.

That part of her that would never die might get her through the ordeal that faced her now.

Chapter 25

As Storm Rider slowly awakened, he smiled and reached out to draw Talking Rain into his arms for an early morning of lovemaking. It was hard to believe that finally he had a woman to warm his blankets and body each morning and night—and not just any woman, but someone so very special.

Talking Rain. Ah, how even thinking of her sent a sensual thrill through his body.

He could feel the heat rush into his loins at the thought of making love to her again, after the three times last night.

He remembered falling asleep the most contented he had been in years. It was she who had brought this contentment into his heart and life.

"Talking Rain, wife, where are you?" Storm Rider asked.

She did not respond, so he sat up and turned to see where she might be. When he did not see her, he smiled. She must have gone to Yellow Flower's lodge to get the morning meal that Yellow Flower had said she would prepare for them. Talking Rain would not want Yellow Flower to have to go to the trouble of bringing it to their lodge after having already spent time preparing it for Storm Rider and his bride.

Yawning and stretching his arms above his head, he gazed up at the smoke hole. He was glad to see the sun shining through the slowly rising smoke. He had been afraid that the last evening's hint of snow might have foretold what he could expect today—snow, and then more snow. He did not look forward to the time of snows and cold winds. Life became more of a challenge then.

But he was ready for this sort of challenge. He had enough firewood cut and piled outside. His hunt had been good, and he had much smoked meat ready for the meals, as did he have enough warm pelts to share with his wife.

"Wife," he said, loving the sound of that word as it crossed his lips.

He rose from his plush bed of pelts and blankets. His eyebrows rose when he saw that the feathers and flowers still lay strewn across the floor of his lodge. It puzzled him that they would be, for Talking Rain had told him just prior to his going to sleep that she would collect the feathers first thing this morning and save them forever in a parfleche bag. She had told him that she would press many of the flowers for memories of their wedding night, as well. She had said that she would do this upon first arising so that no more of them would be spoiled from walking on them.

He glanced toward the closed entrance flap. Then he again puzzled at the strewn feathers and flowers.

Had she forgotten to do as she had said? Had she been too eager to have their morning meal ready for him when he awakened?

Wanting answers, especially since she was still gone after he had dressed in his buckskin attire and warm ankle-high moccasins, he left the lodge and frowned when he saw that snow had come during the night.

Then he lifted his eyes and smiled when he saw the children enjoying their first substantial snow of the season. They romped, rolled, and threw snowballs playfully at one another. He spoke to one and then another as he walked toward Yellow Flower's tepee. He reached it and called Yellow Flower's name through her closed entrance flap. Waiting, he turned and observed the other activity at his village. Although it seemed strange to see a mixture of Crow and Assiniboine, it warmed his heart to know that the Crow people were adapting well to their new home . . . and adjusting to having lost their own.

He wanted their stay there to be one of a gentle peace. He wanted them to be able to relax, although he knew that it might be hard to feel anything but gloom and sadness over having lost so much in their lives: not only their homes, but so many of their loved ones.

The winter would be longer for them than the Assiniboine, because the Crow had plans to make about their future and where they would go to start life anew.

He had told them that they could stay with him and his people, but he had understood when the Crow people as a whole said that they wished to make their own home elsewhere, so that they could grow again as a people.

They wanted their independence, as the Assiniboine had theirs.

"Storm Rider?"

Yellow Flower's soft, sweet voice drew Storm Rider around.

He smiled and looked past her as she held the entrance flap aside. "Is my wife ready to come home?" he asked, confused when he did not see Talking Rain in Yellow Flower's tepee.

"She is not here," Yellow Flower said. Her long hair hung over one shoulder. Her deft fingers were finishing the last touches on her long braid.

"I expect her soon, though," she added quickly.

"If she is not here, where is she?" Storm Rider said, his smile turning quickly to a frown. He gazed with concern into Yellow Flower's eyes. "You have truly not seen her this morning?"

"No, she has not been here at all," Yellow Flower

said. She flipped her completed braid over her shoulder so that it hung long down her back.

She looked past him at the river, then smiled at Storm Rider. "Surely she has gone to the river for water," she suggested.

Storm Rider turned and looked at the river. His spine stiffened when he saw no signs of anyone there, much less his wife.

His eyes moved slowly through the people as they moved about, preparing for their day's chores.

There was still no sign of Talking Rain . . . anywhere.

He sighed heavily and turned back to Yellow Flower. "I must go now and search for my wife," he said. "But should she come, perhaps after having stopped to visit one of her people before coming to your lodge, will you tell her that I am looking for her?"

"Yes, I will do that for you," Yellow Flower said.

Little Beaver came to his mother's side. "What is wrong, Mother?" he asked, then gazed up at Storm Rider.

"Storm Rider is looking for Talking Rain," Yellow Flower said. She reached and playfully tousled her son's thick black hair. "Might you go and help? Ask around. See if anyone has seen her."

"Yes, Mother, I would be glad to do that for you," he said. He smiled up at Storm Rider. "You, too, Chief Storm Rider."

In warm buckskin attire and moccasins, Little Beaver hurried away from them.

Storm Rider watched him. "I am so glad that he is well," he said, again reminded of his wife. Because of her, the child was alive.

"And he will never forget how your wife saved his life," Yellow Flower said. "He will do what he can to find Talking Rain."

Storm Rider turned and watched Little Beaver running from lodge to lodge, asking about Talking Rain. As each person told him that they knew nothing about Talking Rain, Storm Rider's concern grew.

If she wasn't at the river, or at Yellow Flower's lodge, or anywhere at all to be seen, then where was she, and why had she left without telling him first that she was going to leave?

He thought back to having found the lodge undisturbed, with the feathers and flowers still strewn along the floor. Again he recalled her saying that she would pick them up first thing today.

So why hadn't she? Suddenly he went back to his lodge and stopped just outside the entranceway. He knelt down onto his haunches and studied the footprints in the snow. He knew that they were made by his wife's moccasins. Her feet were smaller than any he had seen before, so her tracks were easily discernible from the others there.

His eyes followed the direction of her prints. They went toward the river. He moved to his feet and slowly followed the footprints until he came to the river. He saw that they made a sharp turn left and went alongside the river. He followed them.

When he saw that they were going farther than he thought she would go, especially alone, his hopes waned of finding her unharmed.

Yet there were no other footprints with hers.

Thus far, at this point, she was still alone.

"No one has seen Talking Rain today," Little Beaver shouted as he came running up behind Storm Rider.

Not wanting the young brave to mar the footprints that continued to lead alongside the river, Storm Rider stopped and reached a hand out for Little Beaver. "Stay beside me," he said tightly. "Do not go on ahead."

Little Beaver gazed downward. "These are her footprints?" he asked, then looked up at Storm Rider. "Where do you think she is going?"

"I am not certain about anything at this moment," Storm Rider grumbled. "I am not certain if she made these prints this morning, or . . . possibly last night. As I recall, she was not yet asleep when I drifted off. She seemed too restless to sleep."

"Restless enough to take a walk in the moonlight?" Little Beaver asked, frowning. "She would not leave for a walk and go this far at night, would she?"

"I cannot tell how fresh these footprints are, so I do

not know when she made them . . . last night or this morning," Storm Rider said, moving slowly ahead again. Little Beaver stayed beside him, his eyes also following the prints.

"She came way too far alone," Little Beaver suddenly blurted out. "The Snake. What if the Snake saw her?"

That thought sent spirals of dread through Storm Rider. "Yes, I would have thought she knew the dangers too well to have done something as foolish as this, yet she was feeling so good about life last night, she might have forgotten," he said, his voice drawn. "She . . ."

His heart seemed to drop to his feet when he saw that suddenly Talking Rain's prints were mixed with others.

They were much larger. They were obviously a man's.

And as he knelt and studied the prints, he saw that his wife's footprints disappeared, and in their place he could see the outline of her body.

She had been obviously wrestled or thrown to the ground and forced to lie on her back, while someone apparently held her there by force.

"I also see what you see," Little Beaver said, moving to his knees beside Storm Rider. "Do you think the Snake took her captive?"

Storm Rider was too involved in his concern for his wife to even hear the child asking him questions.

He stood slowly and saw that the footprints led away from where Talking Rain had been forced to the ground. But there were only one set of prints.

Whoever had found Talking Rain alone had grabbed her up into his arms and . . .

The footprints led to the river.

He could then see the imprint of where a canoe had been beached, and then footprints that led into the water. He saw marks where the canoe had obviously been dragged into the river.

"She was taken away by canoe . . ." Storm Rider said, his voice dry. "It was surely the Snake. He abducted my wife."

The howling of wolves in the distance brought Storm Rider quickly to his feet.

He gazed in the direction of the wolves, then felt something tugging at the sleeve of his shirt.

"I hear the wolves," Little Beaver said, his voice small and tight. "I remember something about that day I was bitten."

"What do you remember?" Storm Rider said, turning to gaze down at Little Beaver.

"The cave," Little Beaver said. "There was more than one wolf at the cave. It was as though they might be guarding something."

"What are you saying?" Storm Rider said, placing his hands on the child's shoulders.

"I should have told you sooner," Little Beaver said, swallowing hard. "But I did not want to get in trouble with my mother by saying how far I traveled from the village. Storm Rider, that is the only reason I did not tell anyone what I am now going to tell you. My mother was angry enough about my disobeying her. She would have been really angry if she had known just how far Four Winds and I had gone. His mother, too, would punish him. We both would have never been allowed to go out on our own again alone."

"Little Beaver, you are trying to tell me something," Storm Rider said. "Say it!"

"I have thought about it since Dancing Wings and Young Elk were found, and I believe that they were taken to the very cave where I was bitten by the wolf. That cave might be a haven for not only the Snake, but those renegades who are now captive at our village. It might be their stronghold."

"And why would you think that?" Storm Rider asked urgently.

"Because the cave was purposely hidden behind loose brush and limbs," Little Beaver said. "You see, Four Winds and I moved them to get into the cave. That is when we saw the wolves. There were six or seven of them. They stayed just inside the cave. It was as though they were guarding something. Only the sick wolf came out of the cave."

Storm Rider's spine stiffened. "And so you believe that the cave is possibly a stronghold for the Snake, and you did not tell anyone earlier?" he asked angrily. "Even though Talking Rain's brother and sister were missing and held captive somewhere?"

Little Beaver lowered his eyes. "I was wrong," he gulped out. "So was Four Wings."

He looked up wild-eyed at Storm Rider. "We made a pact to keep silent," he rushed out. "We love exploring. We love adventure. Had we told our mothers how far we went in our exploring, our weapons would be denied us now, as would the hunt. We thought of ourselves, when we should have thought of others. I am sorry, Storm Rider, if what I am thinking is true and I did not tell you earlier."

Little Beaver swallowed hard. "We traveled by canoe that day," he choked out, "to keep anyone from knowing how far we had traveled. With Four Wings's help, I managed to get to the canoe. We traveled far before the Crow and Assiniboine warriors found us."

"Take me to the cave," Storm Rider said, his eyes narrowing angrily. "*Now . . .*"

Little Beaver nodded.

Storm Rider started to leave immediately with Little Beaver, then thought better of going with only the child. Although all of the Snake's renegades were either dead or held captive at his village, there might be more renegades who had not been with the Snake that night. That meant that they might be wherever the Snake had taken Talking Rain.

Yes, he must take many warriors to assure that no

errors were made in the handling of the Snake. This time, if he was found, he would not walk away to spread his evil again, anywhere.

"Let us hurry back to the village and gather up warriors to accompany us to the cave," Storm Rider said, breaking into a quick run, Little Beaver beside him.

"Do you have to tell my mother what I told you?" Little Beaver asked, his eyes wavering. "Do you?"

Storm Rider turned a dark frown down at the child.

Little Beaver ducked his head. "Yes, I know that you must," he said, tears filling his eyes.

"You had just better hope that nothing has happened to my wife, or you will forever regret having kept such a secret to yourself," Storm Rider said angrily.

Little Beaver swallowed back a sob that had momentarily lodged in his throat. "I am very sorry for what I have done," he choked out. "I shall prove myself to you as a valiant warrior someday so that you can forget my bad decision."

"Taking me to my wife is the best thing that you can do," Storm Rider said. "If she is found alive and well, you will be rewarded for your honesty, however late."

Little Beaver smiled awkwardly up at Storm Rider.

Chapter 26

Talking Rain's captivity had taken a turn for the worse. When she could see what the Snake was doing, she had felt some promise of having her life spared. He had said that he had abducted her because he wanted her for his wife, and was tired of his marauding ways and no longer going to live the life of a killer. But after she had had time to think about it, she had truly found all of that ludicrous.

Telling her such lies was just a part of his madman's plan, and drawing Storm Rider and his men into a trap was no doubt the major part of the plot.

A moth drawn to flame died a painful death in its fire, and she was being used as a flame—one that would draw her husband and his men into a death trap.

What confused her was why the Snake had taken her farther into the cave. He had placed her in total darkness in one of the rooms that lined the many tunnels in the cave.

As she was being led to this far-off hole that he

had made into a room, Talking Rain grew more amazed by the vastness of his stronghold. Numerous tunnels connected rooms filled with items that he had stolen from both innocent travelers and people of his own skin color.

When she had asked about his horse, where it was kept, he had told her that his horse was safe, but would not tell her where.

He had proceeded to explain why no horses had ever been stolen during his raids. It was impossible to house them in his cave, and he did not want to leave them outside, for if someone found them, he could quite possibly discover the cave, too.

That had explained why neither he nor his warriors had stolen her people's horses after raiding her village, which had puzzled her at the time, since stealing was considered a valorous act.

But her main concern now was why the Snake had placed her farther back in the cave, alone and in the dark.

She truly felt that she might be living her last moments on earth. After having found what she knew was her happiness in life, she found it so unfair that it would now be denied her.

She felt many emotions now. She was angry that she could have allowed such a thing to happen to her. Yet she was afraid, too, as she wondered just how the Snake planned to kill her.

Taking her to this isolated place in the cave was a

part of his sordid plan, and would eventually lead to her death.

Never had she felt so helpless . . . or so alone.

"I can't allow this to happen," she whispered angrily to herself.

She had to find a way to get free. Time was running out on her. And not only was she in mortal danger, but Storm Rider would be soon as well, because she knew that he would turn this area upside down to find her. He would not leave a stone unturned, nor a leaf . . . nor a snowflake. . . .

He was an intelligent warrior. He was keen in all of his senses, certainly now that his woman was missing. But there was one factor that worked against his finding her: She had been taken away in a canoe. There were no traces left in water for him to follow, as there would be tracks in the snow.

Even though Storm Rider was an astute leader, if he did find her now it would be by sheer chance. And the chances were slim that Storm Rider would ever find this cave. He was new in this land and did not know the secret hollows or caves.

Nor had her people known about this cave, or if they had, saw little importance in it.

"Little Beaver," she whispered, her eyes widening. "Four Wings."

The young braves had found a cave, and surely it was this one.

The wolves! It must have been one of the Snake's wolves that had bitten Little Beaver.

The fact that the young braves had left for their adventure that day in a canoe instead of on horseback meant that possibly it had been this cave that they had discovered.

If it was this cave, and the young braves thought to tell Storm Rider about it, then her husband and many warriors could be on their way even now to save her.

But the wolves! They guarded this cave viciously. Had the young braves ventured farther into the cave that day, Little Beaver would have not only suffered the bite of a hydrophobic wolf, but both boys might have been torn apart by the other wolves.

If Storm Rider came searching for her in this cave, he and his men would not realize the dangers that awaited them. Many of the warriors might be attacked and mauled before Storm Rider and his men could kill the wolves.

"I have to do something," Talking Rain whispered. She couldn't just sit there and wait for something terrible to happen to her husband! Now was the time for her to use all of the skills that she had learned as a warrior-woman. Although she had planned to leave that part of her behind her, she must one more time reach deeply inside herself to figure out a way to out best the Snake and escape!

"But how . . . ?" she whispered.

Her wrists were snugly bound. How could she get them free?

In her mind's eye, she remembered one of the rooms in this cave, where all sorts of weapons were stored.

A knife! If she could find that room and get a knife, she could cut the bindings at her wrists. Then she would choose a weapon to use on the murderous renegade. That might be her only chance at saving not only her life, but her husband's, as well.

But she was sitting in total darkness. She had no idea where to go!

And would the wolves sense that she was moving about in the cave if she did try to find the weapons room? Would she suddenly see the shine of their eyes in the dark? Would they then attack and kill her?

Despite the terrible possibilities, and no matter how much her hands were shaking and her heart was thumping from fright, she moved to her knees.

She had planned to crawl, because she was not sure of the height of the ceiling of rock, but realized that with her wrists bound, there was no way that she could crawl on all fours.

She moved slowly to a standing position just in case the ceiling was too low and she might crack her head on the rock. When she found that she could fully stand, she slowly began making her way around the room as she tried to find the passageway that led from it. After bumping into a solid wall of rock several times, she finally found the opening that led out into a tunnel that was as dark as the room in which she had been taken.

But she was too determined to do what she could to escape not to go on and try to find where the knives and other weapons were stored.

Her knees trembling, she left the room and made a sharp turn right. She walked slowly onward, almost letting out a cry of pain when she suddenly hit her head on a lower ceiling of rock.

But that made her know where she was!

When the Snake had taken her on a "tour" of his hideout, she recalled how they had had to stoop lower right before he had led her into the room where he proudly showed her, by the light of his torch, his stash of stolen weapons.

Talking Rain stopped. This part of the cave had a lower ceiling, and she paused to try to get her bearings and estimate just how far she and the Snake had gone before they reached the weapons room.

Then she remembered. She smiled.

"The weapons are at the very far end of this tunnel," she whispered to herself.

Hunkered low, she moved onward. Still she feared that the wolves might sense her movements and come after her.

When she envisioned a wolf at her throat, its

long, sharp fangs ready to sink into her jugular vein, a shudder raced through her body. She made herself stop thinking such things and focus on the task at hand.

She knew that the Snake could discover what she was doing at any moment. Then he might kill her in a more terrible way than the wolves would.

Her heart pounding in her chest, she moved forward.

Then she ran into a body of rock. She turned slowly to one side, and then another, to find where the passage went . . . to the left? Or to the right?

When she felt an opening at her right she smiled, for she recalled having taken a right turn at the very end of this passageway. It had taken her and the Snake directly into the weapons room!

Her hopes were high now of being able to free herself of this madman. Reaching the room, she smiled and hurried inside.

She reached her bound hands around her until she found a pile of sharp knives that were luckily not sheathed.

She took a knife with one of her hands, secured it between a pile of rifles with the sharp edge sticking upward, then began sawing at the ropes until they fell apart and her wrists were free.

Her heart pounding, she grabbed the knife and cut the rest of the ropes away from each wrist. Then she felt around her until she found a sheathed knife. She secured it at her side.

She was excited that she was using her skills as a warrior, yet knew that if she did get free and returned to her husband, this would most definitely be the last time. Hopefully she would not have *cause* to use them again.

She felt around until she found a small revolver and ammunition, which she placed inside its chambers. She slipped this into the pocket of her buckskin dress.

Then she found a more substantial weapon, one she might have to use not only on the Snake, but on the wolves as well, to save herself from their deadly fangs. She lifted the rifle and made sure it was loaded. Then, feeling triumphant, at least for the moment, she made her way out of the weapons room.

She kept low until she made her way to the part of the tunnel that gave her more space to stand.

She then moved onward, careful not to stir up the rock at her feet and alert the Snake and the wolves to her movements.

When she finally saw the faint glow of a campfire ahead, she stopped and inhaled a nervous breath.

"*Wah-con-tun-ga*, Great Medicine, oh, God, the God that my true parents taught me about, please give me the courage to do what I must to get free," she whispered.

Yes, it was all up to her now. She was in charge of her own destiny. And she was confident that she could pull this off, for she felt the courage and strength that had gotten her through many danger-ous moments riding with the Crow warriors after a horse-stealing expedition.

Although they were skilled at what they did, they had had some close calls and had almost been caught.

Talking Rain drew from that inner courage that had been instilled in her on the day of her white parents' deaths. Knowing then that she must be stronger than they had been, especially her mother, Talking Rain crept forward.

Suddenly she stumbled on something on the cave floor and almost lost her balance. She had to grab hard to the rifle as it nearly slipped from her hand.

After she steadied herself, she bent low to see what she had tripped over. She gasped and jerked her hand back when she felt the cold body of a wolf. It was dead! But how?

The possibility of hydrophobia came to mind. Had more than one of the wolves contracted the dis-ease and only now died of it?

Shivering from dread, she stepped cautiously over the wolf, then took only a few more steps be-fore her feet made contact with something else.

Almost afraid to see what, she hesitated.

If it was another wolf, surely hydrophobia would not be the cause of its death, or the other's.

They had been killed. But who would do that?

"Storm Rider?" she whispered, her eyes widening.

Had he arrived? Had he killed the wolves as he tried to find her?

She leaned down onto her knees and felt around on the wolf. She drew her hand quickly away when she felt a wetness that had to be blood. Whoever had killed the wolf had done it with the silent strike of a knife!

Talking Rain was unsure of what to do now, because someone was in the cave killing wolves, and it certainly was not the Snake, who had trained them. She stepped away from this wolf and gazed ahead of her.

This cave was too quiet for her husband to have arrived with his warriors to save her. That had to mean that the only person there with her was the Snake!

But why would he kill the wolves? she thought desperately to herself.

Afraid to go on, but afraid to wait for the Snake to possibly slice her throat, as well, Talking Rain inched her way along the rocky wall. She could see by the glow of the fire as she grew closer to it that more wolves were lying on the earthen, rocky floor, dead. That had to mean that they all had been killed.

That had to mean that she was next!

She was even more careful now not to make any noise as she inched her way forward to the main section of the cave where the Snake kept a fire burning and had luxurious pallets of furs placed around the fire. When she finally caught sight of the evil man, her heart dropped, it seemed, to her toes.

Earlier he had gloated as he showed her explosives in one of the storage rooms. At this moment he was spreading explosives around the room and into the corridor that eventually led to the entrance of the cave.

Talking Rain felt the color rush from her face when she realized what he was up to. He was obviously setting a trap for Storm Rider when he came to rescue her.

He actually expected Storm Rider to find her. And if the Snake was leaving the cave to live elsewhere, he did not mind destroying it, and everything and everyone in it. He would no doubt set up the explosives so that he could stand guard outside the cave and ignite them just as Storm Rider entered with his warriors.

It was then that she saw the remaining wolves. They lay along the far wall. All were dead.

That truly confused Talking Rain. She could not

see the purpose in killing the wolves, especially after they had been so loyal to the man.

Almost too afraid to move and uncertain just how sensitive the explosives were, Talking Rain knew only that she must stop the man's madness before her husband stepped into the trap. She leveled the rifle at the Snake's back. She knew that she could kill him now, but she could not find it in herself to shoot him in the back.

And if he dropped the explosives as he fell? What then?

She had no choice but to face him. She just could not allow him to get away with this latest plan. She was in charge of her own destiny, and her husband's, as well.

"Snake, slowly turn around," Talking Rain said.

She stepped out into the open so that when the Snake did turn, he would see her instantly.

"Be careful, Snake," she said solemnly. "Don't do anything foolish, like setting off that explosive. I believe you value your life too much to do that."

Hearing her voice, the Snake stiffened.

Then she heard him give a low, sinister laugh, and was puzzled. He must know that he would blow himself up along with her if he set off the explosives. So what did he find so amusing?

Slowly he turned and faced her.

"You are more clever than I thought you were," the Snake said, his hands still holding the explosive.

"I should have known that ropes couldn't stop you. I should have paid more attention to your reputation."

He chuckled. "What a waste," he said. "Most men would die to have a woman as beautiful as you in their blankets with them. But I doubt many would want someone who behaves so manly."

"And you were planning to take me away and force marriage on me?" Talking Rain asked, her voice harsh.

"No, that was not in my plans," the Snake said, his eyes gleaming. "Do you truly believe that I did all of this to have you as a wife?" He laughed sarcastically. "It was never my intent to take you anywhere with me. Telling you that was just a part of my plan."

"And you do not think I figured that out already?" Talking Rain said, laughing. "But there is one thing that truly confuses me about what you have done."

"And that is?"

"The wolves," she said, still feeling the coldness of their bodies and the wetness of their blood against her fingertips. "Why did you kill the wolves?"

"They are no longer of any use to me," the Snake said, idly shrugging. "They were trained to keep intruders from my cave. Now I *want* intruders. I am counting on Storm Rider and Brave Shield coming for you. In one blast they will be dead, as will you."

He took a slow step toward her. "And so will I be just as dead, for I plan to die with you," he said tightly. "My time on this earth is over. I will die with pride, though, as I take my enemies with me."

"You are sicker than anyone imagined," Talking Rain said, her voice breaking.

Then she took a step closer to him, her rifle still aimed at his gut. "Your plans have just changed," she said. "You are going to die, all right, as will I. But not Storm Rider or Brave Shield. If it is necessary, I will die to save them."

She swallowed hard. "Either lay down that explosive, or I will shoot it while you hold it and you will be the first to die," she said, even as she prayed that she would not have to die that way.

Suddenly an arrow whizzed through the air and the Snake's body lurched with the impact of it. His free hand grabbed at the arrow that pierced his chest.

Talking Rain saw him let go of the explosive just as Storm Rider came into view.

"No!" she screamed, expecting the explosive to go off the moment it hit the floor, killing her beloved husband and everyone else in the cave.

But it didn't explode.

Apparently it was not set to explode unless the wick was lit.

Her gaze turned again. She watched the Snake fall to his knees, his eyes wide as he looked back at her. Then he fell forward onto the arrow, his last breath a strange sort of gurgle.

Talking Rain stared at the dead man, knowing just how close she had come to losing everything because of him. She felt a keen relief that finally he was dead.

He would never again cause fear in anyone's heart. He would not kill.

She was free . . . free of him!

So was Storm Rider.

So were their people!

She dropped the rifle just as Storm Rider came to her and drew her into his embrace.

"Talking Rain," he said, as she sobbed and clung to him. "My Talking Rain."

"I am all right," she murmured between sobs. Still she clung to him. She did not want to let him go! She had come so close to losing him.

The other warriors, along with Brave Shield, entered the cave.

Storm Rider gently held Talking Rain away from him. His gaze slowly moved over her, and then stopped as his eyes held hers.

"Did he . . . harm you in any way?" he asked.

Knowing what he was referring to, she smiled and shook her head. "No, I am truly fine," she murmured. "It is an experience that I wish never happened, yet in the end perhaps it was worth it."

She turned and gazed down at the dead man. "He is finally dead," she said solemnly. "He is no longer a threat to anyone."

Then she turned to Storm Rider. "How did you know to find me here?" she asked.

Little Beaver and Four Wings stepped into view.

"We told him," Little Beaver said. "This is the cave that we found while we were exploring. If it had not been for the wolves, we would have found the stronghold and we could have reported it to Storm Rider."

Little Beaver hung his head, swallowed hard, then gazed over at Storm Rider. "I am sorry that I did not tell the full truth about the cave earlier."

He paused. "Had we been honest enough to tell you about finding this cave, perhaps you would have known to come and investigate it, and none of this would have happened," he said.

Then Little Beaver looked up at Talking Rain. "What puzzles me is that there were no wolves this time," he said, his eyes innocent and wide.

"That is because they are dead," Talking Rain said.

"Dead?" Little Beaver said. "Did you kill them?"

"No, not I," Talking Rain said, looking over her shoulder in the direction of the dead wolves. She again gazed at the child. "They outlived their use-fulness," she murmured. "The Snake killed them."

She then proceeded to tell them all about the plot, and how they had almost walked into a trap of the Snake's making.

"I am taking you home," Storm Rider said after she finished. "It is best that we put all this from our minds."

"Let's not leave just yet," Talking Rain said. She took one of Storm Rider's hands. She looked at Brave Shield, then nodded toward the unlit torches that lay against the far wall. "Light a torch. I have something to show you."

She took them through the entire stronghold. They were all amazed at the extent of the caves. And they were shocked at how much the evil man had taken from innocent people.

"There are many valuable pelts and weapons, even food, that can be put to good use," Talking Rain said. "I think we should help ourselves to all of this. We can build several travois and take it home with us. All of these items can go to those who lost so much in the ambush."

"And it would be you who would think of help-ing people in such a way," Storm Rider said, gently touching her cheek. "My *mitawin*, you are all heart."

"Do you still see me as all woman after what I did today?" Talking Rain asked.

She watched his eyes, trying to read his feelings.

She was glad when she saw a quiet sort of humor, and then pride.

"You are all woman, every inch of you," he said, laughing softly. Then he placed his hands on both of her cheeks. "But it was good that you used the survival skills you know so well, or—"

"Let us not think of what might have been, but of what is," Talking Rain said, moving into his embrace. "We still have our happiness."

"Forever," Storm Rider said, holding her even closer.

"And soon there will be someone else to share in that happiness," Talking Rain said, only now remembering that she had gone past the time, by several days, when her monthly was due.

Storm Rider placed his hands on her shoulders and held her away from him. "You are saying that . . . ?"

"That, yes, I might be with child," she said, her eyes filled with a bright happiness. "Yours . . . mine . . . *ours.*"

With an endearing carefulness, he again drew her into his arms. "*Wah-con-tun-ga* has been good to us," he murmured.

"Very," Talking Rain said. "Very good."

Then she smiled at him. "So has the God that I knew before I learned about yours," she said.

Chapter 27

Years Later

Talking Rain's Crow people had moved, but had not gone far. They built their new village close to the Assiniboine's, and the bands worked together as one entity in the hunt, celebrations, and all else, making both villages thrive.

There had been many weddings between the Assiniboine and Crow people, making the bond of these two bands even stronger.

Even the Crow chief Dark Horse had come in friendship and joined the council with Brave Shield and Storm Rider.

Should anyone try to take advantage of these three bands, as the Snake did, their warriors would come together as one heartbeat to destroy the culprit long before he could begin a game of terrorizing, much less take lives.

It was a good, comfortable peace shared between the Assiniboine and the Crow, and Talking Rain thrived on this. She was so proud that she had had a role in bringing this about for the people she had loved since the day Chief Blue Thunder had taken her into his strong arms, and into the lives of his tribe. Then falling in love with Storm Rider and marrying him had brought her Crow people into a lasting relationship with the Assiniboine.

A new trading post had been established nearby, and Talking Rain and Storm Rider were on their way home from a healthy trade with the whites.

As they rode beside each other on horseback, Talking Rain smiled and glanced behind Storm Rider.

A travois attached to the back of his steed was piled high with provisions for the coming winter months.

She turned farther around and regarded the travois behind her own horse.

Asleep on this travois were her and Storm Rider's two children.

Rushing Waters, their daughter, was now eight, and except for her dark skin color, she was the exact image of her mother. Her long, golden locks of hair contrasted beautifully against her smooth, copper face. Her features were delicate. Her eyes were sky blue.

And she had a personality that Talking Rain felt torn about. Her daughter often displayed the same traits that Talking Rain had at the same age. Rushing Waters was too often interested in challenging the boys her age . . . sometimes in games, and sometimes in begging to go on the actual hunt with them.

Whereas at other times she was quiet, sweet, and all girl. She would play with dolls that Talking Rain had traded for at the trading post.

Talking Rain was not sure which side would win out over the other, but she had tried to direct her daughter toward the skills that she felt would benefit Rushing Waters the most . . . those of being a girl who would grow up into a beautiful woman.

She glanced then at her son, Brown Elk, who lay asleep beside his sister. He was only three, and how he did look like his father in every way. And even at his young age, he already displayed the same courage and leadership as Storm Rider.

He had long, black hair, beautiful smooth, copper skin, and long legs that seemed to grow more every time she looked at him.

Yes, she was proud of her daughter and her son.

And she was anxious to know whether her next child would be a boy or girl, for she was now five months into her next pregnancy.

She smiled over at Storm Rider. When she had told him that she was with child again, his eyes had beamed with pride and happiness.

He was the sort of man who loved hearing children's laughter in his home, and the more, the better, he had always said.

And because their family was growing, the lodge they all shared was twice the size of the one Storm Rider had lived in before he brought a wife and children into his home and heart. It had taken many more poles and buffalo hides to make this larger lodge.

Talking Rain had everything her heart desired, and she scarcely ever recalled that day when she had lost her true parents in the river.

She had made certain that her children knew about their grandparents. Of course, she had had to tell them the way they had died in order to explain why their mother was white, yet lived with Indians.

But she talked more about the love her father and mother had for her, explaining that that love would have been theirs, had her parents still lived.

She had told them not only about her parents who were white, but also those who had opened their hearts to her oh, so long ago and made her their daughter.

And Storm Rider had also told them about his parents.

Although they had no grandparents alive who could take them onto their laps and tell them stories, the children had their grandparents in their hearts forever.

"*Mitawin,* you are so quiet," Storm Rider said as he gazed over at Talking Rain. "What is on your mind?"

"Our children," Talking Rain murmured. "Us. I am so happy, Storm Rider. I am so content. I am so very, very proud of our children."

"As am I," he said. His gaze moved to her swollen tummy. "And soon there will be one more of us. It is good to have a large family. I missed that as a child."

"I did, as well, until my adopted parents had the twins," Talking Rain said, recalling the day when her siblings were born, and how wonderful it had been to hold one in each arm. "Would not it be fun to have twins of our own?"

"That is rare among my people, but yes, it would be a wonderful thing to behold," Storm Rider said. He gazed ahead, where he could now see his village. It sat nestled among aspen trees and up from the river enough to be safe from spring floods.

"Our home, Talking Rain," he said, gesturing toward the village. "It is always good to return home and see that things have remained the same."

"The Snake, and the destruction he spread across this lovely land, are only memories . . . dark, ugly memories," Talking Rain said. "It is good that with each year the thoughts of that renegade grow dimmer and dimmer in all our hearts and minds. One day he will not be remembered at all."

"Yes, that is so," Storm Rider said. He reached a hand out for Talking Rain, and she placed hers in his.

"The trade was good today, wife," he said, smiling, and obviously stopping talk of the man who had brought so much sadness into his people's lives, as well as his and Talking Rain's.

"Yes, good," Talking Rain said, smiling back at him, and knowing that he was purposely leading their conversation away from the Snake.

But no matter how they talked about forgetting the Snake, she knew that they would never totally forget that such a man had existed, for there was always someone else as mean, as cruel, and as scheming, who would enjoy interfering in the happiness of the Crow and Assiniboine people.

Yes, it was easy to say that in the future the evil man would be no longer even a memory, but in truth, that could never be so. It was best to remember him and the evil that he wrought, so that they did not let down their guard and allow someone else to take his place.

But for now, all was well.

Talking Rain and Storm Rider led a contented life, as did their children.

Each day, Talking Rain and Storm Rider's love for one another grew. Theirs was a never-ending love.

"*Tecihila,* I love you," she said, smiling at her husband.

"As I love you," he said, bringing her hand to his lips and kissing it.

As it was that first time he had kissed her, a blissful warmth spread through Talking Rain. He was her happiness . . . her everything!

Letter to the Reader

Dear Readers:

I hope you enjoyed reading *Storm Rider*. The next book in my Signet Indian series that I am writing exclusively for NAL/Signet is *Racing Moon*. This book is about the Chitimacha Indian tribe of Louisiana, and is filled with much passion, intrigue, and adventure.

Those of you who are collecting all of my Indian romance novels and want to hear more about the series and my entire backlist of Indian books can send for my latest newsletter, bookmark, autographed photograph, and fan club information. For a prompt reply, please send a stamped, self-addressed, legal-size envelope to

Cassie Edwards
6709 North Country Club Road
Mattoon, IL 61938

You can also visit my Web site at:
www.cassieedwards.com
Thank you for your support of my Indian series.
I love researching and writing about our country's
beloved Native Americans, our country's first
people.

Always,

Cassie Edwards